I'LL LOVE YOU TILL I DIE

MEG O'BRIEN

SMP

ST. MARTIN'S PAPERBACKS

I'LL LOVE YOU TILL I DIE

ISBN: 0-312-95586-3

Printed in the United States of America

St. Martin's Paperbacks edition/August 1995

10 9 8 7 6 5 4 3 2 1

This one's for Robin, Greg, Amy, Kevin and Kaiti, with deepest love.

I would like to remember, too, my aunt, Marie Catherine Moore, who turned moments of childhood pain into joy, and who, though departing far too soon, has remained ever close to my heart.

ACKNOWLEDGMENTS

With love and appreciation to Roland Deighton, whose assistance—both in terms of stories told, and his excellent book, *For My Girls: A Cornish Boyhood . . . and Beyond*—provided much of the Cornish background for this book. Grateful acknowledgment is also made to Daphne du Maurier, whose *Vanishing Cornwall* gave me a wealth of superstitions and locale details to draw from.

Deepest appreciation as well to Ginny Crossley, who generously read the early manuscript and assisted all along with British details, spelling, and idiom. To Bill Damon, too, who along with Ginny has been a good neighbor, providing me with wonderful nights off that included good food, good music, good conversation, and excellent wine.

I would also like to especially thank my agent, Nancy Yost, and my editor, Jennifer Enderlin—both of whom threw their excitement and support behind this book and cheered me every step of the way.

A writer's path is more often than not strewn with many challenges, and there are many angels in the form of people who have assisted me over the years to meet these challenges through their love, encouragement, and healing. To them I send a huge thank you and lots of love and light. To new friends and neighbors: Cathie Inglis, Peter Murphy, Jeff Girkout, and especially Christine Switalski, she of the generous heart and helping hands. To old friends, tried and true: Maylon Hamilton, Mona Horwitz, Anne Wilson, Sherryl Woods, Bernadette Reichardt Taylor, Margie Ford, Tammy Ford, Lu Wilcox, Cathy Landrum, Randy Landrum, Pat Myers, Read Myers, Toni Fuller, Robert G. Lenerd (the keeper of the flame, who made all things possible), Maureen and Frank Havens, LaUna Huffines, Michael "Riz" Rizza, Ramona Boothroyd, Tom and Terri

Doria, and to Sid Nyhus, who writes the greatest fan letters in the world.

As always, to Peggy, Tiffany, Josh, Darrell, Constance, Becky, and Scott.

To the healers: Barbara Stone, Pindéy Shahi, Steve Roseboro, Steve Lockard and Barbara Caserta.

There is one very wonderful group of people any writer is blessed to know—the independent bookstore owners. I can't name all who have supported me with enthusiastic applause through my last eight books, but a few come to mind easily: Helen Strodl of Cheshire Cat Books in Sausalito, California; Hut Landon of Landon Books in Mill Valley, California; Terry Baker of the Mystery Annex of Small World Books, Venice, California; Bruce Taylor of Mystery Books in San Francisco; and Beth Caswell of Sherlock's Home, Long Beach, California.

I am sure I've left out many other angels who have assisted me along the way. To them I offer apologies and the promise of remembrance in my heart.

Finally, I would like to thank M.B., without whose love, enthusiasm, and gift for play I might never have written a word.

CHAPTER 1

They say that to love another selflessly, without holding back, is the most noble act of the human soul. They say it has its own reward.

But who exactly says that? I don't know. Certainly not I, not anymore. As I seek beyond the vast, empty landscape of my soul today, I see only that the clouds are moving in again.

I see them above the drift of hill where David and I first met. I feel their cold mist surround me, just as it surrounded me on certain summer days in that meadow there, beyond our house. Can you see it, our house? It's ramshackle now, its broken windows like gaping eyes that have shattered from witnessing too much pain in too short a span of time. One can handle terrible things, I believe, if they don't come rushing at one like a runaway train barrelling down a track with no shoulder on either side. If there's a place to jump off and catch one's breath, one can remember the platitudes, perhaps, and stay the course. *"Ah, yes, 'tis a terrible thing,"* one might say, *"but then God never gives us more than we can handle at any given time."*

When the Dark Train comes hurtling down that track without warning, however—when there is no place to run for a bit and hide—we can only stand and allow ourselves to be run down. Even then, of course, people will come at you with their platitudes. *"God's will,"* they will cluck with a sorrowful air. *"God's will."*

* * *

Pennoryn. I see it now in my mind's eye, around that bend of Cornish road. It nestles between hills that form a soft, velvety *V,* much like the coming together of a woman's body. This is fitting somehow. I came together for the first time as a woman in that house. My body opened to David with little persuasion needed, as if it had waited all my twenty-eight years for that moment only, waited and known that it would come.

When I first saw David, tears leapt to my eyes. They say it is like that with soul mates. They say you "know." That everything about you knows: your mind, your heart, your very being.

It was like that for me. I looked at David that first time and I saw us together in a house just like the one he built for us there by that meadow, alongside our hill. I saw us working side by side in a garden of primroses and daisies, of hollyhocks and giant lilac trees. I pictured us sitting on a porch swing, holding hands on gentle spring evenings, and I imagined us swatting at gnats and scratching behind the ears of a friendly old hound with soulful eyes. I dreamt. . . .

Well, enough. As I have said, I "knew."

Shortly before we were married, David built our house; he and a small crew of workmen down from Fowey. I would bring him ice-cold bottles of his favourite dandelion and burdock drink, and then I would sit on the cob wall nearby and watch him, his muscles rippling with strength, his longish blond hair bleached by the sun. I never tired of watching David. I was like one of those politicians' wives you see, who hangs on every word.

But then when our house was finished and we turned to the garden, David wrote books while I trimmed the daisies. I wanted one of the two bedrooms as a nursery; David claimed it for his study. He took to sleeping there often after working on his pages at night.

That David and I would come to sleep apart more times than not, I did not "know." I did not foresee this as our future. There is much I did not see.

* * *

The doctor here has said that I lived on the wing of a dream. I say I lived on the breath of a prayer. From my earliest days of childhood, I can remember wanting someone "just like David." Someone with whom to share deep secrets, with whom to laugh and do mad, crazy things. David and I would burst into song together on the merest whim—loud, boisterous song of the type one learns in school: *"Row, row, row your boat, gently down the stream . . ."*

David brought me so much joy. I had only to look into his eyes, hear him speak my name, and I'd have done anything, become anything.

The doctor says that's why I'm here. That loving David so recklessly brought me pain as well.

I know the doctor is right. I see this as clearly as I still see, in my mind's eye, Pennoryn—the house we built—though it's been close on eight months now. I see the pond off to the side, and the ducklings that were born each spring. I hear the skylarks singing in the elms that scratched the windows above our bed. I see David kneeling before the big stone fireplace that final evening, adding a heavy oak log, his handsome face flushed with red from the flame.

I see the knife flashing down, sinking into his back. Blood gushes. I hear myself scream, "No!" I feel my own life leave my body and my soul meet with his. I feel us touch, come together as one flame, bonded together in death. Then I feel him wrenched away, and my flesh coming back to life. I see myself fighting it, wanting to die, to disappear, to be nothing, and in my mind I get smaller and smaller, till I am no more than a pinpoint in some vast, black tunnel. At the other end of that tunnel stands David, his hand outstretched and covered with blood. He tries to reach me, to pull me with him, but there are winds all about me now, and the winds have voices, and they tell me I have no choice this time, I cannot go.

Since then, I have lived a shadow life in this hospital—not ill, as in coma, yet not alive. For months they moved me, clothed, and fed me. They say I helped, that I knew enough to chew and slip my arms into the proper holes.

Yet I remember it not at all. It is as if, in my head, I slept. "Withdrawn," they say. A mental thing. But then little by little, there were glimpses of light. Of memory. I began to see David's face. I heard his voice as I hear it now, and it was calling to me then as now: "Joanna. Joanna come to me."

This time there are no winds, no tunnel, only my heart telling me to get out of here. Get home. There are things I must know, and the answers are all at Pennoryn.

CHAPTER 2

"What is your most vivid memory of childhood?" the examiner asks.

I answer with false excitement, knowing what they are looking for: something normal, something not laced with the kind of pain that pops out like an "inappropriate laugh" and puts one back in the bin.

I sit forward on my straight wooden chair. "I loved growing up here in Cornwall. And Mevagissey is on the coast, you know. The inner harbour was built in the early 1400s, and the town was called Lavorrick, or possibly Lammorrick, then. Of course, there are T-shirt and ice cream shops all over the place, but when I was a child—"

The examiners glance at each other. I am talking too much. *Slow down.*

"You've been to Mevagissey recently?" asks a somber man in black who looks more like an undertaker than a doctor. "Before you came here, that is?"

It has been eight months total since I arrived at Whitehurst: six of them spent in that withdrawn state, and the past two "coming back," struggling to remember what occurred in the weeks before David's death. I remember most. Still, there are huge dark holes, and when I begin to explore them I feel quite faint.

I don't tell the examiners this, of course. It's their job to either approve or disapprove the doctor's recommendation that I be allowed to leave.

"I haven't been to Mevagissey since shortly after I married," I say. "Over a year and a half now, that would be? But I have a friend there, an artist. He sends me postcards at times."

A third man with short manicured nails picks up a file and pages through it. "I see you have family in Mevagissey, as well. If you leave here, will you be going back to them?"

"No." My answer is blurted out, and again they glance at each other. "I would like to go home," I amend, with only a small tremor in my voice.

"To your house, you mean, to Pennoryn?"

"Yes."

There is a heavy silence. These men . . . these men hold my life in their hands. Without their approval to leave I am a prisoner here.

I struggle to make it sound as if my going home makes sense.

"I love Pennoryn. It's smallish and quiet, and there are trees and flowers and birds, and I can finish getting well."

"You don't feel that you're well now?"

"Oh, I didn't mean that," I rush to assure them. "I just meant that I can work my way back into ordinary life there without too much stress. Doctor Shahi advised that. Even he agrees that Pennoryn seems the perfect place."

"You were . . . disassociated for a good six months," the man with the manicure says, choosing the word carefully. I notice that a thumb nail is bitten to the quick. "You should be with people who know you, have someone to talk to."

"That won't be a problem. I have neighbours nearby."

"Charlotte Dean?"

I look up, surprised.

"Her name is in the police report," he explains. "Tell me, what do you remember of how your husband died?"

This is what I remember of the way David died, I say: I remember the knife flashing down, the terrible red gleam of firelight on steel, the almost physical plunge through my own heart. After that, nothing.

"Dr. Shahi thinks it will all come back in due time," I tell them.

"I understand the police have not closed the case . . ." a man with a yellowish bald spot says. The words dangle as he sucks his tongue, and he makes a puzzled frown, as if the bald spot were a lemon and the bitterness has seeped down.

"No. They have not."

A police inspector named Goff visited me here in the hospital the morning I "came back." He was eager to hear my story of that night, he said, as he'd been on the case from the first and only waiting for such an occasion. (They always suspect the wife or husband first in these things, or so I've heard.) But I had no memory, no story. I could not give him anything with which to trip me up, and with this he seemed displeased.

Well, one would think common sense would have sent him looking elsewhere. I'd been attacked as well, left unconscious, and there was no murder weapon about.

Furthermore, Charlotte and Henry—the Inspector himself told me—had spotted someone in dark clothes running along the road as they drove to Pennoryn for a visit that night. Police reports confirmed that there had been a burglary in the area earlier that week, at a farmhouse not more than three miles from mine.

"I believe they've decided for now that it must have been a burglar," I say.

"So we understand," the man with the yellowish bald spot answers. "And that does concern us. If the killer is still at large and learns that your memory is coming back . . . that you might now identify him . . ."

"At the slightest hint of trouble," I assure him, "I'll call the police. I won't confront anyone."

Dr. Shahi and I have been through all this: what is appropriate and what is not. In the past two months since I came back, they've had me in therapy of one sort or another all the time. So I've had to watch myself, keep on my toes.

"I'm sure Dr. Shahi told you that although you were struck on the head, your condition wasn't caused by that?"

"Yes. He said it was shock that made me withdraw from reality, into my mind."

"Tell us more about your childhood," the "undertaker" interrupts.

Anger flares. That's all they ever think about here. For two months now: "Tell us about your childhood, your childhood, your childhood." With each telling those days become smoother yet more removed, like a manuscript that is polished so often the life is wrung out, leaving it boneless and dry.

"It was a wonderful childhood," I say, trying again for animation. "I remember Mevagissey Primary, with prayers and hymns each morning, and learning to count with small shells. I remember clouds of chalk dust from the blackboard dusters, and little china wells for ink set into the desk." I lean forward, my voice rising a bit. "Down on Tregony Hill there was a pilchard factory, and the smell from it was awful. The pilchard's a horribly oily fish, you know, and we children used to sneak in after school and watch them cut off the heads and dig out the guts. Then we'd play in the wooden packing boxes. They were encrusted with scales and congealed blood . . ."

I'm satisfied to see a grimace of distaste on one pale face. "Children hardly notice those things, of course," I add with an innocent smile.

"Indeed."

There is much shifting in seats and clearing of throats.

"And your family?" the somber one asks.

"Our house was on the quay. It was centuries old, and built on a steep hill. Our front door was actually in the roof. You came in that way and walked downstairs to the living room. The banister rails were short at the top and longer at the bottom. You could run a stick along them as you descended, and the pitch would change like a xylophone."

A heavy sigh. "Mrs. Carr, this is all very fascinating. But quite frankly, what we're looking for is a psychiatric history. What was your mother like? Your father?" Another rustle of paper. "You were the youngest of four, I see. Three older brothers. Were you happy?"

I hesitate only a moment, folding my hands and leaning back in my chair. "What do you mean by happy?"

The voice rises in irritation. "Did your parents make you feel secure? Did they treat you well? Did you have close friends?"

"I had Michael."

"Michael . . . ?"

"My friend, Michael Lamb. We met at school when we were six, and stuck together from then on. Against the other children, you know."

"The others treated you badly?"

"I think they treated Michael worse than me, because his family was poor."

"Is this Michael the one who sends you the postcards?"

Their job, I remember, is to collect details like this and stick them to my chart by a pin. If I'm not careful all my memories could dry and shrivel there, like the wings of a moth. I protect them as best I can.

"Yes. Michael is an artist. He owns a gallery in Mevagissey."

I glance out the window, to grey buildings beneath a brilliant blue sky. The air is soft, and I long to be at Pennoryn. I long to lie in the meadow beneath the sun and remember . . .

I remember I had planted a bed of primroses beneath the kitchen window, and Michael came out to Pennoryn for the first time—shortly after my marriage—bringing with him a wedding gift, a stone hare. "A little friend to keep you company while you're working in the garden," he said, kneeling down on the grass beside me. "I couldn't bear to wrap him in paper. He seems to need plenty of sunshine and fresh air."

He grinned at me, his blue eyes twinkling mischievously, the way they did when we were children. And then he nuzzled my nose with that of the hare.

I laughed, so glad to see him after so long a time, and tousled his unruly black hair. We had set the stone hare amongst the primroses with his little nose and ears sticking out, and agreed that he looked rather happy there. David was working in his study and had asked not to be disturbed. When he saw the hare later he gave it only a glance. "From Michael Lamb, you say? Has he been coming here often?"

"Not at all. This is the first time."

I could see my husband wasn't happy, even so. We had fought that morning about the long hours he spent cooped away in his study. Married only three months, I was feeling neglected. Still, I wanted him to succeed. I found things to busy myself . . . the garden, the birds. We seldom had people over. "I love you, Joanna. I want you all to myself for a while," my husband would say.

An important thing, I've learned—perhaps the most important in life—is learning to read between the lines of love. There are messages there, and if we don't listen with our brains as well as our hearts, we risk not hearing them at all.

"Mrs. Carr?"

The examiner with the bald spot is speaking to me. I bring my attention back. "Yes?"

"You never did tell us about Charlotte Dean."

Strangely, there is a taste of fear on my tongue. I clear my throat. "What would you like to know? Charlotte's my friend."

"According to the police report, she and her husband were first on the scene after the incident. They found your husband dead on the floor, and you lying near the door unconscious, a wound to the head."

"Yes." *In a red negligee,* the inspector had said. Covered nicely with a small blanket I'd kept on the sofa. They don't mention that—though personally, if I were them, I'd find it quite odd I'd been covered so thoughtfully, as if by someone who cared.

"Mrs. Dean is the one who signed you in here," the examiner continues.

"Yes." Charlotte signed me into Whitehurst that night. It was my mother, wouldn't you know, who came up later and gave them the right to keep me here.

"Mrs. Dean has been here several times to see you. Do you remember any of her visits?"

"Only one, shortly after I, uh . . . came back." I still feel awkward referring to my return to conscious life.

"That was two months ago, Mrs. Carr. She hasn't returned since?"

"I . . . no."

"Yet you feel you can count on her support if we release you? If you're allowed to go home?"

"Absolutely. Charlotte's been my friend for years. I'm sure she's simply busy lately."

Still, there's a tremor in my stomach that won't go away. I'm not sure of anything any longer, and that's the truth. I simply have to *appear* certain if I'm ever to get out of here.

Mrs. Rimes, the nurse, helps me to pack. "Dr. Shahi said he'd pop in to see you," she tells me, her ruddy face folding into a bittersweet smile. "I've got to say I'll miss you, Mrs. Carr."

I give her a hug. "You never did learn to call me Joanna."

She picks up a brush, and I sit on the stiff-backed chair as she begins to run it gently through my hair. This is a daily routine, begun shortly after I came here, she has told me. "Look how long it's grown," she says now. "And only one or two grey hairs, after all you've been through. Imagine."

"One or two is a lot for thirty, Mrs. Rimes."

"Not at all. I had plenty of grey by that time. My daughter, too."

"Well, I guess I haven't really been through all that much lately, sitting here with my head in some other world. It's been rather peaceful in there."

I can see us in the dresser mirror, the kind, grandmotherly woman behind me, and my long brown hair haloed by sunlight. It is like a painting, and I remember that before I married David, I not only worked at a gallery, but haunted other galleries and museums on my days off.

My body in the mirror is still slender, but blurred, I think. I can't wait to get back to my meadow and walk. My complexion for the most part is smooth over adequate cheekbones, and I remember David saying, "You have the kind of face that will never grow old."

I lean forward and squint into the mirror. There are fine lines around the eyes, and a slight puffiness in the lids. None of this was here a year ago. I touch the lines, wondering.

There is a sound at the door, and I turn to see Dr. Shahi. He is looking pleased, as if he has pulled me back from the precipice all by himself—as in fact he nearly has. He is the one doctor here I respect. The others think the answers are in the head; Dr. Shahi looks into the heart, where he knows they hide like a frightened badger until someone risks a bite and drags them into the light.

"You look lovely, Joanna."

He is tall and dark-complexioned, with a face that is younger than his fifty years, and greying black hair that keeps springing up, no matter how many times he tries to smooth it down. His English is rather precise, with only a trace of accent remaining from his childhood years in Punjab. I have come to think of Dr. Shahi as a father, or perhaps an older brother. I return his smile. "Thank you. I'm so glad to be going home." A true flush of excitement warms my cheeks.

"As you know, your house hasn't been kept up."

"Yes. Charlotte told me, it's been held by a trustee. Without my approval no one could order repairs."

"One thing, you'll be all right financially for a while. We looked into that."

I nod. Though my personal savings account, begun years before I married David, is all but gone, the money he left me has been earning interest while I've been here.

"Remember, I'll want to see you in three weeks," he says gently. "And you've promised to call me every Friday morning at ten." This is a condition of my release, and Dr. Shahi is sensitive enough to know how much the constraint bothers me.

"I'll check in," I promise.

"And any other time, if you feel you need to talk."

"I will."

He frowns, hands in his white coat pockets. Beneath the

coat are black trousers, and on his rather small feet are highly polished black shoes. He stands with them neatly together, as if he's been taught that in school and never forgot.

"I'm just a bit worried that this may be too soon," he says.

My heart plummets. "You wouldn't—"

"Reverse my recommendation that you leave? No. But Joanna, I know how you can hide things. You and I both know that you fooled the examiners to some extent."

My nervous glance flicks away, then back. "You know this, and you're letting me go?"

"I believe it's time. Now that you're stronger physically, there's really no reason to keep you. And Joanna . . . being back at Pennoryn may help you to remember. You may need to do that before you can forget."

I laugh with only a trace of bitterness.

He smiles. "Ironic, true. But it's in your subconscious, doing unknown damage."

I sigh. "Like woodworm, I know—invisible until the house collapses." This, too, we have gone over before.

"You understand, if things don't work out . . ."

He doesn't say it, but I know. *You'll have to come back.*

He holds out his hand, and in it is a small white pouch. "A little going-away present. Lavender," he says, "for your bath." I smile and hold it to my nose, inhaling its calming scent. Dr. Shahi has a greenhouse window in his office, and every shelf is lined with herbs. He is always giving them away to patients. "It will relax you," he says.

"Thank you." I slip it into my suitcase. Mrs. Rimes bustles about, snapping the case shut, and pulling my old green coat from the closet. She sniffles.

"Take care," Dr. Shahi says.

"I will."

Part of me hates to say good-bye. The other part is like a race horse, stamping and huffing, anxious for the gates to open wide.

CHAPTER 3

It's a forty-minute drive south along the coast to Pennoryn, and the hired Ford takes the road fairly well. I relax at the wheel, relieved that Dr. Shahi has taken me out driving before this, getting me used to the feel again. Around me are the green hills and cliffs of Cornwall, to me the most beautiful sight in the world. I am so happy to be free, so light, I feel as if I and the car might rise right up and fly the rest of the way.

But—and this startles me, as it comes at me suddenly in the midst of such rosy thoughts—my husband is dead. I am going home to our house, and for the first time he will not be there. How can I feel anything other than sad? I do, however. I am elated, my spirits tossed high by this freedom. And there is something . . . something I don't quite remember nibbling at the edges of my brain. A confused sense that the freedom I celebrate is for my liberation from more than Whitehurst.

Nor is this anything new. Over and over I have said to Dr. Shahi in our sessions, "I don't understand. Why do I think of David with joy one moment, and depression the next?"

"It will come back if it's meant to," he has answered. "Meanwhile, focus on the present. Fill it with joy."

This business of focussing on the present has irritated me no end at times, but I also believe it is all that has kept me afloat. "Sufficient to the day . . . ," the Christians would say, while Dr. Shahi exhorts one to "live in the now," and I can only believe that since so many people of so many differing persuasions teach it, there must be something to it. On my better days I've nearly managed to do it.

Nibbling at soda biscuits on the seat beside me, I remember that there will be no groceries in the house. Still, I have the two pints of milk Mrs. Rimes insisted I bring, stealing them and the biscuits from the hospital kitchen. In the morning, I think, I'll go into the village. Gas and electricity were arranged from the hospital, but the telephone must be tended to in person. Afterwards, I can shop for provisions.

"You might call for a housekeeper to do things up ahead of time," Dr. Shahi suggested.

"No. I don't want anyone there just yet. I need to reclaim my home first."

The examiners found my intensity over this matter odd but not necessarily alarming. Dr. Shahi understood completely.

The sun is an hour or two over the western horizon as I take the turn inland to Pennoryn. Within ten minutes I begin to see a familiar swell of green hill, and my heart beats fast. My hands grow damp on the wheel. I press hard on the accelerator and the Ford eats up the distance. Soon I can see the tops of the elm trees that shelter our house, and then, around one last bend, Pennoryn itself. My mouth is dry.

A rambling stone cottage, Pennoryn is one storey high, with an attic. Its tall windows are trimmed in white and, like a picture postcard, it sits nestled in that gentle valley. Beside it on the left is the duckling pond, the last rays of sun casting pink upon the tall reeds that rise from it, trembling in a warm breeze.

Excitement makes every inch of me quiver, just like those reeds. *I'm home.*

I pull into the gravel drive, thrilled with the familiar crunch beneath the tyres. Parking, I jump out and stand motionless, absorbing the scene before me. My heart, I think, will burst from my chest.

It is much like the pictures Charlotte brought to me in the hospital: a front window broken by storms, the white trim flaking, weeds grown high. But I'm here. This is my house and David's, this is where our love began. I can curl up within these walls and feel my husband around me once more. I can rummage through closets and find his old flannel shirt, hold it to my breast, smell his scent and pretend he's still alive.

I run onto the porch and stand at the door, my key in a trembling hand. I turn the key and push the door open, hearing it creak. The hinges need oiling, I think. Tomorrow I'll have a glazier come out and replace the window, and after that—

I stand in the living room, looking about. In corners are cobwebs, and on the bare oak floor is powdery dust. The red-flocked wallpaper that David chose is mildewed where rain has seeped through the broken window and run down, and the curtains are faded. One is shredded along the bottom, as if some small animal has been biting at it.

I feel a sudden weight. My eyes are drawn to the floor in front of the big stone fireplace. It has long ago been scrubbed clean of blood; Charlotte saw to that when the police were finished. Still, I cannot face it yet. *Think of something simple,* I remind myself. *What needs to be done?*

On that one visit to the hospital after I "came back," Charlotte told me she had stored small valuables away in the attic. "I've locked it up to discourage any would-be thieves." Only the tables, sofa, and chairs remain down here, their faded red fabric a testimony to happier days. I can still see David reading, a cup of tea at his side, his long legs stretched out . . .

My mouth opens of its own volition and I call out, unable to stop myself: "David?" He should be hunched over the typewriter in his study. He should call back, "In a minute, Joanna," while he finishes a line or paragraph, and then he will come to help me carry the shopping, kiss me on the cheek, ask me what we are having for dinner. This I remember from our early days together—that bright honeymoon.

"David?" I call again, before the tears begin. They rush down my cheeks in a sudden torrent, like a spring river overburdened with months of accumulated snow. "Oh, David . . . where are you?"

I stumble down the hall to his study, knocking over a small table along the wall. I know my husband isn't here. I am not delusional, I'm sane. But I have to touch his desk, his chair, his things.

I fling open a door and I'm inside the room David worked in day after day, and I remember how I complained that I didn't see him enough, that he never came out. Now I think I would give anything to have him here. I'd never complain again. *Dear God, let him be here.*

It's true, I suppose, that we never know what we've got until it's gone. We pick and pick at our fortunes, finding fault, thinking that's our right. Then the gods speak. They thunder and roar, and they snatch what we've got away— often, I believe, just to show us who's in charge.

If I were to erect a sign above every door in the world, it would say: "BEWARE, ALL YE WHO ENTER HERE. JUST WHEN WE THINK WE KNOW WHAT'S WHAT . . . THEY SHOW US THAT IT'S NOT."

David's study is as thick with dust as the rest of the house. His desk faces the window overlooking my garden of primroses, and the panes are unbroken but filmed with grime. There are still manuscript papers piled beside his typewriter and scattered on the floor, overflowing the wastebasket. A red pen lies uncapped.

Why didn't Charlotte clean up in here? I wonder. She told me she took care of things—yet I feel I've entered a house of wax, where the scenes have been preserved as if the people were living in them still.

I touch the dry tip of David's red pen, remembering how ruthless he could be in destroying his work, how he'd go into dark moods afterwards, unhappy with everything, no less me. I'd come in with a cup of tea and he'd turn his back, not even looking my way.

"The boiler isn't working properly," I remember saying once. "I thought you might like this to warm you up."

"You'll use any excuse to interrupt me, won't you?" he had raged. "Why can't you take care of the boiler? For

God's sake, Joanna, call a plumber. Don't bother me with these things."

I felt terrible; I had made a major blunder in my marriage. My job as the wife of a creative person, a writer, was to protect him from the irritating, everyday details. How could he possibly create otherwise? And as for David's moods—one moment dark, the next whimsical—these were the hallmark of any great artist, were they not?

We were married three months the day we argued over the boiler, and I longed so much to be a good wife, and hopefully, to get back to the way things were when first we met. David was on holiday from London when we met, touring, and I had run from Mevagissey one day, tearing off into the countryside for a moment of peace from all the summer crowds. David's tyre had gone flat and I stopped to help, even though I'd been warned from childhood not to stop for strangers by the road. Something dark in me that day welcomed the potential danger. *Perhaps this is the way it will end,* I thought fancifully, *my body in the bracken. And people will say, "Well, I always knew she'd end that way."*

The other, saner half wished for a weapon beside me on the imitation leather seat.

As it turned out, I didn't need the weapon, but I did have a jug of cool water to offer. We sat beneath a tree at the edge of what came to be our meadow and took turns drinking from that jug. David wore jeans and a blue denim shirt. His straight blond hair was short and he wore it slicked back, in a simple cut. I remember thinking he could have been a model for men's sportswear. Still, I felt more comfortable with him than any of the London men who came to Mevagissey in business suits, carrying briefcases even while on holiday.

He told me he owned a modest bookstore in London, and I told him I worked in a gallery in Mevagissey, but little more. Questions about family I deflected with care. We talked on and on—about books we both liked, about films we'd hated. At one point David did something very funny. He stood and ran into the meadow, pulling up an old PROPERTY FOR SALE sign and slinging it over his shoulder

like a gun. Then, in imitation of a mad Peter Sellers in one
of his early movies, I can't remember which, he marched
around singing at the top of his lungs. He did it so well I
laughed until my cheeks ached.

I fell in love that day.

After a while, I reluctantly said I should go. The sun was
low and red behind the hill, and there would be incessant
questions if I returned home late.

"Perhaps I'll see you in Mevagissey," David said.
"Where exactly do you work?"

I didn't want this beautiful, exceptional man in Mevagissey around people I knew. Already he and the day had
assumed both fictional and romantic proportions in my
mind. For David Carr to walk into Morley's—for the other
clerks to whisper behind their hands and perhaps make
something dirty of what for me was somehow sacred—was
unthinkable.

If I never see him in Mevagissey, I thought, he can remain untarnished in my memory forever.

"I'll be too busy at work," I said quickly. "But if you're
staying nearby, I might see you here again tomorrow. Say
around five?"

I was startled by my forwardness, but David didn't seem
to mind. And in fact he did show up at the meadow the
next day . . . and the next.

"If you were mine, Joanna," he said at the end of that
week, his warm lips at my temple; "I would buy this land
and build you a house, right here. We'd never have to leave
each other. Would you like that, my love?"

And that was how it began.

Every weekend for seven months—right up to the January day we married—David travelled down from London
to help the workmen with our house. I pitched in, too, and
now and then David would look up from a hammer or saw
and catch my eyes on him, a pulse that I couldn't hide
beating in my throat. A flush would rise to his handsome
face, and he'd wet his lips, dropping whatever he was doing.

I had been celibate for years before David, a virgin in my
heart if not in fact. Love came belatedly at twenty-eight,

but once begun I couldn't stop. We made love the first time within the open framework of our house, with the scent of pine, cedar, and oak about us, and nettles stinging our backs. I remember spitting on a dock leaf and rubbing it on the welts on David's back—healing him, even as my other hand slid down his front, bringing back his desire so we could begin again.

"You're insatiable," he had said, laughing. But there was a fullness in his voice; David himself was insatiable then. There came a time when the lowly nettle became part of our passion, first the exquisite torture of a fine wisp drawn over the skin, causing the weals to rise, then the dock-leaf healing.

"Harder, love," David would whisper, his breath catching. "Don't use such a light hand." My fingers would shake, for I never wanted to hurt him in any way. But I would do as he asked, drawing the nettles over his shoulders, his stomach, everywhere he directed . . . and his muscles would tense, his ardour rising along with the faint pinkish welts.

When the house was finished, we married. The night before our vows David announced he was selling his shop, that he'd always wanted to write. I was surprised, but thrilled to have him home with me every day. It was the perfect wedding gift.

He needed room to work, of course, so my tentative plans for turning the second bedroom into a nursery fell by the wayside. "We need to be alone for a while anyway," David said. "Children can always come later."

We were on a modest budget, so we furnished the study with odds and ends of unmatched secondhand furniture, putting the lion's share of the pot into David's typewriter. On our first anniversary I bought him a new lamp. The old one had a broken switch, and you had to turn it on and off by twisting the bulb. Many nights I lay in our room and heard David swear as he unscrewed that bulb and burnt his hand. Then I'd listen for the study door to open, his footsteps crossing the hall.

After the first few weeks there were often no footsteps,

only my own irregular heartbeat pounding in my ears as I acknowledged that he wasn't coming, again.

There was an early spring night, however, when David did come to share our bed. He lay with his arms around me, my back against his chest. Rain tapped at the window, and the elm trees scratched overhead. David's fingers stroked my breast; his tongue played with my ear. My skin seemed on fire, every nerve bathed in heat. It had been weeks, and I turned hungrily to open my body over his. Somewhere nearby cats were mating, the fierce howl of the female like a baby's cry.

"I want your baby," I whispered urgently, drawing my husband in. "Give me your baby, David, *please.*"

Even now I can feel him pull back, feel the cold chasm of distance. I asked for too much, had too high expectations of what for him was only a moment of desire. I feel stupid and ashamed. I would cut out my tongue if it would change things, because all I wanted then was to hold him, not to feel him inching away, his eyes focused on the ceiling in that awful cold stare. "I can't give you that," he said harshly. "Drop it, Joanna."

Remembering this, the pain I felt then returns, flooding my bones. I shake myself, and wiping a finger over David's typewriter, I draw his initials in the dust: D.A.C., for David Allingham Carr.

There is a pall, now, over my homecoming. Drawn back to the parlour, I stand before the fireplace at last, to face the only memory I have of my final night with David and the terrible thing that happened here.

CHAPTER 4

The stone hearth and the floor reveal only grime, yet I fancy I can still see the stains, as one might with those tests the police now have. They spray a chemical, turn off the lights, and the hideous splashes of blood appear as if they've never been washed off at all.

I read that somewhere. I became a prolific reader while married to David, devouring books, newspapers, and journals—filling my head with trivia to keep myself from thinking that things weren't all they should be. When I read about that chemical, I thought, *It's that way in life. Just when you think your sins are washed away, some evil trickster god comes along with one of those cans and reveals them for all to see.*

I wish now there were a chemical one could spray over old events, attaching itself to any remaining auras, and frame by frame, showing one the scene. It might reveal what really happened here that night.

When I came back to myself two months ago, the hospital called the police as a matter of form. That was when the inspector, Goff, came to question me about the night David died. He sat beside my bed, a hard-faced, heavy-set man with hands that belonged more to a lorry driver than a policeman.

"Your husband was stabbed," he told me, "several times with a sharp instrument. The weapon was never found, but we believe it to have been a serrated knife, perhaps eight inches long. There was a great deal of blood. The front door had been left open, and friends of yours"—he checked a small notebook—"a Charlotte and Henry Dean found you by the door, unconscious. No blood on you, no wounds, but you'd been struck on the head."

I had learned from Dr. Shahi only that morning that David was dead. He broke it to me gently over a cup of tea, the sun shining warm on my face. Yet the thrust to my heart had a nightmarish quality; I wanted to believe I'd wake up yet again and find that none of it was true. As the inspector talked, I couldn't keep my mouth or chin from trembling. His stony gaze fixed on that as if it were a clue. I felt guilty, though I couldn't for the life of me think what I might have to hide.

"Did you or your husband have any enemies?" he asked. "Anyone who might do this?"

I shook my head. "No one. No one at all that I can think of."

"Would you know? If your husband had enemies, that is. Were you close enough to know?"

"I . . . well, of course." Oddly, I didn't feel quite certain this was true.

"Well, times have been difficult in the cities," Inspector Goff said. "More and more people out of work. Many are coming to the country looking for handouts—or worse."

He leaned forward then, his eyes seeming to scour mine in search of secrets. "On the other hand, the attack on your husband was especially vicious. Why you were spared, and to be left that way, covered over with a blanket . . ." He shook his head and seemed to wait for an explanation.

I glanced about my hospital room, my window looking out on its treeless yard. "I wasn't spared," I said.

Hours have passed. I stretch my cramped arms, which have cradled my head as I've huddled on the hearthstone, trying to force that evening back. My eyes are swollen from tears, my brain numb. I still see only the knife slashing down, and I hear only my screams.

"Go about a normal day, an ordinary routine," Dr. Shahi has advised. "Don't force it. The familiar surroundings will help. It should come back, though of course we can't be sure. You may have to live with that possibility, Joanna."

Never to remember? Never to know what happened? I cannot accept that. I would go finally, irreversibly, mad.

I haven't said this to Dr. Shahi or the examiners, of course. They wouldn't have let me out.

I haven't yet seen the kitchen, or the upstairs, the attic. I've heard slight scurryings, and know there must be a field mouse or two. We once had a whole family, the babies all pink and no larger than my little finger. David and I discovered them one day and spent half an hour oohing and aahing as if they were children of our own. I can still see David lifting one tiny baby ever so carefully, and holding it gently in his palm, then against his cheek.

"Oh, let me see!" I cried, and he leaned over and held it to my breast, bare above my shirt. The tiny feet pummeled my skin, sending an unbearably sweet thrust to my heart that was strangely like arousal. "Oh, David, this is what our baby would feel like," I said.

By evening, the field mice were gone.

As I've sat here, I've heard the cooing of pigeons as well. They must have returned to nest in the small recesses of our cob wall. I would like to walk out through the garden, swing my legs over that wall and explore the meadow— perhaps lie in the coarse grass in the dark, plotting the stars the way I so often did. But then, I think, I will wonder why the light isn't on in David's study as it always was, and I'll begin to believe that he may come out and join me at any time.

Of course he seldom did.

Brushing dust from my jeans in irritation, I turn toward our room—David's and mine—thinking I'll save the meadow for tomorrow, when the sun is low and red beyond the hill.

But our room is wall-to-wall with ghosts. I tiptoe in so as not to disturb them, for I feel I've had all I can stand for one night. I go straight to the old mahogany wardrobe where David kept his clothes. In its mirrored door I see myself, gaunt and strained, not at all the same woman who last looked into this glass. Behind me I see our bed, its four dusty posts topped with carvings of the four heads of Eros, god of love and the suffering brought on by the pangs of love. I'd always found those four heads to be frightening, but David embraced them as art.

I look for his favourite flannel shirt and cannot find it. For long anxious moments I toss things aside—jeans, work clothes, sweaters—needing to feel that shirt, to press it to my nose and sleep.

Then I remember. David was wearing it the night he died.

It takes me a while after that, but I choose, finally, an old leather jacket, smelling a bit of mildew, and stiff now from dampness and the passage of time. Most of my own clothes had been brought to me in hospital by Charlotte, and I've left them in the car along with toiletries and such. Too tired to get them out, I hear Dr. Shahi say, "Don't push yourself. Do what makes sense and no more."

It makes sense now to lie on this bed with David's jacket held against my cheek, and believe I can still smell his essence mingled with the must of time.

The hour is late, after two A.M., I think, judging by the position of the moon. It glances over the bed, casting shadows from the elms that resemble thin, waving arms. I wonder what awakened me. Then I remember that I was dreaming about Whitehurst, and hearing the soft bells that paged the doctors for their rounds.

I can still hear them, in fact, the way you can sometimes hear a radio just after you've turned it off. I wonder if the hospital bells will always be with me now—if I'll never forget them as long as I live.

CHAPTER 5

In the morning things are better. There is sun, and finches are chattering in the lilac trees. Looking out the side kitchen window I see the duck pond, deep green water shimmering in widening circles as a mallard head bobs down, looking for food.

Though the restless night has drained me of energy, I can't wait to start settling in. Grabbing a quick breakfast of soda biscuits and milk, I decide to pretend that I've simply returned from a long holiday, and now must put things in order. I drag my cases from the car, shower and dress in clean jeans and a shirt, then rummage through the attic for items Charlotte stored away.

There isn't a great deal of value. Most of my savings from before marriage were used to build Pennoryn, and afterwards, David insisted we live off the proceeds from his book shop. I'd have continued to work, either at Morley's in Mevagissey or somewhere in our village, but David wouldn't have it. "I've got my pride, you know, and I won't have people saying I can't take care of my wife."

I didn't argue. I was far too happy then. We lived on a small budget—small, because David watched every penny, though in fact he'd come out of the sale of his shop with a tidy sum. "One never knows what might happen," he said, and I understood that, having grown up in an orphanage, he worried there might never be enough. I stretched every pound and we ate simple meals, made do with clothes we brought to our marriage, and only a handful of times went up to London to the theatre.

David's ancient record player sits on a shelf in a corner, and beside it are stacks of his collectors' albums. He began collecting before we were married, his favourites being hit songs from the forties in the U.S. I plug the record player in, put a record on without looking at it, and turn the switch. The turntable spins, the arm drops, and I hear Margaret Whiting's clear-as-a-bell tones. She tells us about lost love, and how the lovers carved the words "I'll love you till I die" on a tree when first they met, words lovers everywhere tell each other when first they meet and fall in love.

When David and I were still building our house we would sit some nights before the finished hearth with a picnic and wine, a hearty log crackling. The old record player would be beside us, all but its pristine needle battered and worn.

I remember David saying one night as this song played, "Joanna . . . I will love you till I die."

With an angry flick of my hand I knock the record player arm. The needle flies across the grooves, screeching to a halt. *You lied!* I think. *Damn you, you lied!*

And again there is that heavy, confusing weight all about me.

Like clouds moving in.

CHAPTER 6

The rest of the morning I busy myself with knocking down cobwebs, sweeping, making a list of things to be done and provisions needed. That afternoon I don a soft pink dress that I've found in the attic, and feel I'm almost back to normal as I walk slowly through the village near Pennoryn.

The changes here are few on the surface. However, Charlotte told me that day when she came to Whitehurst that there are many newcomers, people from the Midlands finding our out-of-the-way town at last and moving in. There are more young women with babies in strollers, and the harbour has been widened. There are several leisure craft in sight, yet it's still a working port. The fishing boats are the same old toshers I remember—old-timers trying to keep their trade alive.

Two new shops have opened, I note. One is a yarn shop featuring Christian de Falbe, Lister, and Rowan, according to a sign in its window. The other is a small art gallery: "Harbourside." It looks much like Morley's in Mevagissey, the gallery I worked in before marrying David. There are oil paintings and watercolors in the window, and a large model of a sailing ship.

A particular seascape catches my eye. The waves are filled with a tender light, the kind seen in Cornwall only on rare July evenings when the heat has been warming the cliffs for a day. The waves seem to rise from their canvas and roll gently toward me as if alive.

I feel a tug, a welling of love untainted by loss, something joyous that has been missing from my heart for a very long time. *Michael.*

Leaning forward, I squint, my nose against the glass. Yes, there it is, the bold scrawl in the lower right corner of the canvas: *M. Lamb.*

I am more thrilled than surprised to see it here. Michael's paintings have been shown in galleries everywhere, from London to New York. But his work in this window today is like a special welcome home.

I wander inside, eager for more. There are three, all depictions of Mevagissey. They take up an entire wall. One is of Hitler's Walk, the grassy cliffs from which they say you could see the flames of Plymouth during Hitler's Luftwaffe raids. The others are of the port: the old fish cellars, the inner and outer harbours with boats bobbing at anchor, the ancient stone houses climbing the hill.

Looking more closely I am surprised to see that my own family's house by the quay is missing. One can see it clearly on picture postcards. Yet on his canvas, Michael has painted in trees.

"May I help you?" the shop assistant enquires. He is young, with glasses, and rather thin.

"These paintings. Do you know the artist?"

The clerk nods and pushes the glasses up on his nose with a finger. "Michael Lamb. Fabulous work, don't you think?"

"Yes. Have you met him? Has he been here personally?"

"Only once that I remember, when we first opened up. But he'd be in touch with the owner, I should think. That'd be Mr. Talbert. He's off on a buying trip today."

I continue to stare at the third painting, curious about those trees.

"Are you interested in buying?" the clerk asks. "There's another one, over there." He motions to the wall behind me.

I turn, expecting another scene of Mevagissey—and freeze. Blood rushes to my face.

Centered on the wall is a large portrait of me at eleven. *But no, it can't be me. Everything is wrong.* The girl on the canvas is fresh, she is innocent. She smiles angelically at a small bird she holds cupped in her hands. Her hair is golden brown; it falls to her waist in glossy waves. She wears a shimmery, pale-blue dress that tells one somehow that she is cared for and loved, that she will go to school dances and have wonderful dates, and that there will be good men constantly after her hand.

This isn't me. Yet it surely is meant to be. The features and hair are mine as a child, and there is a familiar ring fashioned of sea grasses, entwined, on the third finger of the girl's left hand. Michael made that ring for me when I was thirteen. He placed it on my finger the day—

My heart begins to pound. Without so much as a thank-you, I run from the gallery, the clerk's concerned queries following me through the door. "Is something wrong? Miss, are you all right?"

I stand for a moment in too-bright sunlight and wish to be anywhere but here, here on this street, unprotected, alone. The way my heart is hammering, I believe I might die.

Beside the grocery shop is a public phone. I run for it, jamming a hand in my bag, looking for change. "If it gets to be too much," I hear Dr. Shahi say, "ring me. I'll be here." My hand touches the receiver, grabbing it up. I feel the cold weight and try to formulate my plea: "I'm not doing well. I'm confused—and afraid."

But then I know he will say, "It's all right, Joanna, calm down," and I know he'll reassure me and remind me that I can always come back.

He may even insist I come back.

Deliberately, I slow my breathing and replace the receiver on its hook. Through the glass I see old Mrs. Garber standing in front of her dry goods shop, a broom in hand, eyeing me curiously. "Is that you?" she asks, peering myopically my way.

"Good morning, Mrs. Garber," I answer, calmer now. I come round the booth, taking a tissue from my bag and dabbing at the perspiration on my upper lip. "Yes, it's me, Joanna."

"Good heavens. I didn't know you were home."

Her tone conveys that she isn't at all sure I should be, and I know that for the next hour or more she will be on her party line, spreading the word.

"Are you better now?" she asks, her voice quavering. "You aren't mad anymore?"

I can't help smiling. In days past Mrs. Garber would ask me about David. "Did he sell that book yet?" she'd heckle, knowing full well that if he had, a check would have come and Mr. Barty, the postmaster, would tell everyone in town.

"I thought he was foolin' himself," Mr. Barty would say, *"him so snooty and keepin' to 'imself as he does. But bugger me, looks like he's done it!"*

"I wasn't mad, Mrs. Garber," I say. "Just sort of away. And yes, I'm better. That's why they let me out."

For the moment, I almost believe it's true.

I see to having the telephone connected and then shop for provisions with all the fervour of one who has been denied the pleasure for far too long. Putting flour and butter in a basket, I follow them with lean meat, crispy-fresh carrots, and two large potatoes. I pick up a brown onion and sniff it, hoping it's sweet. I remember Mrs. Rimes, my nurse, saying that one can put up with a lot in pasties—a limp crust, a meat that isn't as tender as you like—if the seasoning is sweet. "Same thing with a man," she added, pleased when I laughed.

I add the onion to my bounty and hear my name called out. "Joanna!"

With a start, I turn to see Charlotte just behind me, a head of cabbage looking out of place in her delicate, ring-bejeweled hand. Her blonde hair is pulled into a stylish twist, as if she's just had it done.

"I can't believe it's you!" She drops the cabbage into the bin and stands with arms slack at her sides, looking confused, perhaps even hurt. "What are you doing here? Why didn't you call? I'd have come for you . . ."

I cannot say, *Thinking of you makes me afraid, and I don't know why.* I have felt this since the examiners asked me about her. *She hasn't been to see you in two months,* they said. The implication being, *Are you certain you can rely on her? Is she truly a friend?*

Though I defended her then, I felt fear, and I am oddly nervous and evasive with her now. I run through excuses, trying to make them sound true to someone who knows me better than I sometimes know myself.

"The doctor said it would be good for me to do it alone, Char. And I thought you might be busy."

"Busy! Joanna, for God's sake . . ."

"It's all right, really. It's been fine."

Further meaningless words are bandied about, and finally she throws her arms around me and hugs me. "Oh, never mind. I'm just so glad to see you! Can we go somewhere? Have you had lunch?"

Her sea-green eyes are bright with tears that I can only believe are from joy.

"Yes," I say. "Lunch would be fine."

Our table at the Gull Cafe overlooks the harbour. Sunshine glints off blue water, and rainbows bounce from Charlotte's wedding ring as she lifts her glass of wine.

"How is Henry?" I ask.

"Same as ever—an old dear. Henry's never been anything but."

"You're a very lucky woman." Henry is her friend, her defender in all things.

"I am," she agrees. "Of course, nothing is ever perfect . . ." She gives a delicate shrug.

"You're not having trouble?"

Glancing away briefly, she says, "No . . . no, not at all. It's only that Henry's seventy now. I worry about his health."

"Have you been abroad lately?"

"Only to Greece, a few months ago. We didn't stay long." She looks embarrassed, possibly at having had a good time on holiday while I was ill.

We order salads, and seeing my friend again, I wish I had spent the past two months eating berries and twigs. She is thirty, the same age as I, yet her cheeks are still fashionably hollow, and she wears a flowing white dress

with a narrow gold belt at a twenty-inch waist. By old habit
I suck my stomach in as we talk. It flattens for a moment,
then betrays me by pouching out in a whoosh when I'm
forced to breathe. It has ever been thus between Charlotte
and me.

"I'm so glad you're back, Joanna. I've missed you."

I search her eyes. "Have you?"

"Of course! And I really don't understand why you
didn't tell me you were coming home. I could have made
things ready for you."

"I . . . I wanted to do it myself."

There is an edge to her voice. "Even so, you might have
called."

My eyes meet hers across the table, and I see the gulf
between us. She has absolutely no understanding of what I
feel, of how it is to return from the dead to a life that's
a'shambles. I can't fault her for this. While I've been gone
for all of eight months, Charlotte has shopped for groceries, lunched with friends, watched news on the telly, made
love in the dark. She has no frame of reference for what
I've been through, or how it feels to be a stranger in your
own land. Driving into the village it was as if I'd been gone
for years, not months; I barely remembered the streets.
Looking about the Gull I note the kitchen has been widened; my favourite table is gone.

And I feel as if people are watching from behind my
back.

Studying me, Charlotte asks, "How are you now,
Joanna? When I last saw you, there were . . . well, certain things missing from your memory." She looks down at
her salad and stares at it intently. "Especially that last
night. Has . . . has anything come back?"

"Of that night? No. And there are other holes. It's
strange, Charlotte. I think I remember most of the past
two years since I married David. But now and then I'll be
thinking of things and it's as if I'm walking into a pit. My
heart plummets, things go dark, and I start to feel afraid."

Charlotte sets her fork aside and sits with her hands
folded under her chin. Her eyes close momentarily as if
she is choosing her next words. Finally she gives a shrug as

if discarding them all and asks instead, "What does your doctor say?"

"He thinks it will all come back, given time, and now that I'm home. Charlotte . . . tell me again. What do you remember about that night?"

She sighs, then takes a sip of wine and sets it down. "Joanna, we went over and over it that day in hospital when you woke up."

"Came back," I say. "I wasn't asleep, so it was more like coming back. Catatonia, it's called. In therapy the past two months they said I was repressing something quite painful, that I probably withdrew because I didn't want to remember that night." I lean forward, fixing her gaze. "Charlotte . . . was there something else, do you think, something besides the obvious—what happened to David—that I might not want to remember?"

Her tone becomes irritable. "How could I know that, Joanna? I wasn't there, how could I possibly—"

"But you found us—you and Henry. You said we had plans at Pennoryn that night for a late dinner, and when you arrived you found us like that. You didn't see anything? Anyone? Something that might be a clue?"

She runs slender fingers through her hair, and a single golden strand falls over her cheek. "I've already told you, and I told the police the same thing that night. There was someone in dark clothes running along the road."

"The burglar, yes I know. Or someone they thought had burgled a house nearby earlier."

"And the police decided it must have been him. He must have broken in and you and David caught him in the act, and he killed David so he wouldn't be able to identify him."

"That's what the police said, yes. I know. But then why didn't he kill me, too?"

She flings out a hand. "For heaven's sake, I don't know! I don't have the answers you need, Joanna. Perhaps David fought with him and the burglar fought back, that's all. And perhaps as he was running out, trying to get away, he knocked you down. We did find you by the door."

I fiddle with my water glass, letting all that sink in. It makes sense, yet . . .

"Charlotte, the inspector who visited me in the hospital said I was in a negligee. A red satin negligee."

Again she lifts the wine and takes a long, deliberate sip. "I . . . well, yes, I suppose so. What of it?"

"Char, if you and Henry were coming to dinner, why wasn't I dressed?"

She blinks, then gives a light, dismissive laugh. "Don't you remember? You often wore a negligee or wrap while you were putting on your makeup to go out, or when guests were coming."

"Still . . . red satin? Ordinarily when I was doing my hair or putting on makeup, I wore something simple and cotton that could be washed."

She gestures irritably with the wine glass and a drop spills onto the white tablecloth. "For God's sake, Joanna! So you did it differently that night. Who knows why?"

"But the inspector said—or perhaps he only insinuated —that David and I were having an 'intimate evening.' We wouldn't have been doing that if you were expected for dinner."

My friend's mouth flattens into a grim line as she sets down her glass. "I really don't think I want to talk about this any longer." She sits straight in her chair, squaring her shoulders. "Joanna, you are my best friend, and we've hardly seen each other in eight months. May we drop this, please, and talk about something more pleasant? Tell me about Pennoryn. Are you finding things all right? Do you need anything?"

I open my mouth to argue and ask one more question, then close it, remembering that this is much the same thing that happened the last time I saw Charlotte at the hospital. I pounced on every word, while she drew away. It must be difficult, I realise, to be so consistently hounded to fill in holes.

"Pennoryn is fine. I'll be fine," I say, going back to my salad. "The gardens are a mess, but it'll be good therapy getting them into shape."

"How are you getting around?"

"I've hired a car until I can pick up the Fiat. I suppose I should come for it soon."

"No hurry. It's just sitting there in the garage, it hasn't been a bother."

"Still, I should turn in the rental car and pick it up. Would Friday be all right?"

"Joanna—" Charlotte looks at me impatiently. "For heaven's sake, you know you can come any time. Just give me a ring first, and we'll give the battery a jump."

She smiles reminiscently. "Do you remember how that stubborn little car wouldn't start, the day you and David were married?"

Colour rises to her cheeks, as she wonders if it was all right to remind me of this.

"Yes," I say with a catch in my throat. "You were my matron of honor . . . and you looked so lovely in that flowered linen dress."

Her smile softens. "I still have it hanging in my attic."

She reaches over and takes my hand. "Joanna, I know things are strained. Let's give it time. My God, we've been friends for years. We'll get back to the way we were."

The catch in my throat becomes a lump. It is difficult to speak. "I'm not sure about that. I'm not sure of so much these days."

Charlotte frowns, her hand tightening over mine. "You'll forget, you'll move on."

"Perhaps."

Releasing my hand, she sits back, her eyes suddenly angry. "You were always far too intense about David, Joanna."

My laughter is defensive. "I was in love. Love is intense." A brief thought races through my mind: If anyone should know about passion, it would be Charlotte. And then a word comes—a word that shocks me to the core, and I cannot even begin to believe I've thought of it in reference to Charlotte. The word is *slut.*

I reach for my water glass again, wrap my fingers around it, and barely restrain myself from throwing it at my friend. The impulse shakes me. *My God—what is wrong?*

"You lost yourself in David," Charlotte continues angrily, oblivious to my confusion. "You lost Joanna."

My fingers tighten on the glass. "That isn't true. He kept to himself all day, every day . . . I nearly lived alone."

"Still, you didn't build a life for yourself—"

"You know damn well I tried! I wanted a baby, but David refused. He said we weren't ready."

My friend looks pointedly at my rigid hand on the ice-cold glass. "Perhaps he was right."

With a difficult exercise of will I tilt the water to my mouth, then set it carefully down. "I wasn't like this back then, Charlotte."

She touches my hand again, a light feathery touch that for some reason chills me, making me pull away.

"I didn't mean to imply you were," Charlotte says with a slight narrowing of her eyes. "I just think you need to move on now as quickly as possible. Put all that business of David behind. Joanna, we cannot do one bloody thing to change the past."

"But I don't want to change it! I only want to *know* about it!"

She glances away.

"What is it?" I say sharply. "What's wrong?"

The green eyes swing back to me. "Just be careful what you ask for, Joanna. Knowing may not be . . . safe."

"And what the bloody hell does that mean?"

The eyes close briefly as she shakes her head. "Why not let all this go? David is dead, Joanna! He's buried in that grave up in London, and he's never coming back!"

"I know that," I snap. "I know it all too well. And I still don't understand why you didn't insist he be buried here."

"Me! I had nothing to say about it, he'd put it in his will. He wanted to be in London."

"Even so, you might have argued it for me."

"Joanna, for God's sake, do you hear yourself? Let it go. Believe me, you're better off."

"Better off? Why do you say that?" Again, the taste of fear, like bitter copper on my tongue.

But Charlotte doesn't answer. While I down a slice of

saffron cake for dessert, she sips black coffee, her disapproving lips barely touching the cup.

An hour later we stand on the grassy bluff outside town, the way we have in times past. The angry words are forgotten for the moment. We hold each other's hands in easy friendship and look down at the village. Gulls wheel and cry above a fleet of fishing boats making their way out to the Channel. Sometime before dawn the boats will return, and the harbour will buzz with life. The fish merchants will toss their flat wooden boxes onto the decks, and using great scoops, the fishermen will fill them. People will come from miles around to inspect the catch and hear tall tales.

It has been this way for over a century or more. For the fishermen in this village, time has stood still.

"I've missed you so much," Charlotte says, and she puts her arm about me, offering love to heal the breach. Her hair has come untwined; long blonde strands blow softly about her face.

"I've missed you too," I say. My own arm slips around her waist. It's as if we were teenagers again, just meeting, and vowing we'd always be friends. That day floods back to me now, more sharp and clear than any memory of recent times: Charlotte, her face flushed and angry, yelling at a threatening bunch of girls at school.

"Give that back! Give it back right now!" she had screamed. She was new, sixteen, and her parents had moved to Mevagissey when her father took an early retirement from his work as a solicitor in London. Charlotte was lovely, but rather standoffish at first—snooty, some of the girls thought—and the two things combined made her a target.

On this particular day a small group of girl bullies cornered her in a desolate area behind the school building and grabbed a notebook from her. It was one of those simple little lined notebooks one buys at any store, but the cover was rather exotic, with brilliant tropical birds amid glossy jungle trees. Up till then the rest of us had been content with our cheap black-and-white-marbled notebooks, and Charlotte was perceived, I suppose, as flaunting both her style and wealth.

I came upon the scene and felt empathy for her immediately. I, too, was an outsider at school, though for other reasons. I saw this girl I barely knew standing there, her back against a brick wall, mouth grim, eyes flashing angrily. Two larger girls held her in place by standing nearly nose-to-nose with her, taunting and jeering as one of their comrades stood off to the side and held the notebook aloft, teasing.

"Give it back, you bloody bitch!" Charlotte yelled. "Give it back right now!"

I remember feeling shock at her language, as it didn't seem to fit that beautiful cool creature at all. I was even further shocked when she raised a fist and swung, punching one of the girls square in the jaw. As her tormentor fell back, Charlotte broke away, going for the notebook. Then she was grabbed by an arm, and the girl with the book began to tear pages out, crumpling and tossing them at Charlotte's face.

It wasn't a fair fight at all, and that's when I entered the fray. I ran at the girl—Phyllis Lye, I remember, a rather solid and mean-spirited lass—taking her by surprise. I grabbed the notebook out of her hand, then threw myself at her friend, who was holding Charlotte fast by the wrist. She lost her grip and Charlotte was free again. The two of us turned on the girls—Charlotte with fists clenched, ready to tangle with them—and me with her wondrous notebook gripped tightly in one hand, my heavy book bag in another.

"Leave her alone!" I hollered, waving the bag by its strap. "Get away! Go on!"

I'm sure Charlotte and I, just the two of us, would have been no match for this bunch under other circumstances. But I was known as being rather quiet and shy, not someone who would ever cause trouble or even enter into it. The girls stood for a moment with their mouths agape. Charlotte took the opportunity to surge forward menacingly. "Get away or I'll kill you!" she yelled, reaching down and grabbing up a rock. I followed right behind swinging that bag, and Phyllis, who seemed to be the ringleader, stared a moment, then gave a careless shrug. "Oh, bloody hell," she muttered, turning to the other girls. "Forget it." With that, they all miraculously turned on their heels and went away.

Charlotte and I looked at each other, shocked that we'd won, and finally we laughed. We sat on the ground, our backs to the brick wall, and caught our breath. I gave her the hapless notebook and said, "Sorry—looks like there's not much left. Was there something important in it?"

"No. It's blank."

I turned and looked at her. "Why didn't you just let them have it, then?"

The stony expression on her face, the tone in her voice, both chilled and somehow thrilled me. "Nobody takes what's bloody mine," she cursed through gritted teeth.

Nobody takes what's mine.

Here was a woman—for that's what she was, even at sixteen—who wasn't afraid to stand up for herself, to protect herself. I admired that, as it was something I needed to do more often in my own life. I also admired Charlotte's style and the educated way she spoke. There was no West Country dialect in her speech at all, and through the next years I worked at removing mine. I patterned myself after Charlotte in other ways as well, reading the same books and studying many of the same subjects. Though Charlotte went away to school the following year, she brought her textbooks and notes home and gave them to me when each term was done. I was ravenous for knowledge, eager to become just a fraction of what I deemed my new, well-bred friend to be.

As for Charlotte, she never got over how I'd leapt to her defense. She admired me for sticking my neck out when I didn't have to. Charlotte's fierce loyalty, and my rather awestruck admiration for her, is what's kept us together, I suppose—even when we've not agreed on things.

"Have you heard from Michael lately?" she asks now, bringing me back.

We begin to walk. "When I came back to myself in hospital, they gave me a shoebox. It was filled with postcards and letters. Michael kept writing, even though no one knew if I'd ever come round."

"Well, he was always devoted to you."

"My nurse, Mrs. Rimes, read Michael's notes to me as they came. She hoped they might filter through."

"Did they?"

"I don't really know. I haven't any memory of it, but they say it's possible I heard and they helped to bring me back. Your visits, too, of course."

I don't ask where she was these past two months, why she stopped visiting abruptly. There is, as earlier, a tiny edge of trepidation, a reluctance to know the truth. That I feel this confuses me, and for the moment I would rather not dwell on it.

"Are you planning to see Michael?" Charlotte asks. There is a tension in her voice that makes me wonder. "Does he know you're out of hospital?"

"No. I haven't told anyone in Mevagissey."

She stops walking and looks at me sharply. "Your mother?"

"No."

"But surely it would be good to work through—"

"No." I frown at her angrily. "That's final, Charlotte."

With that, the moments of closeness are over. We stand on either side of the gulf again, and for the rest of the afternoon we fail to touch.

Back at Pennoryn I put the shopping away, then change into jeans and walking shoes. Taking David's jacket with me, I go out into the garden, which is overgrown with tall weeds and grass that needs to be mown. But the evening sun is warm, and the birds, I am thrilled to see, have come out to greet me; they chatter happily in the trees. A small family of grouse minces off into a dense thicket of yellow furze. One tiny head turns my way, the beak tilting up like a nose, as if its owner is offended to find me here. The grouse have taken over; this is their home now. When I come out here to walk I will be an interloper for a time.

I pass the daisy bed that I tended so carefully, now grown wild, and the tall row of lilacs. They need to be trimmed, and the roses, too. Once heavy with blossom and scent, the roses are smallish and bug-bitten now. A few primroses, however, have fooled nature by struggling through, untended, from last season. They poke through dense weeds. I stop and bend down, remembering the little stone hare that Michael gave me as a wedding gift, three months after my marriage to David.

But the hare isn't here. Its nose isn't poking out of the greenery the way it always did before. I feel a pang, and wonder if some thief has come and carried it away.

Yet it wasn't valuable, except to me. Just to be sure, I push the weeds aside, thinking it may be hiding towards the back. But, no—not even an impression in the ground. The stone hare has been gone for a time.

A feeling of loss overtakes me. There is less pleasure in the garden after that, and I hurry on, knowing what lies ahead. Reaching the cob wall I ease myself over and am on the other side.

With that one small motion I am where I want to be at last.

As in the village, there is little change here in the meadow where David and I met. The wildflowers and herbs that grow at my feet might be the same as then. Unlike people, nature keeps coming back.

Dr. Shahi would say that people do that as well, returning for successive lives. I would like to believe him. But if it's true, I wonder, why can't we recognise the ones we've lost? A rose is still a rose, and clover will always be clover. If David is walking this earth right now, why is it I can't see and know him? I would give the very breath that governs my life for that.

These are the kinds of thoughts I never could have shared with the examiners, or even Dr. Shahi—though Michael would understand.

Michael. The portrait in town is still sharp in my mind. Of all people, for Michael to have painted me that way.

I find my old spot beneath the huge oak tree where David and I had our picnics, and where we so often made love in those early days. Dropping his jacket to the ground,

I rest my head on its leathery cushion and stare up at the sky, feeling the last rays of sun steal in from the horizon, gently warming my face. My thoughts move back to Michael and the sea-grass ring. Alone, with no one to see, I am able to remember it now—that day I turned thirteen—and the dark, hellish days before it.

There had been finger-pointing all my life, for Mevagissey was a small town, not quite so built up or invaded by tourists as now. Everyone knew what went on behind their neighbours' closed doors, not that they'd do anything to stop it, even if it were criminal. People kept to themselves that way. That's why it had to be Michael who finally saved me.

Growing up with three brothers, I played with boys much of the time. Besides the pilchard factory, we spent hours around the boatyards. I was ambivalent about that, for my father had worked at Tommy Mayhew's. One day an unskilled apprentice drilled up from beneath a deck, and the bit went straight through my father's knee. He was crippled from then on, unable to work, and that's when the drinking began.

Tommy Mayhew's was an old boatyard, with an ancient timber frame that was warped and twisted from salt air and time. Hundreds of small holes in the roof allowed in circles of light, illuminating the dusty air. On a sunny day one could imagine that a silver ball hung there, the kind you see in dance halls. As gulls passed over, the circles of light would caper and prance, and the entire ugly place became a rustic fairyland.

My brothers, needing to stay out of our father's reach as much as I, used Mayhew's as a hiding place. They discovered an isolated corner behind huge stacks of timber, where we wouldn't be seen. We would sit there for hours, my brothers sneaking a smoke, and me daydreaming, or reading a book. As they grew older, my brothers would sometimes bring in ale. For a while the only danger at Tommy Mayhew's was that we might be caught and our father told, and then we'd be beaten—or worse, not allowed to return. Little did I know how relatively tame a danger that would prove to be.

It was painfully embarrassing when at ten my body began to change. Up to then I had been more comfortable with boys than girls. Michael was my best friend from first grade on, and I'd always felt at ease with him. He never judged me for having a drunken father, never indulged in gossip the way girls did. And despite his family's poverty, Michael had a good mind. He was finer than my teenaged brothers, who seldom washed or changed their clothes, running wild behind the back of a mother who had escaped into a world of food and Cornish mead, growing ever and ever duller in mind as the years went by. She was shunned by all our neighbours, finally; and I had no friends except for Michael, who looked beyond my chagrin about my family to the "normal" child I struggled so hard to be.

Then my body betrayed me; it began to change. I was startled that it happened so early, and there was no talking to my mum. I took to wearing heavy sweaters, thinking to hide the fact. But in summer I had to shed all that wool, and finally it was Michael who said, "I think you should be careful, Joanna. You shouldn't wear that shirt. It's much too small."

Michael was my age, only ten, but he was quiet and thoughtful, wise beyond his years. And once he pointed out the dangers, I began to see things that till then had gone by my head. That following day I looked up from my book at Tommy Mayhew's and saw my brothers' eyes on me. Ian was the boldest, and the one with the most ale in him, ordinarily. I think it was he who stirred up Denny and Joseph.

I never suspected a thing.

"Are ya doin' it with that little boyfriend of yours?" Ian said that day, his voice slurring.

"What?" I asked, bewildered. I truly did not understand.

"You know, are ya doin' it with your little boyfriend, Michael?"

He laughed derisively, catching my brother Joseph's eye. "Bet the kid doesn't have one—or if he does, he can't figure out what to do with it."

The taunting went on, with me growing ever more

ashamed and red-faced, for now I did understand. This was something that was talked about behind closed doors in our village, or snickered about behind children's hands.

". . . teach her how, don't you think?" Ian said to Joseph and Denny, downing his bottle of ale.

He slipped over beside me, putting a hand behind my neck. His breath smelled of malt and leftover lunch—sausages it was that day. His other hand slid inside my cotton shirt, grabbing my breast and rubbing. I shrank away, feeling hot, then cold, so embarrassed and afraid I could hardly speak.

"Don't, Ian!" I scrabbled backwards, and as my brother laughed I realised I had backed up into Joseph, who had always been my ally in times of trouble. He would help me, I knew. But Joseph's rough workman hands came down on my shoulders and pushed me to the floor. His breath, too, was sour with ale. His face moved above me, and I saw his eyes, unfocussed, bleary. His mouth came down, fastening on mine.

The mood changed quickly, then, from teasing to dark, and innocent as I was, I knew that there would be no stopping my brothers, no going back to even five minutes before. From that day on, nothing would ever be the same.

When it was over they made me sit up and say I was all right, that I didn't mind, and wouldn't tell anyone. I remember I felt terrible physical pain, and that I was screaming inside, and later I wondered why I hadn't screamed on the outside as well, and brought the boatyard workers running. Oddly, I was the one who felt guilty, who couldn't meet anyone's eyes.

My brothers left me there and went back to work. I huddled in a corner. Sun-motes came through the holes in the ceiling and danced over my arms, but they didn't lighten my heart as they had before.

It went on that way for the next three years, from once to several times a week. My brothers would order me to come to the boatyard, and I'd obey—for I'd learned that if I didn't, they would find me wherever I hid, and then it would be worse. Finally they did it even at home, with our father looking on and applauding their manliness, a kitchen tumbler full of whiskey in one hand and himself in the other. I don't know where my mother was.

There was no one I could tell. Not even Michael; I was too mortified for that. But then the day came when I turned thirteen, and my brothers invited several of their friends to help me "celebrate" that landmark occasion at an isolated spot on the cliffs. If Michael hadn't somehow heard about it, hadn't got there in time, I doubt I'd be alive today. If they'd left me breathing, I'm certain I would have jumped from those cliffs to my death.

Michael, I think, *dear Michael. You, of all people, know the ugly truth behind that falsely radiant, child-like face you painted in oils.*

Thinking of this, I lie all night in the rough grass of the meadow, missing my friend. I must call him. In the morning, I will.

With that resolved, I begin to feel at peace. But then, drifting into that netherworld before sleep, some terrible shift takes place in time. I feel David's hands on me suddenly, and the words in my ear frighten now, rather than entice. David's mouth swoops down on mine, biting hard as he draws a handful of nettles over my breast. They hurt, and I hear myself crying, "No, David, please don't do that, please, it hurts," and I hear his soft laughter, his voice persuading, "You'll liked it, Joanna, trust me, you will."

But I never liked it, I remember now. Not ever. And the nettles were only the beginning. There was so much more.

Angry, I push my dead husband's jacket away and close my eyes, wishing David away as well.

In the morning there is a cold, dank fog. I am cramped and stiff, and tears have left salt on my cheeks. I rise and slip my arms into David's jacket, having nothing else for warmth. Stuffing my hands into the pockets for the first time, I feel a piece of paper and draw it out.

On yellowed parchment is a note. *David,* it reads, *I can't keep on with this charade. I must see you. Meet me in the meadow after Joanna leaves for town.*

The signature is clear, and matches the flowery handwriting of the note, a handwriting I've known for fifteen years. *Charlotte*. The note is to David—from Charlotte.

CHAPTER 7

It is too much, suddenly. Too much pain, and too many questions. I feel I am in one of those nightmares where you think you're awake but your vision is skewed; everything is topsy-turvy, blurred, and not even walls are where you expect them to be.

But the question batters my mind, it must be let out. *Were Charlotte and David having an affair?*

I cannot believe it. Yet the note in my hand is evidence of some sort of collusion. And it is a measure of the distance between Charlotte and me that I am unable to pick up the phone and ask her about it straight out.

I don't know what to do. In time there will be an explanation, I tell myself, one I can accept. Meanwhile, rather than go mad thinking about it, I launch into a massive cleaning of the house, throwing myself into work so that I will not have to think. Work has served to protect me in times past; it will serve me now.

The living room is done. At least, dust has been removed. But I no longer want the dark wallpaper David chose, nor the heavy furniture. Later I will go into town and see about supplies—wallpaper, paint, materials for curtains. I'll buy a paper and scan the advertisements for furniture. It will keep me occupied.

Charlotte never liked David's choice of furnishings, either, I remember. She felt they were depressingly baroque.

Charlotte, David, Charlotte, David. Despite my earlier

resolution, I cannot get them out of my mind. I stand in the kitchen doorway and remember a scene: David with his hand on Charlotte's slender white arm. She turning to him —and what is that on her face? Excitement? I cannot be sure.

David had been showing her round the kitchen. I'd heard him from the dining room where I sat with Henry, going on and on, telling her how he was raised in an orphanage and had always longed for a real home. David's ideas of what constituted a "real home" came largely from decorating magazines and old films from the era of his childhood. Our fridge, while new, resembles an old-fashioned standing icebox, and the white-and-black range has curved legs and a cooktop with an attached oven at eye level on the side, circa 1930.

"Joanna did up the curtains," I heard him say. With those, at least, I'd had my way. I'd chosen a breezy blue and white gingham check, with a matching cloth for the round oak table in the bay window.

I stepped into the kitchen that night and saw through Charlotte's eyes the plants hanging at each window, the copper mold gleaming so brightly, the almost frantic, nostalgic attempt to re-create something one has never, in fact, known.

I wondered if she was laughing at us. Pennoryn, for all our trouble, could not hold a candle to the elegantly appointed Dean mansion.

But then I saw David's hand on her arm, and his mouth at her ear. He was whispering something, and I saw her look up at him. A dull red flush began at her neck above the slim white dress, rising to her face. I had only that one brief moment to assess her reaction before they saw me. David dropped his arm, turned to me and smiled. "We were just talking about you," he said. "Complimenting your taste. Weren't we, Charlotte?"

She smoothed her blonde coil of hair. "Yes," she said, smiling, though her voice was unsteady.

And then Henry came up behind me, and we all stood in the kitchen together, admiring my taste.

* * *

The windows in the kitchen are grimy but unbroken. There is only dust on the cupboards and a light layer of old grease on the range. The fridge has a musty smell; Charlotte unplugged it eight months ago, turning it on again only recently. I wipe the inside down with a wet rag and baking soda to absorb the odour. Then I tackle the whole room with a bucket of water and cleanser, a scrubbing brush and sponge, getting into every corner. This takes me a bit more than an hour, and when I finish I stand looking about, feeling better. David and Charlotte are not gone, but they are, for the moment, diminished.

I have worked up an appetite, and I stand at the kitchen sink munching an apple, looking out. Far off over the hill a hawk soars, and closer in I hear the loud cawing of crows. I am reminded that I haven't done anything yet about feeding the birds. They were always the first thing I thought of in the morning; I never fed myself before them. Since coming home, however, I've left little space in my cluttered mind for the care and feeding of birds. I feel ashamed, and make a vow to stock up on seed. Meanwhile, I can fill the birdbath in the garden, take them out some bread.

The loaf I've bought is a good hearty wheat, and I cut off several slices. Stepping outside the kitchen door I am on the path that leads through the gardens. There are weeds up to my knees and dead flower stalks all around. The place is a mess. But I built the birds' feeding table with my own hands, and it is still here in the kitchen garden; eight feet high on a slim metal pole, it is safely out of reach of the neighbour's cat, who lives a mile down the road. I break up the bread and, using a system of pullies, fill the feeder. In less than five seconds I hear an excited clamour from the trees. It begins close by, then spreads to the willows and oaks round the pond. I've always fancied them spreading the word, "She's home! There's food!"

It has been eight months, and many of these birds were here last year. Some are messengers—advance men—and they will call out the ecstatic word that there are sunflower seeds when I return from town. Yet they won't come close for a while. They must be certain this isn't a trap, and their caution overshadows hunger.

I leave them to it and finish my inspection of the garden. It is truly awful, and I cannot bear it. I decide to go into the village today and buy as many pots of bright flowers as can be fitted into the boot of the car. I will line the path with them, to lift my spirits as I'm weeding. Then I can set them into the ground.

But it will take me forever to put everything back in order. I am bewildered that Charlotte didn't do something about this. She might have hired a gardener to keep things up; surely she knew I'd repay her.

There are so many things I don't understand now about Charlotte. And suddenly my resolution to work and not think is abandoned; I cannot keep her—or David—out of my mind.

After the shopping today, I think, I'll invite myself for tea. I'll say I've come to see about the Fiat and Charlotte and I will talk. Perhaps something will come out. Some small clue as to why she wrote that note.

Meanwhile, I am noticing something—how little I feel of anger, or even jealousy at the thought of Charlotte and David together. This startles me. I am more upset, I think, at the thought that Charlotte betrayed me.

I am at Abbott's Nursery, paying for my purchases at the counter. "Will you be needing any help, Mrs. Carr?"

Mr. Abbott is a very old man, certainly over ninety, and only helping out his son at the register. I can't imagine him lifting a leaf, he seems so frail.

"Help?" I ask.

"Out at the house. Old Robert might help you put these in. He's not at all expensive, you know."

"Old Robert . . . Oh, yes, I remember him. He works for you?"

"Well, now, he's never in fact been hired on. Just sort of hangs about, you know. Likes working with the plants."

"Old Robert . . ." As I recall, he must not be a day over fifty. Mr. Abbott could be his father twice over. But Robert's slow and he hunches over a bit when he walks. That's what inspired his nickname with people about town.

I remember something else about Old Robert. According to people in the village, he's loonier than me.

Perfect, I think. "Does he mind pulling weeds?"

"Not at all."

"Then do send him round."

We leave it that Mr. Abbott will talk to him, and if he's able, Old Robert will come to the house the next morning. I leave feeling a bit lighter, as if part of the burden of all that cleanup has already been lifted from my shoulders.

Charlotte's house is less than fifteen minutes from Pennoryn, but the land is different here. The road runs along the river Fal, where Tristan, disguised as a pilgrim, is said to have waited by the Mal Pas Ford for his queen to pass over into Carlyon. Rather than farms there are rolling green hills here, streams, and thick woods.

Fallston, the Dean manor house, stands tall and graceful on a wooded hill. There are large wings on either side, one the library, another a room with windows on all three sides, overlooking a garden of lilacs, azaleas, and prize roses. The manor house was in Henry's family for centuries, going back to a great-great-great-grandfather who owned most of the land in these parts. When Charlotte married Henry she took on ancestors and history, much of which is recorded in family annals in their library.

I've often wondered if Charlotte, young as she was, married Henry for his money, but it is not something I ever felt I could ask. It would be like saying that I thought less of her by simply thinking it might be true. And too, there are things we would rather not know about our friends. Boundaries we draw, like fences, to keep a flowering friendship safe and unpleasant truths away.

If, however, Charlotte did at first marry Henry for his money, she at least seemed to truly love him in recent years. Henry is a rather short, bumbling fellow with a shiny pate and soft grey eyes that peer at one through a myriad of tiny wrinkles. His mouth is nearly always curved in a slight smile, as if he's thinking more of some wonderful new hybrid rose than whatever conversation is going on, as indeed he generally is. I have always loved Henry, in the way that one cannot help loving someone who is kind, whose intent is only to be held harmless, to bring good to those he loves. Over the years, I watched Charlotte soften with Henry. They seem the perfect couple.

Rather than pulling all the way along their circular drive to the front door, I stop down the road at the garages. Two of the three stalls are open, one revealing an empty spot where Henry's beloved and well-kept Morris generally resides. He must be out, I think, and wonder if Charlotte has gone with him. Part of me feels relief. The truth is, now that I'm here I would as soon forget the whole thing and go home.

In the other stall is David's red Fiat. I pull to a stop and sit for a moment with my window down, remembering drives we took through the countryside when first we met —up to Fowey, down to Land's End, now and again off to London, packing lunches and stopping along the way in someone's field. The sense memories are strong: hot sun, the scent of it resting on overly ripe peaches, the heady wine. And afterward, David driving with one hand, his other in mine at first, then sliding onto my knee. Little by little he would inch his fingers along my thigh, reaching the hem of my skirt and stopping there, teasing, always teasing, making me want him until my breath was nearly gone, my legs parting. I loved the silky feel of David's fingers sliding along my stockings, and the excitement that would flush through me as his hand would find—

I am astonished that I feel him now, that my juices are flowing as they haven't in months. In truth, I had thought my body dead as well as my mind.

My mouth on the other hand is dry as a bone. It is trembling, but not from passion. From fear. For long moments I rest my head on my hands, which grip the steering wheel. Then I slide from the car and stand on the drive, my knees shaking. Grasping the open door I hold myself upright there, waiting for this terrible feeling of dread to subside.

The sun moves, casting light inside the stall and shining on the bonnet of the red Fiat. It seems to wink, to move, to flow like thick, old blood. I see myself riding beside David, and I hear him say to me, "Don't be a sissy, Joanna," as he veers recklessly around corners, up hill and down. "I'm in control," he would say. But one night we were tail-ended by another car, a green Ford, when David stopped too quickly on a mountain road. The driver was following too closely, and David muttered something like, ". . . teach him a lesson." He slammed on the Fiat's brakes. The tyres on the other car squealed furiously as the driver tried to swerve and failed. He came upon us like a runaway truck, metal clashing, glass shrieking as it flew in every direction. The boom from our two cars connecting was so loud I was certain the Ford would plow straight through us. But it was small, lightweight, and somehow, miraculously, the Fiat's rear bumper held. David and I were thrown forward, slammed against the seat belts, and came to rest finally by the side of the road. We both had numerous aches for months, while the other driver suffered whiplash.

I was shaky after that incident, afraid that every car that approached was coming directly at me. I begged David to drive more slowly when I was with him. *"Wheeee,"* he would cry instead, like a child with one of those little cars one sees at the fair, laughing as he zoomed over bumps and ruts, the blood-red Fiat rattling and rising into the sky as I hugged my seat belt, terrified.

I realise I am hugging myself now. When Charlotte speaks from behind me I am startled that I haven't heard her approach.

"Poor Joanna. Why didn't you just tell him you wouldn't ride with him anymore?"

As she so often does, she has read my mind. "I don't know," I say. "I don't know." I look into those enigmatic eyes and wonder why I've never been able to read her as well.

"You did, didn't you?" I say. "You refused to ride with him ever."

Or so I thought. Did you and David take secret jaunts into the countryside? Did you have tête-à-têtes *I knew nothing about?*

"He was a maniac behind the wheel," she says. "David . . ." She shakes her head and falls silent, putting a hand on my shoulder. "Let's not talk about him, all right? You're just in time for lunch. We can have it on the terrace."

"Where is Henry? I see his car's not here."

She smiles and takes my arm, leading me up the flagstone path to the house. "He's gone to town with a neighbour to meet with the owner of a horse he wants to buy. Bright Lady. He'll be back soon."

"Henry's racing horses now?" It seems so out of character, the vision of fragile Henry Dean shouting from a grandstand, waving betting tickets in the air. I have to smile.

"It's just a hobby," Charlotte says, "He needed something to do, a new outlet. Retirement hasn't been easy for my husband."

Unlike some of his ancestors, Henry had worked every day for forty years in the family business, before retiring at sixty—ten years ago—at Charlotte's insistence. "I didn't marry you only to sit around this big house alone," I remember her saying. "We've got places to go, Henry, things to do."

If it was true that she had softened under his love, it was also true that Charlotte had brought energy into Henry Dean's life. A somewhat stick-in-the-mud banker who wore stiff collars all his life, he had allowed himself instead to be rousted out of the dark corridors of the family bank and carried off to strange, exotic shores. He and Charlotte travelled several months out of the year. They always came back with tans, a few more fine lines from the sun, and loaded down with expensive *objets d'art.* To my knowledge, Henry has never complained about this state of affairs; rather, he has gone along with Charlotte like a happy puppy. Charlotte has seemed content, too.

Why, then, would she become involved with my husband?

David, of course, could be persuasive. I have only to look back upon our first days together to know that. Still, walking up to her house with my arm in hers, I find it hard to believe that Charlotte's note meant what I read into it. There must be another explanation.

* * *

Henry has returned, and we three sit on the terrace around a large glass table with a white wicker frame. The chairs are wicker as well and thickly padded with a bright blue chintz—but that does nothing to add to my comfort. There is something wrong. I saw it the moment Henry walked through the terrace door. His back stiffened, and tension settled in his generally beaming face. A wariness overtook his eyes. As quickly as I saw this, however, it disappeared.

Now Charlotte turns to Henry and says, "Joanna came for David's car." A look flashes between them. Then it too disappears.

"Really?" Henry says. "I would think . . ." He lets it go, but I know what he has meant to say.

"You're right, Henry," I agree. "I've just now decided. The Fiat's best left here till I can sell it. If that's all right with both of you, of course. I believe I'll look for a good secondhand car. Something that's more my style."

Charlotte picks up on this almost gratefully. "Wonderful! I'll drive you, Joanna. Tomorrow? We can make a day of it. We'll have lunch in St. Austell and then go looking, and when you find what you want you can just drive it home."

For a brief moment Henry's smile fades, but then he nods. "I'll put an advertisement in the newspaper for the Fiat if you'd like, Joanna. I'd be happy to show it for you."

I set my salad fork on my plate. "Thank you, Henry. And you, Charlotte. But as for tomorrow, I believe I'll go into Mevagissey and run some errands. The car can wait for now."

Charlotte frowns. As in the past, she's way ahead. "He isn't always at the gallery these days," she says disapprovingly. "Michael travels, setting up showings, you know. I hear he likes to do that for himself."

Henry looks at her worriedly. "Michael . . . that would be Michael Lamb?"

She ignores his question. "Joanna, please tell me you're not planning to start that up again."

" 'Start it up again?' " My voice takes on an edge. "What

a strange way to put it. Michael and I are friends. Why shouldn't I see him?"

Charlotte makes a sound of distaste and touches her throat.

"What? Charlotte, what on earth is going on?"

She makes an obvious effort to collect herself. "Nothing . . . nothing at all, dear. It's just that you haven't been out of hospital more than a few days, and seeing Michael . . . Well, I can't imagine it would be the best thing for you."

"Why not? Is there something . . ." *Something about Michael I should know?* There is—I know this now in my gut. It fills the room, the presence of it like a huge, black cloud.

Both Charlotte and Henry rush in to rain sunlight over that cloud and disperse it with phony reassurances. "No, certainly not," Henry says quickly, though he looks decidedly worried. And Charlotte follows with, "I just meant, why not take things slowly?" She squeezes my hand, and I feel her bones, brittle and dry, digging into my skin. There is a subtle panic in those bones; it transmits itself to me. My jaw goes rigid, I draw away.

"The doctor says I'm to live a normal life, Charlotte. Tell me why I shouldn't see Michael."

She leans back in her chair and sighs delicately. "You're making too much of this, Joanna. Blowing it out of proportion." The cool green gaze slides up to mine. "Is this . . . this paranoia . . . part of your illness?"

"Charlotte!" Henry is aghast.

I feel heat rise to my cheeks. "Isn't it odd, Charlotte, but I've always thought that word—paranoia—to be hostile, the kind of word people use only when they want to accuse you."

She flushes. The muscles in her neck tighten. "I simply meant that you should get on with life, leave the past where it belongs. Joanna, you are looking for shadows round corners where there are none."

"On the other hand, it's been said that even the paranoid can be followed."

She falls silent. I am shaking, but I cannot let her see it. I keep my hands in my lap below the table until they are reasonably still. Then with more calm than I believe myself capable of, I dab my mouth lightly with my serviette and stand.

"Thank you for lunch, Charlotte. And you, Henry. I really must be going."

"Joanna . . ."

Charlotte half rises, but I ignore her. There is a ticking in my head, as of a bomb that has lain silent in the ground for years, until just now being tripped. I barely hear Henry as he follows me to the door, trying to placate, to smooth things over. ". . . so sorry . . ." he says, ". . . so truly sorry . . . didn't mean . . . do come back . . ."

Henry, in fact, is trying so hard that I barely notice—till I'm outside on the flagstone path and look back to reassure him I will be all right—that Charlotte is not there. Henry stands alone in the doorway, his kindly face drooping with regret.

I rush back down along the drive, and at the car stalls I glance at the Fiat. The blood-red bonnet winks. I climb into the Ford, my hands grip the wheel, and I sit thinking, *Is it paranoia that you didn't come to see me in hospital, Charlotte, for two entire months? Is it paranoia that you and David had a secret you did not share with me?*

I wonder why I did not come straight out and say these things, why I have always felt it so difficult to confront Charlotte. Why do I always feel she will prove me foolish, and herself more reasonable, more sane?

That evening, it rains. I sit in a large overstuffed chair at the living room window and stare at the slate sky, at the tangled wilderness that surrounds me. I think about my initial excitement over coming home; how wonderful it felt in that moment when I first stepped from the car.

But now the wilderness that lies without also lies within. Since coming home from hospital I've begun to remember more bad than good about David, it seems. I shudder with embarrassment, remembering the rosy portrait I drew of him and our marriage only scant days ago.

"David was what every woman dreams of, the one man who could complete, fulfill," I said to Dr. Shahi once in a therapy session. He answered, *"You* are all you need, Joanna. All the joy you will ever want, all the strength you will ever need is *right here with you."*

I would like to believe that. But if it is true, why do I sit here in such utter devastation now, mourning something that never existed?

The truth is—and it's coming back now—it took almost no time at all to realise that David was not as happy living at Pennoryn as I. He found little joy in the warble of a bright new bird finding its way across the gorse (although he'd seemed to share my joy in that, the day we met). Nor did he stand with me, as before we wed, gazing in awe at sunsets that now and then striped a brooding sky with gold, rose, and aquamarine. I came to spend those evenings alone in the meadow, while David worked in his office. I might sit under our tree for hours watching every last fleeting moment of such a rare sunset, not even noticing when my limbs grew stiff and my nose cold. These were the things that gave me joy.

I couldn't expect that of David, however. People are different, he said, and I agreed. David needed more life, more activity than the little village of Pennoryn provided. He would go up to London on business, and I knew he often took in a show or had dinner with old friends. While I would have liked to go with him on these occasions—and sometimes did in the first few weeks—later he would argue that there wouldn't be time for us to be together. It was to be a quick trip; he'd take care of whatever business needed attention, and then be home. After a while I didn't even question him as to what that business was. When I did, he would grow irritated, and I preferred to have our time together free of dissent.

And then slowly, ever so slowly, something new crept in. I cannot quite remember what it was, but there are edges of darkness round my memories now, a feeling that there is something for which I should be horribly ashamed.

I shiver, and draw the small knitted blanket more closely over my legs. The storm is having its way with the elm trees; they scrape the roof and rattle against windows. Wind howls through the eaves. On the porch are pots of flowers waiting to be planted. They looked lively and bright at Abbott's. Here, they grow dim as the last bit of light fades and the weeds encroach.

I feel myself growing dim, like a candle whose wick has burnt out. My limbs are cold as death, and for a moment I think that perhaps it would be all right to simply let go, to cross over to that place of light that people talk about. I have no family that matters, no one to stand and grieve. And on that other side there would be no pain, no lying awake nights thinking who did what, or to whom.

But then the wind gusts, shaking the windows and blowing the pots of flowers on their sides. They roll about the porch, carried here and there by the gale. It is a sad, terrible sight; they look so helpless—and like me, so out of control. Something in me rises up against it. Something makes my every fibre swell with rage. *I cannot let this happen.* Flinging off the blanket I stand and run to the front door, hurling it open. On the porch I chase after the wet rolling pots, gathering them up by the armful and bringing them inside. When they're all safe, I run out again and shake my fist at the teeming sky. "I will not let you do this to me, David! Do you hear? *I will not let you do it!*"

Rain spatters my face; wind tears my hair. I hardly know what I'm saying, or how David got mixed into this. But my rage is full-blown now, and it feels good. It is so much better than fear.

Running back into the house, I track water onto the floor; I even leave the door open. It doesn't matter. Let it all pour in, I think, let a monsoon come; it will wash away the miserable remnants of my married life.

In the bedroom I root determinedly through every stitch of clothing in the closet and remove anything that was David's. Shirts, trousers, jeans, suits—all go into a heap by the door. Like a madwoman, I strip the old brown-and-white sheets that Charlotte has put on the bed. The fitted bottom sheet sticks in one corner and I rip at it angrily, fighting tears. It comes, and I add the sheets to the mess by the door.

Feeling better, I storm up into the attic and find others —linens I bought before marriage and never used because

David didn't like them. They are new, still in the package, all stored away in a trunk. There are shams, a comforter, a matching dust ruffle—all splashed with a riot of soft country roses. They have lain here unused, as neglected as the roses in my garden.

I toss the lot of it down the stairs before me, making one trip of it. Running down, I scoop up the sheets, sham, and dust ruffle, and with my free hand drag the comforter to the bedroom. My energy is vast, like none I have ever known.

An hour later I stand looking around the bedroom, appreciating its new look. There is pink everywhere. I have brought in fresh roses from the garden, and even though they are stunted and bug-bitten, their fragrance graces the room. I have brought another precious find down from the attic: opaque white curtains that I tried to talk David into once, but that he wouldn't have. He liked the windows bare and open to the world, liked making love at night that way, with the lights on and darkness outside. "You never know when someone might be watching," he said. "It gives one an extra bit of an edge—more of a thrill, don't you think?"

The truth is, it frightened me having the windows bare, as I always felt there was someone outside the window peering in. There were nights, in fact, when I was certain of it. But David convinced me my fears were childish, and eventually, under his ministrations, I forgot.

The rain has softened to a whisper, and I've opened the windows part way. The white curtains wave gently in the warm evening breeze. There is very little left in this room now to remind me of my husband. No scent of lotion or cigarettes, no stray comb or cuff link. Everything is in a box by the front door. In the morning I will take it to a church to be divided among the poor.

This is my room, now: *Joanna's.* Even the ugly Eros bedposts have been covered, with small white bags from a kitchen drawer. Tomorrow, I think, I'll get those monstrosities off if I have to chop them with an axe.

Without warning, exhaustion overtakes me. I sink slowly

to the edge of the bed. Yet this is not a bad tiredness, rather the result of a job well done. I lean back slowly, luxuriating in the comfort of my newly-clothed bed. My body relaxes, the bones falling into a comfortable space. After a moment I close my eyes and drift off. In my mind I go to a peaceful valley where all about me are only trees, lush green grass, and a quietly flowing stream. "A place of safety," as Dr. Shahi has called it in therapy. *"Let yourself be guided there . . . a journey into self-discovery."* I imagine that a skylark sings in one of the trees, robins poke about in the grass for seed, and a family of deer—a mother and two fawns—tiptoe past. It is as if they think that if they are silent, I will not see them. I laugh softly at that, and lie on the grass in warm sunshine, letting it seep into my bones. I feel it melt me, my body becoming one with the gathering richness of the earth.

Then I feel something else, something I have not felt before on this journey. It is like the deer; it tiptoes my way as if hoping I will not see it sneaking up on me. My hand, of its own accord, strays to my chest. I touch my right breast through the soft jersey. It feels strange, as if I'm rediscovering it, having forgotten it was there. I touch the nipple, and surprisingly it responds, growing hard under the tickling sensation of my idle, stroking finger. My hand begins to move lazily, more out of curiosity than desire, wandering down, down, my breath tightening almost immediately. *Ah, yes,* I think, *I am still alive.* The awakening I felt earlier in Charlotte's driveway was real.

And even better—I do not need David for it.

The thought is barely out, his name barely bruising my mind, before I am breathing in short, painful gasps, and then suddenly my wrists are burning, my thighs hurting so badly I jerk them together from the intense, shocking pain. *"No!"* I hear myself scream. *"Get away!"* The room echoes with my screams, and without thought or plan I jump from the bed and flee, running until I am in the middle of the living room staring at the fireplace and the spot where David died.

My gaze swings to the carton of clothes I've set by the front door. Pure, unadulterated hate pours through me, and again without conscious thought I drag the carton to the fireplace and begin to toss clothes in. Running my hand along the mantel I feel for matches, find a box, and light it —the entire box—throwing it on top of the clothes. The matches flare, then die. The fireplace is damp and cold. The heavy materials will not burn.

I race to the kitchen, scrambling about in a drawer. Here there is a whole store of long wooden matches—seven, no eight packs. I grab them up, holding them against my chest as I dash back to the living room. There I kneel on the hearth and light pack after pack, adding newspaper, then kindling, until I have a fire that blazes so high, it could, for all I know, burn down the house.

But finally the clothes are gone. David's trousers, his shirts, socks, underwear, his leather jacket. Nothing remains. *It is done.*

Kneeling, I stroke the imaginary stain on the floor by the hearth. "All gone," I whisper consolingly, as if to a child who's drained all his milk. "All gone."

Tomorrow, or the next day, I will start on David's study. For now I stay here, huddled into myself. Sounds fill my house, my mind. They move down corridors and through a maze of ringing bells, of Mrs. Rimes saying, "There, there . . . we've washed it all away, all that nasty business. Are we better now?" I dream I see Dr. Shahi above me, probing my eyes with a light. "Poor Joanna," he is saying. "Fire . . . there is fire everywhere. How will she survive?"

It is all so real, I wake in the morning stiff and cold, thinking it has truly happened—the way one does at times after dreams.

CHAPTER 8

I am not doing well. This I know about my actions of the night before. I am not doing well at all.

I consider calling Dr. Shahi. It is Friday, after all. But no, I will put it off until later. Later I may have more strength.

I drag myself to the kitchen for coffee, making it strong as lead, hoping it will bring me alive. Taking it back into the bedroom I cast a second look at the changes I've wrought, and wonder at the night before. I must have been drugged—drugged with some chemical the brain emits when it's had more than it can stand.

I begin to smile. Actually, looking at all those pink roses, the whole thing seems rather funny. So different from the way David liked it.

And then, burning his clothes.

I see myself last night bending over the fireplace, tossing in all those clothes, my long hair swinging wildly about my face. I look into the mirror and pull a lock forward, studying it. Yes, I did singe a few strands. I wonder if at some point I even quoted Shakespeare. *Out, damned spot!*

I can't help it; I am finding some humour in this. I wonder—is it a sign of improvement?

I am dressing to go into Mevagissey and look for Michael when there is a knock on the door. I look out and see Old Robert standing there. I had almost forgotten he was coming.

* * *

Old Robert and I walk through the jumbled disorder that once was my lovely garden. Deep puddles have formed from the rain, and both of us are in Wellies. "As you can see," I tell him, "there are so many weeds. But there are rather a lot of flowers that would come up, I think, if they could only breathe. And I'd like to plant some new."

He nods and shuffles over to a pitiful stand of peonies. He is tall and skinny, with straggly brown hair to his shoulders. He wears an old white dress shirt with the collar open, and baggy trousers with bright red braces. I think for some reason of a tall Charlie Chaplin—the rather childlike gait, the round face and innocent eyes.

He stoops down to a weed and seems to study it. After a moment he stands, shaking his head glumly. "It's the spirits," he says in a faint West Country dialect. "They'm don't like this, not at all."

I look into his colourless eyes. "The spirits?"

He casts me a glance that says he can't believe I don't know. "They'm that live in the plants."

"Oh. Well, then. Hmmm. What do you think we should do about it?"

He flings his arms out and up, like a prophet. "There's evil here, you know."

I imagine Old Robert knows from the village about David, and the way he died. I also think he is an old Cornish farmer and superstitious to the hilt.

At any rate, I won't be intimidated. "Well, of course I know there's evil here," I say briskly. "But now what do we do about it?"

He shakes his head, and there's that disheartened look again.

I plant my hands on my hips. "Well, there's got to be something. These—these spirits of yours. Surely they'd like it if we weeded a bit."

He walks away and stands with his back to me, hands in his pockets, as if deep in thought. A minute passes . . . two. Just when I'm thinking he's gone into a trance, he turns back.

"We must go about it carefully."

I try not to smile. "Of course."

"You can't yank out weeds like they haven't a heart."

"No, no, you're absolutely right."

"You've got to ask their permission."

"Mmmm." I am deciding that Old Robert is the perfect gardener for me; our shared looniness makes us compatible to a tee.

"Ask their permission?" I say. "And how do we do that?"

"Well, you tell them what you're wantin' to do. You say it's for the common good."

"I see. And will they agree?"

He scans my garden, which is as tangled as my life has been. "Would you be wantin' to live like this?" he asks.

"I . . . no. No, I would not." So there is wisdom behind those eyes.

He nods and bends down to the primrose garden, resting his palm on the ground for a moment. "Something was here. Something with blood."

A chill goes through me. The stone hare, the wedding gift from Michael.

"There was something there," I say. "I . . . don't know about the blood."

He stands and wipes his hand on his baggy trousers. A bee lands on his nose, and he lifts a hand and gently removes it, letting it rest on his palm before it flies away.

"We'll start here," he says. "First, I'll be needin' a pint of dark rum."

I frown. "Rum? Look, I really . . . I'd rather you didn't drink on the job. Afterwards, of course . . ."

He sighs. "For the *potion*. The potion must be poured into the ground at twelve points, twenty-three paces apart."

"Oh."

"We'll be needin' the rum, three droppin's from a lark, and the eye of a bat."

Again I plant my hands on my hips. This really is going too far. "Now, wait a minute. Where on earth would I find all that?"

He shakes his head and sighs again, thoroughly disenchanted with me now. "I'll see to it, never you worry. I'll see to it all."

I head for Mevagissey, wondering if Old Robert is truly loony, or simply more knowledgeable about such things than I. After this morning I am willing to believe either way. Meanwhile, I do feel better, somehow. I've got an extra hand to help, and I can start getting Pennoryn, and my life, back on track.

The truth is, I rather like Old Robert. For his first chore of the day, he has agreed to speak with the weeds. If all goes well with them, he will drive his rusted lorry back to the village and pick up everything he needs for his potions. I have even trusted him enough to leave money with him for the rum.

The eye of the bat is quite another thing. I try not to think of my new gardener lurking outside some cave at sunset, prepared to pounce. Or the talk that will go round the village if all this gets out.

In Mevagissey I pass up the car-park on the outskirts and follow one of the few lanes accessible to automobiles. It is one the delivery lorries use, and it goes right by The Blue Swan gallery.

I haven't phoned ahead. Some inner sense tells me Michael will be here. I don't, however, go too quickly, too eagerly, to the gallery, partly because the prospect of seeing Michael is something I would like to savour. It is also true that I am nervous. It has been a long time. Largely to stall, then, I park at the end of the lane and get out and walk, glancing at shops I remember from childhood and many that are new. I do not go near my family's home, which stands as it always did above the quay. Although my father is long gone, they live there still, my mother and brothers.

In hospital I remembered having seen them shortly after marrying David. He and I were having troubles already, and I blamed myself for too many fears. I suppose I hoped that something at home had changed, that in the time since I'd married there might be some glimmer of remorse from any one of them. In that way I might put the past to rest, and forget.

It was not meant to be. I left my mother that day rocking in her old stuffed chair, staring off into space. Heavy drapes were pulled against the grey winter light, and the room had a smell of old fish, a sickish odour of decay from all the years of my father and brothers tramping in with their boots on, having taken the shortcut through the fish factory. They would carry in bits and pieces of fish guts on their soles, which would seep into the carpet, then down through the cracks of the floor. Impossible to remove with either broom or mop, there they would remain.

That day I visited after marrying David, my mother scratched idly at the thick scar on her left cheek, a gift from my father on one of his binges. If she felt any interest in the state of my marriage, or even an ounce of remorse for what had been done to me as a child, she gave no sign.

My brothers, on the other hand, cast sly looks my way. "Does he know you're used goods?" Ian had said, laughing.

I looked from one to the other and said sharply, "I told him about you, if that's what you mean. Watch he doesn't come after you."

In truth, it was the hardest thing I'd ever done, telling David about the horrors of my past. But he was calm about it, sympathetic, even pressing for me to tell him everything I could remember. I didn't want to dwell on it, but David was insistent. And so I told him, dragging out details until finally I was so repulsed by the telling of it, I could tell no more.

My brothers fell silent with the knowledge that my husband knew. When threatened with someone their own size, they were inveterate cowards. I learned this on the day of my thirteenth year, when Michael found them raping me out on the cliffs. I remember him appearing as if out of nowhere, a young man of not more than thirteen himself. Nevertheless he stood tall and strong against the churning winds. His black hair was down to his shoulders, then, his blue eyes dark with loathing. Every muscle quivered with rage. "You bastards!" he shouted. "I'll cut your filthy black

hearts out!" With that he yanked a fish-gutting knife from
his belt and went after Ian's throat. Ian paled, stumbling
back against Denny. Joseph was not there that day, but
their two friends who'd come along for the fun, ran. My
bruised thighs ached as I struggled to get up from the
ground. I pulled at my blouse to cover my torn undershirt
and bare breasts, and I cried out to Michael, "Don't, they
aren't worth it!" I didn't want their blood on his conscience; it was bad enough I would carry the memory of
that ugly day with me the rest of my life.

But Michael had the rough serrated knife at Ian's throat,
and he was murmuring softly, "It'd be so easy, wouldn't it,
now? Just t'gut you like a fish, pull your sorry heart out and
throw it over these cliffs."

"No, Michael!" I cried again. "Please!"

Abruptly, he shoved Ian away, causing him to half knock
Denny over. Michael stepped back and spat on the ground
at Ian's feet. "She's right. You're not worth dullin' the
blade."

Ian looked dazed. But he recovered quickly and began
to smile, a cocky, instant bravado, thinking he'd won out.
"She wanted it, y'know. Asked for it."

In a flash, Michael was on him again. This time he drew
blood beneath Ian's chin. "I swear by all that's holy, if
either of you ever touches her again I'll kill you. Do you
hear me? I'll kill you, and I won't think twice."

His words frightened me, as I could see he meant every
one. I had never seen Michael like this; always with me he
had been gentle, soft-spoken, kind. Even when faced with
bullies in the school yard, he seldom fought back with his
fists, but with words. He won people over with reason.

At this moment, however, I could barely get through to
him. I put a hand on his arm and it felt like stone. I tugged
at it. "Michael, let's go. Please, let's go."

He turned to me blindly at first, then focussing. His gaze
swept the cliffs, the dull grey sky, the frightened faces of
my brothers. Rain began to spit, landing on his face, and it
seemed somehow to dissolve the rage. He lowered the
knife and his face softened, the eyes returning to their nat-

ural shade. "Jo . . ." he said, as if for long moments he'd forgotten I was there.

"Come, let's go," I said softly. He let me take his hand, which was shaking, and draw him away.

We left my brothers standing sullenly on the trail, rubbing sweat from their brows, and muttering face-saving threats of retaliation. I shall never forget the feelings that rushed through me as Michael and I left that sorry place, his hand clasped firmly in mine.

First, of course, relief. I had a champion now. Michael had saved me, and I dared to think he might even in the future protect me. At the same time I felt deeply embarrassed that my friend had seen me that way—that he knew the type of person that in secret I'd become.

If Michael felt any differently about me, however, he didn't show it as we trudged hand in hand along the barren cliffs, hurrying to put as much distance between us and my brothers as we could. Though we didn't speak of it, we both knew they might get back their courage and come after us. Finally we came to a fissure, a wide break in the cliff, with a track leading down to a small cove. We ran to the cove and fell weakly to the ground beneath a cropping of trees. Michael's hands were trembling, his face pale, and I knew what the violence had cost him.

"We can rest here a few minutes," he said, breathing heavily. "You can collect yourself before you go home."

I drew up my knees and buried my face in my arms. "I can't go home. I just can't."

He patted my shoulder awkwardly. "They won't hurt you there, Jo. Not with your mum and dad around."

Tears caught in my throat, and I was silent, shaking my head.

Michael's hand tightened on my shoulder. He turned me to face him. "They wouldn't . . . your mum and dad wouldn't let them do this to you again." But there was a question in his voice.

I looked away, at my muddy shoes and torn skirt, and the blood that now coursed down my legs, for it seemed my brothers' brutality had started my monthly flowing. I quickly pulled my hem down before Michael could see, but his next horrified question brought even more shame to my heart. "Jo, don't tell me they know what your brothers have been doing to you!"

"It's . . . all right," I said. "I'm almost used to it now."

An astounding thing happened then. I had never seen a man or boy cry; I never knew they could. But Michael's eyes filled with tears. He pulled my head against his chest and began to croon something Irish and grieving, the sort of sound one might hear at a wake. I buried my nose in the roughness of his shirt. "How long?" he said. "How long have they been doing this to you?"

I shook my head. I couldn't tell him. *Three years. Three hellish years since that first day at Tommy Mayhew's boatyard.*

There had been days when I'd wanted to kill my brothers, and other days when my shame went so deep I wanted only to die. The only thing that kept me alive was my friendship with Michael, knowing I'd be seeing him after school, that we'd pack a sandwich and take a walk on his mother's farm, or sit on the seawall watching the boats pass into the Channel. It mattered not to me what we did; the only thing that mattered was that I felt safe with him.

Even in those days Michael was different from most boys. Rather than hunt or play games of sport, he drew sketches of birds, of trees, of the wild winter cliffs. Once he drew a sketch of me, a very simple drawing, as he was still learning his skills. But the result was dark—the eyes haunted, the face that of someone quite tired with life. Michael never meant it to be unflattering; he was striving for truth. But it disturbed me that anyone could see so clearly into my soul. I asked him never to draw me that way again.

It occurs to me suddenly: Is that why he painted me so differently in that portrait at Harbourside Gallery? A make-believe me, one that never existed? The kind of pure, delicate child—or woman—he wished, perhaps, that I'd been?

I see I've circled the block and come round to a spot just across from The Blue Swan gallery. It nestles between a cluster of shops with thatched roofs on the one side, and

Michael's small white cottage on the other. Michael has lived here since purchasing the gallery five years ago, and although he could surely afford better now, the cottage is perfect for him. He keeps it clean and neat but quite bare, with only a painting or two of his own on the gleaming white walls. "I can focus on my work this way," Michael said when he first moved in. "There's not so much to distract me."

As if in afterthought he added, "Besides, I can see the entire town from here." His gaze swept from this lane to the quay, and then left to mid-cove, to the hill where my family's house stands. There it had rested with a brief tense flicker.

At this time we were both twenty-five. I still lived at home, but things had changed. I touched Michael's hand. "I'm all right now," I said quietly. "You know that. Thanks to you, I've been all right."

"Still . . ." His eyes had narrowed. "I feel sometimes we're sitting on a powder keg, Jo."

"But it's been years."

"That's just it. Years. Yet nothing's changed with them. Not one whit."

"*I've* changed," I said. "I'm stronger now. They can't hurt me anymore."

Michael's brow creased with worry.

"You don't think they'd come after me again?"

"I just . . . Jo, I'll be travelling a lot now. I want you to promise me you'll be cautious when I'm not here."

I knew Michael's worry came from the fact that he cared. And it was true my brothers still treated me like some object they had lost and couldn't wait to find again. But the physical abuse had ended that day on the cliffs. Returning home that day, and for the next several days, I spent as much time as possible away from the house. I took long walks in the country, exploring the beaches even though it was a cold and miserable summer. Then on the third night I came upon Ian, Denny, and my father in the kitchen, drinking their ale and picking at chicken bones, deep in angry conversation. As I entered the room they looked at me, then away. They stopped talking abruptly.

My father made a scornful sound in his throat and muttered something about "not enough sense to keep it in the family." The next day a child welfare worker arrived at the door—clearly by appointment—and everyone had known she was coming but me.

It was a Saturday morning, shortly after breakfast, and we were all at home. The worker interviewed each of us separately, asking questions. When it was my turn she sent everyone to the kitchen, closed the door behind them, and sat on a dining-room chair across from me. She had received an anonymous call, she told me kindly. Was it from me? I shook my head no, still bewildered as to why she was here. Was there anything I wanted to tell her? she asked. Any trouble in the family? And then I knew.

"N-n-no," I stuttered, horrified by this turn of events, unheard of in those days when families kept these things to themselves. I shook my head. "No problems in the family at all?" she pressed. "Excess drinking? Anything at all that makes you afraid?"

With each question I could feel myself growing truly afraid. Soon my spine was plastered so far back against the straight wooden chair, I wondered if it might break right through. And the more the woman asked—the closer she came to the truth—the more I denied everything. My fear of what might happen if the authorities moved in was greater than my fear of my brothers. They were the known; the other was a terrible, frightening unknown.

The worker left finally, unsatisfied but defeated. Afterwards, I expected angry words from my family—retaliation of some sort from at least Ian. Instead, a thick silence filled every room. Finally I grabbed my coat and ran to the other side of town to Michael, who lived then with his widowed mother on a farm on Tressany Road.

Pulling him outside to the porch steps I told him in a rush of words what had happened. "Did you call her?" I demanded, knowing he must have, for who else would? When he admitted it, I was even more angry. "How could you *do* that, Michael? How could you tell outsiders such a horrible thing about me?"

"Jo, I'm sorry. I felt I had to. It was the only way to protect you, don't you see?"

"No, I don't see! Why did you do it? It was awful! She sat there asking me the most ugly questions, about whether anyone had . . . had touched me, done things to me . . ."

Michael's face clouded with pain. "I thought about it a long time, Jo. It was the only way I knew to help."

"But you already did that! The other day, you *did* that—"

Michael took my cold hand in his. "They won't be stopped by my threats for long. You'll see, Jo. If nothing else, there's been some light thrown on it. Things'll be better now."

I was angry with him the rest of that afternoon. I wasn't sure anything would be better, ever again. But Michael was right. My brothers never touched me after that.

It took me a while to give myself part of the credit for that. But along the way I did gain a certain strength of my own. It began with making a more determined effort to stay out of my brothers' sight, and thus hopefully out of their minds. At first my mother complained that I was never at home to clean anymore, and as my walks became longer, my hikes into the countryside more frequent, it took no time at all for the entire house to begin to fill with dirty dishes, unwashed linens, and, of course, empty bottles. I couldn't live like that myself, so I began what would become a routine: Each morning after cooking breakfast for the family, I would tear through both stories in a frenzy of dusting, mopping, making or changing the beds. Then before going to school—and when I was seventeen, work— I would prepare food that could be popped into the oven for dinner. That way I had no need to be at home until late in the evening. Once home, if anyone so much as looked at me askance, I would cast them a look so heaped with contempt they were forced to glance away.

Over time a subtle change began to take place; I achieved some measure of power, even ordering my brothers about. "Pick up those shoes," I would demand. "Put them where they belong—*right now.*" And to my initial amazement, they would obey. I began to feel that my family feared me, in fact. It wasn't perfect, but better than their previous scorn.

In time the memories of my childhood faded. My brothers left school and went to work at the boatyard. Ian and Denny found girlfriends. Not girls from town, but a couple of sisters with purple and orange streaks in their hair, who'd come down from London in the summer. I finished school and worked as a clerk in a yard goods store. When I was twenty the opportunity to clerk at Morley's gallery arose, and I grabbed it. A year later my father died.

It was odd that even with his depressive presence gone, very little changed. My mother still drank her mead, growing ever and ever fatter until one day she could walk no more. My brothers had to lift her into her bath. One night the water was too hot, and she screamed as the scalding water covered her skin. I ran to the bathroom when I heard—just in time to see Ian and Denny hesitate for a second or two before pulling her out. I yelled at them, *"Get her out, get her out!"* By this time they had, pretending, of course, it was all a big mistake.

Now that I am older I often wonder if my mother drinks to remove herself from the knowledge of the monsters she gave birth to. For indeed, she was never truly present in any meaningful way. And after the scalding, she grew even worse. Last time I saw her she was twisting thick, bloated fingers in her yellowing grey hair and talking to herself.

Standing across the road from the gallery now, I see that the front windows of Michael's cottage are wide open, as is the top half of the double door leading into The Blue Swan. My heart begins to pound. It has been so long since I've seen Michael. Since that day three months after my marriage. He never came to see me at Pennoryn again.

What will he be like now? I wonder. The postcards he sent to me in hospital were casual, breezy: *"Here I am in Paris again, the City of Lights. They say if you sit in this certain cafe, everyone you know will pass at one time or another. I keep wishing for you. Tomorrow I'm off to Notre Dame. Be well . . . Love, Michael."*

Mrs. Rimes told me that as she read them to me—even

though I was still unconscious—she would try to put as much feeling into that word "love" as possible. I tried to tell her that there was only friendship between Michael and me, but she would have none of it. "I know a man in love when I see one."

"You've seen him? Michael's been here?"

"Quite a bit for a man not in love, I'd say."

I turn and see myself in a shop window, my long hair windblown and tossed. Reaching into my bag, I pull out my cosmetic case, open a mirrored compact and study my face. Quickly, I drift powder over my nose and cheeks, which are shiny and much too pink.

CHAPTER 9

The Blue Swan has changed rather a lot. Michael's wonderful paintings still line the gallery walls, and I recognise a few of them. But there are new oils, many of them, and even several watercolours. He's been busy in the time I've been gone.

That is not the major difference, however. The gallery is more richly appointed now. In a back corner beneath track lighting there is a simple black orchid on a small white desk that is trimmed in gold. The desk is new, as is the carpeting, which is a soft dove grey.

No sooner do I enter than a young, lovely woman comes from the back, which is now shut off by a door rather than the curtain Michael hung five years ago. There must be a silent alarm, I think, to announce customers. Michael has come up in the world.

The woman's black hair is silky, it grazes her shoulders, and her eyes are cobalt blue. She wears a white dress in a fluid-like material that I surmise is silk jersey. The neck is scooped low, the sleeves long. The effect—half demure, half sensual—is stunning.

The woman's smile is relaxed, her demeanour not that of a clerk, but of one who belongs. The message is subtle—in the bearing, perhaps. A thought arises, and with it a pang that surprises me: Has Michael married, or become involved, in the time I've been gone? Is that what Charlotte didn't want to tell me? I look quickly down to the woman's slender hands, but see no ring.

"May I help you?" she asks.

"I . . . yes. Is Michael here?"

"Sorry, no. Is there something I can do?" She makes a gesture around the gallery, as if I'm there to buy.

"Not at the moment, thank you. Is he out of town?"

She hesitates. The dark blue eyes assess me.

"We're friends," I explain, oddly nervous. "I just stopped by. I hoped he was here."

"Oh." She looks at me curiously now, and holds out her hand. "I'm Annette Bower."

I take the hand and shake it. "Joanna. Joanna Carr."

A slight frown puckers her brow, and the friendliness fades. The woman drops my hand as if startled to find she's holding a mouse. "One moment."

She turns away and I watch her walk to an ornate telephone on the desk and lift the receiver. Her hips sway beneath the jersey dress. She keeps her back to me as she presses a button and speaks. After a moment she turns, smiling, but a tightness around her mouth tells me she is not pleased.

"Michael is working in his cottage. Do you know the way?"

"Yes, I do. Thank you."

I feel her eyes on me as I cross back to the front door, lift the latch, and step onto the pavement. I am relieved to be out of there and in the bright sunlight again.

Rounding the gallery on the right, I take the brick path that leads through Michael's small vegetable garden. He has always grown fresh vegetables in season, as he likes to cook. From where I stand I can see three kinds of lettuce, some wonderfully large tomatoes, and a small plot of herbs. There are a few weeds cropping up in the herb bed. Automatically I bend down to pull one up. A scent of rosemary reaches my nostrils, and I am swept so far back in time that when I hear my name spoken I believe it to be a memory. But then again I hear it, "Jo . . ." and there is gentle laughter in the voice.

I look up, smiling.

"You never could leave my weeds alone," Michael says. He is standing in the kitchen doorway wiping paint from his hands with a rag and smiling. It is the same Michael: longish dark hair combed back neatly, then twisting into curls at his neck. A slightly crooked nose in a thin face that seems to radiate energy. In jeans and a faded blue work shirt he looks as lean as ever, as comforting and strong.

"I'm afraid things have gone to seed out here without you." He gestures towards the garden.

"Indeed they have," I agree, feeling oddly constrained.

A brief shadow crosses his face. "I've missed you. Are you all right?"

"I . . . yes. I'm all right."

With that he starts down the steps and, dropping the rag, extends both arms. As if I've just been set loose from some horrible bond, I run towards him, hugging him so tight he is forced to pull back, laughing. "Jo, you're breaking my ribs!"

I laugh, too. And I realise this is the first I've laughed this way in a very long time. The words come out in a rush. "I'm just so glad to see you. I got all your postcards. Mrs. Rimes, my nurse, read them to me even when I couldn't hear, although the doctor says I probably did hear anyway, and Mrs. Rimes thinks they helped me to come back from wherever I was, and then when I did come back, I read each and every one . . ."

By this time Michael is shaking his head. "You don't have to tell me everything at once! We have all the time in the world."

He turns and leads me up the stairs into the kitchen. The screen door swings shut behind us. Releasing my hand, he settles me into a kitchen chair. The furnishings are the same: polar white, their simplicity soothing. Here and there are touches of royal blue. At the window are white mini-blinds, pulled all the way up now to let in dappled sunlight from a wisteria vine.

"Let me get you something," Michael says. "Coffee? Is that still your drink of choice? And what about a salad? I've got French bread—"

I laugh. "You don't have to feed me, you know. But yes, I'd like coffee. I do prefer tea now at night, or when it's cold and damp, and there are times when I love a glass of wine . . ."

He looks at me and I smile. I am still rambling, I know, wanting to tell him so much, so many little things that are of no importance at all, but that we used to share.

"It's all right, go on," he says. "I want to hear it all." He turns to rinse out the pot, and I see from his rather clumsy movements that he feels awkward with me as well. He takes a package of coffee beans from the fridge and drops it on the floor, and when he picks it up he gives me a rueful grin. "I don't know why, but I feel all thumbs with you sitting there."

I smile. "I know. It's been so long."

"And you seem older somehow."

"Thanks." It's all I need to hear; I'll be thirty-one in a fortnight.

"I didn't mean that. Steadier, perhaps?"

"Hmmm. You think so?" A good thing he didn't see me last night.

"Yes," he says, tossing beans into the grinder. "Tell me how you feel, what you're doing now. Where are you staying? And how long have you been home? Why didn't you phone me?"

I raise my voice over the whine and rattle. A strong scent of freshly ground coffee fills the air. "I've only been home three days. I don't know how I feel yet, and I suppose that's why I didn't phone. I'm at the house. At Pennoryn."

He spoons coffee into the filter. "Pennoryn?" His hand pauses, and his voice seems oddly stiff. "Is that a good idea?"

"I don't see why not. It's my home."

"Even so . . ." He finishes with the coffee, switches on the pot, and turns to me. "Jo, if you'd like to rent a little place here in town, I could help you find a house agent, and then get settled in. Wouldn't you rather be away from there?"

"No. Michael, I need to be there—to remember."

He frowns, but is silent.

"I still have no memory of the night David died," I explain. "The doctor thinks I won't be truly well till I know what happened."

Michael sits across from me and says worriedly, "I don't know if I agree. Quite honestly, Jo, I think it might be best if you never remembered. Why relive all that?"

"Well . . . it's true I get tired thinking about it. Sometimes I wish I could just wipe the whole thing out of my mind forever. But things are going on, things I don't understand. First Charlotte and Henry act strangely every time I talk about that night—"

"Charlotte!" he interrupts, his voice laced with contempt. "You aren't seeing her again, are you?"

I am as bewildered as when she spoke this way of him. "Charlotte? Why not? She's my friend."

The coffee bubbles, it is finished. Michael stands and fills two large blue mugs. He hands me one and takes a seat across from me again.

"Michael, is there something being kept from me? Something about that night?"

His blue eyes flicker, the way they always did when he was being evasive. I remember when he was a boy, his mother calling out to him from the front porch as we'd be going off somewhere. "Michael, did you wash up first? I don't want you going out without washing up." And there would be that flicker as he'd look back and say, "Yes, Mum. I washed up," when he'd only done his hands, not his face. Then he'd grin at me.

He doesn't grin now.

"Michael?"

He shakes his head. "I don't know anything, Jo. I would just stay away from Charlotte."

"That's funny," I can only think to respond pointedly. "She said the same about you."

We sit at a wrought-iron table in a secluded area of Michael's vegetable garden, well back from the road. A thick hedge lends privacy from passersby on the walk, and muffles the sound of traffic. Overhead the fronds of several palm trees drift slowly back and forth, pushed by a zephyr of air. The palms were trucked into Mevagissey long before Michael and I were born. A bronze fountain, however, is new.

My irritation at his warning about Charlotte fades in these tranquil surroundings. "You've created quite an oasis here," I say.

His smile is wry. "A quite expensive little oasis, and I'm paying through the nose for it now. But Annette thought— well, actually, *I* thought it as well—that I needed a place of quiet in the midst of the day. The gallery sometimes gets to be . . . oh, too much a business."

"And Annette?"

"A godsend. She's here every day now, and she keeps things going while I'm out of town. It was Annette's idea to do things over a bit, especially in the gallery itself. She thought it would be good for business to spruce the place up."

"It is quite different from the last time I saw it. Rather *fawncy* for the struggling young artist I knew."

Again that ironic grin. "I'll admit it took some getting used to. But now that I have, I find I rather like it. One thing, Annette is a wonder at paperwork, and with her handling the accounts I've more time to paint. I'd say we make a good team. We're even thinking of starting up another gallery in London soon."

"Mmmm." The beautiful Annette: *quite a wonder.*

"And you?" Michael looks at me over the rim of his cup. "What have you been doing since you got home?"

"Oh, the usual. Shopping, cleaning, burning my husband's clothes."

He chokes and sputters as I laugh.

"You burned David's clothes?" he says with a wondering tone.

"Every stitch."

"I . . ." He looks blank. "I guess I don't know what to say."

I sigh and set my coffee down. "I just felt so . . . so *angry* all of a sudden."

He leans forward on his elbows. "Jo, how much do you actually remember?"

"Of my marriage? It's coming back rather quickly. Bits and pieces, here and there."

"And that last night?"

"Very little. Certainly not who did it."

A butterfly comes to visit a basket of fuchsia, and we watch it skip from one bright pink-and-blue flower to another. Then off it goes, a shimmering gold flicker against the azure sky. "Why can't life be like that?" I say. "We come, we taste, we fly away."

Michael searches my face. "Would you like to fly away?"

"At times. There are moments when I would like to spread my wings and leave all this behind. This town, my past."

"You remember the past, then?"

"My childhood?" I laugh softly, bitterly. "Oh, yes. Indeed I do."

He frowns. "I'm sorry. I almost wish you'd forgotten all that, as well—for good."

"Me, too."

"Jo . . . remember that one time I came out to Pennoryn after you were married?"

"When you brought me the stone hare? Of course."

"I didn't feel comfortable talking about this then, but I've always wanted to ask. When you married David— when I was away in Paris—did anything happen? Is that why you married, for protection?"

"From my brothers, you mean? No, nothing happened, not like that."

"But you married so quickly."

I arch a brow, and my voice, I am certain, has that age-old tone that women use when men have been thick-headed and unaware. "It may have seemed that way to you, perhaps. You were in Paris having a grand old time. I was here . . ." *Ah, well . . . Let it go.*

He fumbles with his cup. "I just thought . . . I know now I was being unrealistic, of course. I just thought you might wait."

I look at him, puzzled. "Wait? I don't understand." Then I meet the look in his eyes and am stunned. "For *you*, you mean?"

I remember with a pang the day he left for Paris just a few months before I met David. Michael had got a grant to study with one of the country's foremost teachers of Renaissance art, and was letting out the gallery for a year. I drove him to the train station and stood there as he boarded, then watched every window till he appeared. When I saw him in that car, waving from that window—when I saw that train pulling away—I thought my heart would break.

Michael left in March. In June I met David, and by then I was feeling foolish for mooning over someone who'd never hinted at anything but friendship, not once in all the twenty-one years I'd known him. Foolish—and incredibly lonely.

By July, David and I were building our house. All that summer, autumn, and winter we worked on Pennoryn, laying the foundation, erecting the walls and roof, then turning to the indoors as the weather got bad. And in all that time, not a word from Michael.

My voice is unsteady. "I still don't understand. Why didn't you tell me? You never said a *thing*."

He frowns. "But I *did*. I wrote every week, all summer long, even after I got your letter saying you were getting married. I can't tell you what a shock that was. I asked you to wait, to give it some time, but in your letters back you never mentioned it. I thought, 'Well, I've been the fool. She must not feel for me at all.'"

"Michael, I never got those letters! The first I heard from you—from July on—was when you came to Pennoryn the following March and gave me the stone hare. I was quite hurt. And angry. Up till then, I thought you'd forgotten me."

He fists his hands together so tightly, the knuckles turn white. "Bloody hell. I should have known something was wrong when you didn't at least acknowledge my letters. But yours kept coming—and you seemed so damned happy."

"I . . ."

"What?" He fixes his gaze on mine. "You were, weren't you? Happy?"

"I . . . yes. Yes, of course."

I run a hand through my hair, and the truth is, I'm feeling a bit of a shock and close to tears. Though I never admitted it to anyone else and barely ever to myself, I had loved Michael with all my being since childhood. Even when he went away and I met and fell in love with David, there was a small, secret part of me that waited to hear from Michael that summer, waited to hear him say, "No, don't do it, don't marry him. You belong to me." One word might have turned things around, one word to show that he missed me, cared for me more than he'd realised.

When no letter came, not even a card, I finally gave it up. The man of my dreams was right there before me, wasn't he? We had built our home together. Pennoryn was finished; we were to be married in January and begin a wonderful life there.

Why spit in the eye of God?

My anger of the night before returns. It is like a sea of blackness, washing over me—and I cannot help it, I direct it at Michael. "I don't know what happened to those letters. But more than that, I don't understand why you didn't tell me how you felt, long before you left for Paris. Michael, we knew each other for years! For heaven's sake, why didn't you say something?"

He shakes his head. "I see now I should have. I simply never felt I could. I hadn't enough money to take care of you, especially in the beginning, when I was struggling. My dad had died, and my mother couldn't manage alone. Then when the grant came to study in Paris, I had only that and a bit saved for expenses—"

"But that wouldn't have mattered to me! If I'd only known . . ."

If I'd known . . . so much might have been different.

Michael grabs my hand. "You're shaking. What are you thinking?"

"I don't know. I . . . there's this horrible blackness, and I feel so terribly angry. I feel as if . . . as if I want to kill someone."

Michael pales. "For God's sake, Jo, don't say that aloud to anyone else—not ever. Promise me, do you hear? Never even *think it* again."

By mutual consent we put the past aside, as well as any talk of our feelings in the present. I don't think either of us knows what more to say. There is a processing of information going on; I see it in Michael's eyes, and I am sure he must see it in mine. *What now? What next?*

With poorly hidden determination, then, we set about making the remainder of this extraordinary afternoon as ordinary as possible. Michael goes with me to St. Austell to find a car, following in his Range Rover. I pick out a dark green two-seater at Ryan's, and we drop off the rental. Michael insists I return to the cottage; he would like to cook dinner for me. "Fettucine Alfredo with lemon zest, and a fresh salad from the garden," he says.

I am easily persuaded; it is almost like old times.

Still, there are tensions that were never there before. We don't seem to know how to behave with each other now. Every word, every movement, is fraught with new and wonderful—but perhaps also frightening—possibilities.

After dinner the fog comes in, and we sit before the low, modern fireplace drinking the last of a bottle of wine. We say awkward things like: "Lovely time of year, isn't it?"

"Marvelous . . . the sun staying up so late, and all those wonderful flowers."

"Excellent lettuce in that salad, too."

"Yes, the weather's been perfect for it."

When we've finally outdone ourselves in terms of vapidity, and even the birds have wrung out their last song, I remember the odd portrait that hangs in the Harbourside Gallery.

I set my glass on a low table next to the fire. "Michael, the first day I was home I stopped into the new gallery in the village near Pennoryn. Harbourside. There's a portrait just inside, on the wall."

He smiles. "The one of you?"

"It *is* of me, then? I must say, it gave me a bit of a start. The ring on the girl's finger is like the one you made for me of sea grass, that awful day on the cliffs. But the girl isn't me, Michael."

"No?"

"Don't be silly, she's far too innocent. I wasn't anything at all like that."

"You were exactly like that," he says.

I get up and begin to pace, irritated. "Michael, I know what and who I was. Who I *am.*"

His voice takes on an edge. "And what is that? What are you, Jo?"

I can't say it. Ugly, I think sometimes. Defiled.

"You don't see me clearly," I say. "You never have."

He laughs softly. "Beauty is in the eye of the beholder? That must tell you something."

"What? What are you saying?"

"Jo, who are you going to believe? Them or me?"

"I . . ."

"Your brothers," he insists gently, "or me?"

My face flames, and he comes and takes me by the shoulders. "Listen to me, Jo. That portrait—that's the way I've always seen you. But I see you that way because that's who you *are.* I would do anything—anything at all—to convince you of that." He pulls me against him, holding me tight. "Sweetheart, let's not waste any more time. Marry me! Marry me now!"

I yank back, nearly speechless. "Marry—?"

"Why not? We should have done it years ago! If we had . . . dear God, Jo, if we had, none of this would ever have happened."

"Michael, what are you saying? None of what?"

"I . . ." Again that evasive flicker. But then it's gone, and Michael pulls me close. "There's simply been too much wasted time, Jo. And I feel so responsible. You never should have been in that hospital . . ." He pulls back, his eyes pleading. "Jo, let me take care of things now. Let me see to it no one ever hurts you again."

"But . . ."

The truth is, I am so caught off-stride, I can't think what to say. I touch his cheek, lightly reassuring. "Michael, things have changed. No one's going to hurt me now."

His brow creases with worry.

"You don't agree?" I ask.

"Remember that powder keg, Jo? The one I spoke of years ago? I feel sometimes it's about to explode."

CHAPTER 10

It is three days later, and I have bolted like a rabbit to a hole. I have passed the hours since Michael's proposal working in the garden, steaming off old wallpaper in the living room, and painting trim around the windows that have been repaired. I have not left Pennoryn for a moment, at least not in body. My mind is all over the place. *How can I possibly marry Michael?* I natter on and on. *Or anyone, for that matter, with so many questions unanswered, so much healing to be done?*

I am up one moment, down the next, still so uncertain about everything.

Meanwhile, there are Michael's feelings of impending doom to contend with. Well, his ancestors were Irish on his mother's side. His father's people were those black-haired moody people believed to have come here from Crete. Michael could give Old Robert a run for his money, when it comes to superstition.

I forgot to telephone Dr. Shahi that day, and he cornered me the next morning. I had been dashing around, my nerves on edge, acting like someone on amphetamines. I must have sounded mad. "I'm painting," I sang with false gaiety into the phone. "Cleaning things up, having a wonderful time."

"Joanna . . ." His tone was disapproving. "You promised to check in every Friday."

"Well, I didn't know it was written in blood!" I answered

rather huffily. "For heaven's sake, I'm up to my knees in mud."

"Mud . . . But I understood you to say you were painting."

"That, too."

He rang off finally, but not before getting in a cautionary word. "Joanna, do go slowly. Take time to meditate, to think."

Time to think. It's all I have, time to think.

"Robert?" I drop my trowel and rise from my knees, brushing loam from my hands on my jeans. Robert has dug shallow trenches on either side of the path, and I've been setting down flowers. There is dirt on my nose; I can see it from the corners of my eyes. Sweat pours down my forehead beneath the old straw hat I found in the garage. I wipe it with my sleeve. "Robert, where are you?"

I am thinking that before he leaves, I would like him to tackle the bedposts. I find him out in the garage, uncovering a white wooden bench that once sat in the rose garden. He motions towards it and I nod. "Perfect." We both grab an end and carry it out into the light. "Let's clean it up and put it in front by the camellias, all right? There's a nice sunny patch there. It'll be perfect for sitting out and having lunch."

He points into a dark corner of the garage, silently indicating a green bench.

"Right. That one goes by the pond."

I get the hose while he sets off across the garden, lugging the green bench behind. In three short days Old Robert and I have fallen into an easy routine. We need very little conversation to get things done, which is just as well, since Robert is a bit thin on conversation. I found myself prattling away at him yesterday, all that nervous energy, and it took me twenty minutes to realise he wasn't answering.

Michael has called several times. He doesn't pressure me, but I know he is anxious. "I'll be here, Jo. Call me when you want to talk. I love you."

It is like a fairy tale. Perhaps that is why I can't answer yes or no. I'm expecting to hear someone say, "And the Prince rode away on his shining white steed. The End."

But what if, I think, it did not happen that way? What if Michael and I married, and we came to live here at Pennoryn? All the dreams that never came true with David could come true now, with Michael. I could be happy here at last.

How far I have come from those first days home, I think. *How far, and how fast. And largely because of Michael. Knowing about his love fills me these days with joy.*

I am still hosing down the bench, deep in thought, when Old Robert speaks.

"You might be wanting to move away from there, Mrs. Carr." I look down and see the ground around me has puddled badly. My feet, in tennies, are soaking wet. But there are rainbows in the water spray.

I look at Robert and laugh. "Isn't it a beautiful day?"

He smiles, but doesn't answer. I am tempted to turn the hose on my gardener and make him yelp. But the sound would be too odd, too foreign. He might never recover.

I have convinced Old Robert to have lunch with me on the bench. The sun is high, and there are bees vying for our food. Now and again he puts out a hand and lets them land on it, as he did the other day. They seem for all the world to be licking his sweat, like fuzzy little dogs.

"Robert, are you married?" I ask as we're finishing our sandwiches. "Do you have a family?"

He wraps his crumbs carefully in his serviette and frowns. "Married once. Not now."

"I'm sorry. What happened?"

His mouth tightens. "Left, she did. Years ago."

"I am sorry. I didn't mean to intrude." I wish now I hadn't brought the subject up. Old Robert's eyes have gone from irritated to vacant, just like that.

He sets his mug of tea on the bench, and for a moment we sit silently. Then he looks into the distance and says emotionally, in a thicker West Country dialect, "They birds . . . must be hundreds of hungry birds in they trees."

"Yes," I agree. They sit on the high branches and watch us. So far, only a few sparrows have been bold enough to visit. The rest chatter to each other about the advisability of venturing near.

Robert points then to an old feeder I've hung at the corner of the garage. I am surprised to see that his jaw is quivering. "Wouldn't 'ee think they'd trust it by now?"

"Well, it does take them a while," I say carefully.

He grunts. "Come here every year, some of 'em, don't they?"

"Yes. Some do. They have their babies and spend the summer here."

"And you feed 'em regular, each year?"

"I suppose." Why is he talking this way?

"But now they're up there a-twitterin' away, like they'm havin' a convention—tryin' t'decide if 'tis safe down here."

I smile at his idea of a bird convention. But I think I understand now. "Is this conversation about birds, Robert?" I ask softly, "Or your wife?"

He sighs, shakes his head, and stands, rubbing the middle of his back. Picking up his rake he says, "Makes no difference. Birds, people. They might learn t'have a bit of trust."

They might learn t'have a bit of trust.

Dr. Shahi has often said that when one needs a message, one will come. It may be in a book that mysteriously falls from the shelf, or in the casual word of a passerby. It may even be in something so ordinary as the conversation of a gardener.

I never did learn what happened in Robert's marriage, or why his wife left. Directly after that dissertation, he ambled off to spray the roses. He's set me to thinking, though —meditating, as Dr. Shahi would call it—on my own state of trust. I am in the kitchen washing dishes and thinking like mad, in fact, when the phone rings. Eagerly, and with soapy hands, I grab the receiver by the sink.

"Michael?" It is out of my mouth before I've time to call it back.

A small silence. "Joanna? It's Charlotte."

"Oh." I find myself at a loss for words. I am not precisely angry with her still, but I can't help it—I am cautious.

"I know you're irritated with me," she says, taking the bull by the horns as she so often does. "And I'm sorry, I wish things were different. But I thought I should ring you up. Something's happened." Her voice rises, high and thin.

"Charlotte? What's wrong?"

"I've just had a visit from a policeman, the one who was in charge the night David died. He asked all kinds of questions. Joanna, I really thought all that was in the past, and I don't at all understand why he's coming round again now. I especially don't want him bothering Henry. He's had enough—well, never mind. But I thought you would want to know."

"A policeman. Was it an Inspector Goff?"

"That's the one. Big, rather heavy-set, walks as if he's got bad knees."

"He came to see me in hospital. What was he saying to you?"

"The same old questions, for the most part. When precisely did we find you? Did we touch anything, move anything? And he asked me again about that blanket, if I'd covered you with it. I told him no, we'd found you that way. He said didn't it seem odd you'd be left that way, covered over so nicely, as it were, as if by some 'gentleman burglar?' That's the way he put it—some gentleman burglar. I told him you'd been bashed on the head, and that didn't seem very gentlemanly to me."

I cannot help smiling.

"Has he come to talk to you, Joanna?"

"No." My smile fades. "Do you think he will? Did he say he means to?"

"No, but it wouldn't surprise me. I thought you might want to be on your guard a bit. They may be thinking of reopening the case."

I stand there with soapsuds dripping down my arm, hearing her words: *Be on your guard a bit.* But why? What have I to hide?

"Char, Michael said much the same thing the other day, that I should be careful what I say. I don't understand. What do either of you think I might say that could hurt me?"

Her laughter is short, uneasy. "Hurt you? Why, nothing, of course, I didn't mean it that way. It's simply that these people try to trip you up. They try to make you say things that seem suspicious, even when they aren't." She hesitates, and before I can speak she asks, "Joanna, what precisely did Michael say?"

"Not much. I said something about feeling I could kill someone—"

"My God! You actually said that? To Michael?"

"Yes, and then he grabbed me and told me not to ever say it or even think it again. Char, I really must ask you. I'm beginning to think . . ." I can barely get the words out, for fear my suspicions may be true. "I . . . do you and Michael think . . . well, you know, that I did something . . . that night?"

Her indrawn breath is sharp. "You mean, do I think you killed David? I . . . ." She falls silent, and there is nothing to be heard but a whoosh of vacant air along the wires.

My stomach tightens. "Char . . . ?"

"My dear, sweet Joanna," she says earnestly, "of course I don't think such a terrible thing. For heaven's sake, even the police don't think it! You were struck on the head, there was no blood on you, no weapon close at hand . . . how could you possibly have done it? As for Michael, damn him for planting an idea like that in your head!"

My fingers tighten on the receiver. "I didn't say he did, Char. There are just so many things I don't understand these days when I'm talking to people. So many undertones . . . and here I am with all these feelings of anger, and people telling me not to *show* it."

"Simply because you wouldn't want anyone getting wrong ideas," Charlotte says more reasonably, collecting herself. "But my God, Joanna, it's not all that abnormal to be angry when someone you love has died. It's as if they've abandoned you, after all. Any fool could tell you that's often the first reaction."

"I know. Dr. Shahi said that as well."

"And again, as to Michael Lamb—I hate to say I told you so, but I did warn you to stay away from him."

"Char—"

"Listen to me, Joanna. Michael has changed. He's been brooding. Quite withdrawn. He hasn't taken my calls for months, and all I've ever wanted was to talk to him about you. Then just yesterday, Henry heard something rather disturbing. He was at Midland Bank having a chat with his old crony, Roger Stone—Stone's been president of Midland forever, you know. And when they were talking, Michael's name came up. He banks there as well, it seems."

"His name 'came up?' " I ask dubiously. "Or did Henry just happen to bring it up?"

"Dear heart, what does it matter? The point is, Michael tried to take out a *loan* last week." Charlotte pauses dramatically, as if this news carries some obvious portent of evil.

"A loan," I repeat, smiling slightly. "And this, you think, is cause for suspicion? For heaven's sake, Charlotte, we all need a bit of extra cash at times."

"One hundred thousand pounds, Joanna? Rather a lot of extra cash, I'd say."

She's right, and I myself am a bit startled at the amount. "I . . . well, of course, it is a lot. But Char, Michael doesn't just sit and doodle with art. He runs a business. In fact, he mentioned wanting to open another gallery in London. That's probably what the loan is for."

She sniffs. "That isn't what he said. He *said* he needed money to pay off improvements to The Blue Swan. And you know who ordered those improvements? That gorgeous young assistant of his, Annette Bower. Henry says she's nearly run Michael into the ground financially. And everyone is saying there's more going on."

"Well everyone is wrong," I snap. "Michael and Annette Bower are business associates and friends. Nothing more."

"Is that so? Are you aware that she's the one who gave Michael his alibi for the night of David's murder? According to her they were together—*all night.*"

"Oh, for heaven's sake, Charlotte. I'm sure they were only working."

"Well, that's what she said, of course. Taking inventory, or some such."

"And you don't believe her? Char, Michael has always

worked nights doing that sort of thing. That way he can paint during the day when he's got the light. And she is his assistant, after all."

"*Now* she is, yes. But think back. Do you ever remember hearing of her, or seeing her at the gallery, before that night?"

"No, but then I didn't see Michael hardly ever when I was married to David. I never went to the gallery."

"Trust me, my dear. Annette Bower and Michael were *close*—to put it delicately—at the time of David's murder. But not as business associates, not until later. Since then, word around town is that she's head over heels in love with Michael. Everyone who even shops at the gallery can see it. And, given their *liaison,* of course she'd say anything to protect him."

My voice rises. "Bloody hell, Charlotte. Are you actually suggesting that Michael might have killed David? And that Annette Bower covered for him? This is going too far, even for you! I know you never liked Michael, but to think—"

"Joanna, *you* think. Michael has had a pattern of protecting you since childhood. What if he walked in on you and David that night having an argument? What if he saw David . . ." Her voice trails off uncertainly.

"Saw what? What in the world might he have seen? Do you know something?"

"No . . . no, of course not. But who else on earth would have covered you with that blanket? Surely that was the mark of someone who cared." I can hear her at the other end of the line, taking a deep breath. "All right, let's say Michael didn't kill David. Let's say he simply walked in after the fact, saw what had happened, and didn't want to get involved. So he covered you with the blanket and left. Joanna, if it happened that way, why hasn't he come forward and said that? It's unconscionable that he hasn't spoken up, when you've got so many questions about this. I would think his silence alone would tell you something."

"It certainly would—*if* it had happened that way," I say testily. "I just don't believe for a moment that Michael would do that to me. Oh, Charlotte, let's just stop this.

Stop it right now. Of all the people in the world I've reason to trust beyond a shadow of a doubt, it's Michael. If anything like that had happened, he'd have told me."

"My dear, people change. You've been away, you can't know—"

"I know I don't want to hear any of this again. And, Charlotte, there's something *you* should know. Michael and I . . . we're getting married."

I touch my cheek, my lips, wondering at the words I've just blurted out. *Michael and I . . .*

It came out abruptly, as if the decision were sudden. Yet it was not. The answer is knocking at my heart, and has been for days. It is saying, *Listen,* and the message it brings is that *this is right.* I have been on a path with Michael since childhood, straying from it only during those months of marriage to David. Now we are back together. We know we love each other as more than friends, and it would be a tragedy to waste any more time.

My three days of pondering amongst the weeds, mud, and paint have paid off. Not to mention Old Robert, with his words of wisdom about trust.

Charlotte, however, is aghast. "Joanna, you don't know what you are saying! When was this decided?"

"Michael asked me a few days ago. I haven't accepted yet, but I intend to. Today."

"Oh, thank God, then, there's time! Listen to me, dear. You cannot possibly do this. You must tell him it's too soon, that you need time to think."

"I'll do nothing of the sort."

"Joanna, doesn't it occur to you that Michael may have more than one agenda in wanting to marry you? I hadn't yet got to this, but that loan—dear, he was turned down. According to Roger Stone, he seemed quite desperate about it. And you have rather a tidy sum in the bank."

I laugh. "Not that much. Only what I've inherited from David. Most of my savings from working at Morley's all those years were spent to build Pennoryn."

"And if you remember, I tried to warn you about that. You wouldn't listen."

"I simply disagreed with you. David and I spent my

money on the house, and afterwards we lived on his savings. It worked out fine. Charlotte, I didn't feel a need for —as you advised—a hidden cache of 'escape money in case something went wrong.' "

There is a small silence on the line, then Charlotte says softly, "If only you knew, my dear, how easily . . ."

"What? How easily things can go wrong? Well, it seems I do, now," I say with some irony. "But what are you getting at, Char? Is there something, some problem, between you and Henry?"

"Between . . . No, not at all. Not now, at least."

I feel her pull back, and I sense I am treading very close to a truth I may not wish to hear.

But Charlotte continues, "Joanna, the only important thing now is for you to be safe. And I really must strongly urge that you be careful about Michael. You're in danger of falling into the same trap with him, you know. You've inherited David's money, and I'm certain Michael knows it. He also knows how giving a person you are. Marriage at this moment to you could only help him."

"Charlotte," I say with exasperation, "why are you trying so hard to make Michael seem suspect? First you've got him being a killer, then a con artist. For God's sake, do you hear yourself? We're talking about *Michael* here! And the fact is, Michael has never, not once in my life, hurt me. You know that! And why you are now choosing to ignore it is beyond me. Why not just give us your blessing and leave it at that?"

"I can't. I cannot give you and Michael my blessing."

I am so angry I can barely speak. I grip the phone to steady myself. "Listen to me, Charlotte. For six months I lay in a hospital bed, virtually senseless. Since then, one person or another has thought they knew what was best for me. I'm sick of it! It's time I took my life in my own hands and got on with things."

"But this *isn't* taking your life in your own hands, don't you see? Surely Michael has talked you into this. I can't believe you even thought of it a week ago. And if you marry him now, he'll be controlling you just as surely as David did."

I cannot talk to her any longer. If I do, I will say things best left unsaid for the moment. I will tell her point-blank about the note I found in David's jacket, and I will ask her if she was having an affair with my husband. I might even say, "Were both of you controlling me in some way I failed to understand, all along? Have you been my enemy—not my friend?"

But I am still weak in many ways from those months in hospital. There are things I can face and things I cannot; there are moments when I've done all I can do. "Charlotte, I really must go," I say wearily.

"Oh, please, Joanna, don't do this, don't withdraw from me now. I can help you, if only you'll let me—"

I leave her talking to an empty line.

CHAPTER 11

That night, when the chores are done and I've more time to think, I begin to see another side to my conversation with Charlotte. Though Charlotte has never much liked Michael, I've always thought that to be a result of the kind of jealousy that sometimes occurs between friends. There were times in past years when I would have plans with Michael that didn't include Charlotte, and I would feel a certain testiness from her. *"I thought we would do something Sunday. Why didn't you check with me first?"*

As I prepare for bed, I remember how eager Charlotte was to help me find a car in St. Austell, and how disappointed she was to learn I was going into Mevagissey, instead, to see Michael. I remember, too, that for all her wealth and sophistication, Charlotte has never had other close women friends. We always had each other, and that seemed enough.

Except that I also had Michael.

Is that what is really bothering her now, I wonder? With David gone, did she think I would have more time for her? And now, hearing I'm to marry Michael, is she upset to have those hopes dashed?

If so, I can understand her feelings, at least to a point. I felt a loss myself when Charlotte first married Henry. There were all those honeymoon months when they travelled and there was no one to talk to about "woman" things. There have been months since, as well, when they travelled and I was lonely, months when Michael was away and there was only David for company.

Still, fear of losing precious time with a friend is not a good reason to all but accuse a man of murder. If I were anyone else—if I were not someone who had known Michael for years and knew him to be honest and trustworthy —the terrible things Charlotte said could be devastating. I do hope I am the only one she has shared these suspicions with. And fast upon that, I wonder: Has she told Michael what she thinks? Is that why he will no longer accept her calls? Why *he* is upset with *her*? This feels right. Michael wouldn't want to tell me this, and perhaps cause trouble between me and a friend.

Whatever the case, Charlotte is being more and more difficult these days, and if this causes a rent between us, I cannot help but feel that she has no one to blame but herself. That I am feeling a loss as well is something I suppose must be lived with, at least till we can patch things up.

Over the next few days, the troublesome talk with Charlotte dulls to a quiet murmur in my mind. She'll come round in time, I tell myself. She'll see we're as close as ever, and that Michael will not even try to come between us. Her fears will be allayed, and perhaps I can bring my two best friends together, for harmony all around.

Meanwhile, I am caught up in a whirlwind—a pre-wedding daze. Michael and I have set the date: two weeks from this coming Saturday. I have told him to leave things to me, that I will make arrangements. He has gratefully accepted, as he's been running back and forth to London quite a bit, preparing for a showing.

"Let's keep it simple, Jo," he said two days ago. "We can have the ceremony at the Registry Office, with just a few friends."

"Not on your life. I've done that before. I want to marry you in a church."

"A church?" I could hear the groan in his voice. "I see an extravaganza coming up."

"Nonsense. We don't know that many people."

It all sounded like so much grand fun when I talked to him three days ago. And it will be, I know. But first there are chores to be done: get the garden finished, do up the house. And so little time. We're to have the reception here after the wedding, and I want everything to be fresh and new—uncontaminated.

Thank God for Old Robert. Despite his slow, deliberate gait, my gardens are being miraculously transformed. He has more energy than I ever dreamed of—perhaps because he wastes so little of it talking.

Michael is due any moment. He's to come by and fetch me for a surprise, something we're to do that he hasn't revealed to me yet. In my bedroom I toss one outfit after another aside, looking for just the right one. I can't wait for this afternoon. I can't wait to see Michael. I bless whatever luck freed me to do this, to be living this life now.

In the next moment I am shocked to have thought that way. I would never, *never* wish for David to have died as he did. When I think about being "free," I am thinking free from the hospital—am I not?

In truth, I cannot say. Thoughts have come at me out of the blue as I've raced about the house, cleaning and polishing. Thoughts about David—and who really might have done it. Who would have wanted him dead? Or *was* it a vagrant and nothing personal, as the police suggested?

But if the police did in fact believe that, why are they reopening the case—and why just now, when I'm out of hospital? *Do they think I did it?*

I may be confused, coming back from hospital with some memory gone, and with so much of my life to put back in order. But I am not a stupid woman. I know that both Charlotte and Michael think I've something to hide. The worst part of it is that I sense they are right, and the thought frightens me. Time after time I find myself pushing it away. There is so much good to look forward to now. Why ruin it with the past?

What if the past affects the future? is the answer that haunts me. I push it away, as well. It seems to me that I have had far too little happiness over the years, and I am determined to grasp what I can with Michael now, and hold on for all I'm worth.

Rummaging through my closet, I think about the red negligee I was wearing the night David died. Mrs. Rimes said it was a bit torn, and one of the nursing assistants, meaning well, tossed it away. I am having a difficult time even remembering it. I do remember that David always liked red, so perhaps the negligee was a gift from him. Certainly I can't remember ever shopping for it myself.

As to that, I should do some shopping, and soon. My clothes are all pre-hospital. In fact, most are pre-marriage to David. My wardrobe badly needs updating. After much ruminating I decide finally on dark green trousers and a white silk blouse. I should also take a sweater, I think, in case the fog doesn't lift. While I'm looking for one in my drawers, I find a lace handkerchief that Charlotte gave me on my twenty-fifth birthday. Holding it to my nose, I feel a stab of sorrow over the trouble with Charlotte. The handkerchief smells of lavender, and beneath it I find another piece of linen, knotted together with a sachet in the middle and my initial *J* embroidered in gold. This, too, is from Charlotte, and I remember that for birthdays and Christmas she always gave me gifts which appealed to the senses. A book with scented pages, an antique porcelain vase burgeoning with flowers. Once she brought me a box of exotic candy from one of her trips. The fragile sugar pieces, shaped like flowers, were delicately flavoured with bergamot, rose, and lilac.

"You have such exquisite taste," I said then with mixed feelings. "Thank you, Charlotte." I had always envied her ability to choose such lovely gifts, and at times I felt overwhelmed by my inability to repay her in kind. Even more, I was embarrassed about my own lack of elegance.

But I knew that Charlotte meant well. She wanted to give me nice things because she saw how I loved and admired them. She wanted to share with me the other side, the great possibilities that life had to offer. And I followed along happily, eager to learn good manners, good style, good speech. . . .

"I only wish I could just pack you up and bring you with me on my adventures," she had said more than once. "Joanna, if only . . ."

If only you hadn't married David. No matter how I tried to convince Charlotte of my happiness in the beginning, she felt certain that David was keeping me from all good things. "I love being alone at Pennoryn," I would say, when David's trips to London became more and more frequent. "I love my quiet little life in the country."

"But how long can that last?" she would begin, or some version of it. And with newlywed fervour I would cut her off, of course, before she could continue with such blasphemy. The subject would be dropped.

Suddenly my grief is overwhelming at the thought of the space that has come between my friend and me.

Through my open window I see the early morning fog just hanging a bit over the hill, and I smell the damp earth around the primroses, the various mingled scents of wet leaves and grass. My eyes scan this room that I have made so bright and lovely, this room from which I have quite determinedly erased all traces of David. Even the hideous bedposts are gone; sawn off and carted away by Old Robert to be cut up for mulch.

I have so much now, and I know with absolute certainty how little it means that Charlotte disapproves of Michael, or even that she and David had some secret I did not share. Dr. Shahi has said that people are constantly being renewed—in their cells, tissues, blood. "The person we held a grudge against last week is not the same person today. That person is gone; there is no one left to begrudge."

I don't know if I believe that or if I will ever be able to feel this high-minded about those who hurt me. But I know there must be a grain of truth in it, and I can begin, I think, with Charlotte. I am so happy about the life I am about to embark upon with Michael, and the only thing that would make it more perfect is having Charlotte back as my friend.

Crossing to the table by my bed, I lift the phone, ringing her number. After several moments, she answers, breathless.

"It's Joanna," I say, a bit nervous and wondering if she'll talk to me at all.

"Joanna! I'm so glad you called." I can hear her collecting herself, taking deep breaths. "Sorry. I ran in from the terrace. Henry's hosting a meeting of the Garden Society. The place is positively teeming with little old ladies and men going on and on about their award-winning roses. Where are you? Would you like to come by?"

My fingers relax on the phone. "I'm sorry, I'd love to, but I can't today, Char. Michael's coming to fetch me for a surprise."

Damn. Why have I blurted it out like this? Was I testing her?

Perhaps so. And it seems she will pass my test, for after only a brief pause she says, "That's lovely, Joanna," clearly forcing a smile into her voice. "The weather's shaping up nicely over here. You should have a bit of a good day before you."

"Yes. Charlotte, I wondered . . . I know you don't necessarily approve of all this, but . . . oh, for heaven's sake, do you think you could put your reservations aside for now and be my matron of honour?"

"Your . . ."

There is another silence, during which I hear voices in the background chattering, and the tinkle of glass. "Well?" I say. "What do you think? I'll forgive what's past . . . if you will."

"What's past?" Charlotte lowers her voice. There is fear; it is palpable, coming through the wires. "Joanna, what are you talking about?"

I had meant our disagreement about Michael. At least, I believe that was my intent in saying what I did. But Charlotte clearly is thinking of something else.

I could cut out my tongue. What if it all spills out suddenly, some horrid little story of how she and David met time after time in the meadow right where he and I fell in love? What if she tells me more than I now want to know?

"I just meant our argument last week," I say quickly.

Her quiet little sigh of relief fills my ears. "Oh. Oh, that, of course."

"What about it, then? Will you be my matron of honour? And do you think Henry might give me away?"

"Well . . . we'll see. There's time, isn't there? Surely you won't be rushing into anything."

"Actually, we—we're getting married two weeks from this Saturday."

"Two . . . weeks!" Her voice falters, and there follows a long silence.

"Char . . ."

"If only you'd give it time."

"Char, let's not do this again," I say irritably. "You've got to accept that I can make my own decisions. Damn it all, anyway, I think I deserve some happiness. I deserve to put what's happened behind me, and get on with things. I need to forget!"

"It may not be easy, Joanna. David—"

"—is gone. *Dead.* No one can bring him back. And you know what, Char? I am so bloody glad!"

I pull the receiver from my ear and stare horrified at it, at the words I've just poured into it. My hand is shaking. I drop the phone on the floor and sink back on the bed, covering my face and weeping. "I'm glad," I say again, over and over, although I can hear the dial tone that tells me Charlotte is no longer there.

CHAPTER 12

Long moments later I rise from my bed and mentally shake myself, drying my eyes. With determination I put the conversation behind me and finish dressing. *It doesn't matter,* I tell myself over and over. *I have Michael now, and none of it matters, not Charlotte, not David—*

Then, sharp and clear, a memory returns. I see it as a picture on a screen, playing out before me. Charlotte stands in this very room, pleading with me to leave David. I see her before me, her hands tightening into fists, her thin face mottled with anger. What her argument was, I do not remember. It is still on the fringes, playing about like an elusive child. Charlotte had come here, and we—

No. A shiver goes through me, and I no longer want to remember that day. I freshen my makeup quickly, not even looking in the glass, then I straighten the bed and glance around to see that everything else is in order. Leaving my room, I am careful to close the door behind me. There is a sense now—an almost physical pressure between my shoulder blades—that if I do not do this David might come from his office across the way, enter my room, and torment me. I know that is crazy. It is not something I would tell Dr. Shahi. But I have developed these little door-closing tricks for keeping ghosts away.

In the living room I set down my purse and glance around, satisfied that things are coming along in here. With Old Robert's help I've finished steaming off the old wallpaper and begun to paint the walls white. Scrapers, buckets of enamel, rollers, and brushes lie everywhere. As for the rest, I've tried to make things warm and cosy. Yesterday in the village I found a new sofa in off-white chintz scattered with tiny burgundy *fleur-de-lis*. Robert carted it out here in his truck, along with two matching armchairs in a soft dusty rose. I also found a silver teapot at a secondhand shop, which I've polished to a sheen. It reflects light from the fire, which has crackled since dawn. One small brass lamp on a table along the wall is surrounded by freshly cut flowers.

In short, I have done everything I could to change this room, just as I did with the bedroom. There is even a wonderfully thick blue and rose rug that covers the imaginary blood stain in the oak-wood floor.

In the kitchen I pour the lemonade I've made earlier into an insulated jug, wash two apples and wrap two homemade pasties for Michael and me to take with us, wherever it is we're going. He's asked me to pack a simple lunch, so I'm guessing we'll be outdoors.

Putting the lunch into a sack, I take both it and the lemonade jug to the front door. As I'm putting them down, I hear Michael's Range Rover in the drive. Flinging the door open, I stand on the porch and wave. "Hullo, I'm ready," I call out as he comes up the walk. On either side is the border of flowers Old Robert and I planted, a velvety white carpet of sweet alyssum at the front, asters and daisies behind. The garden is shaping up to be a virtual fairyland, and I feel oddly as if I'm in an old movie—one of those brides of the forties welcoming her husband home from the war.

Which is to say that there is something not quite real about this scene, and even I know it.

Michael takes the steps two at a time, and I offer my cheek for his kiss. He duly plants one and gives me a hug besides. It's as physical as we've been, awkward, I suppose, about taking things further after so many years. Without even talking about it, we seem to have mutually agreed to wait until the vows are read.

Meanwhile, we make little inroads, small passing stabs at touching.

"Lunch?" Michael says, seeing my sack and jug beside the door.

"You did say simple, didn't you?" For a moment I worry that it's not enough. "Pasties, some fruit . . ."

"Sounds wonderful." He kisses me on the nose.

We step inside and Michael gives me a searching look. "You seem a bit strained. Is anything wrong?"

I wave a dismissive hand. "I've just talked with Charlotte. It stirred things up."

His brow creases. "Charlotte again. Jo . . . that woman . . . why don't you just break things off with her?"

"She means well. She just wants what's best for me."

"I seriously doubt that," he mutters, but at my frown of protest he smiles and puts an arm about my shoulders. "What do you say we don't talk about Charlotte Dean right now? I was hoping you might still have the kettle on. There's a bit of a chill in the air."

I have already cleaned up the kitchen and put things away, but it pleases me to have something to do for Michael. "Tea, is it now?" I say, taking his hand. "We'll see what we can do."

We sit in the living room with our tea, and I try to tell Michael something of the excitement I feel at fixing up Pennoryn. His disapproval is apparent; he would rather that I closed the house and sold it. He expects that we will live in his cottage when we're married.

"But don't you understand," I argue, "I'm exorcising old ghosts. This is *my* house now—not David's and mine." I put my cup down and fold my hands on my knees. "You know, now that I have some distance from everything, I know that Pennoryn never really was David's house. I think that for him the pleasure was in building it, shaping it into what he wanted it to be. When that was done, David was too. He spent so little time here, after all."

"He died here, Jo." Michael looks uncomfortably around the living room. Admittedly it is chilly in here now, despite the fire. The fog has wended its way down the hill, and through the tall front windows one can see the garden as if framed like a painting. In that painting white wisps of vapour crawl over the hedgerow to lick the trees. The trees drip moisture, and the heavy rose-heads bend with it. The ground is sodden with fallen petals.

Michael sips the hot tea, steam rising to his face and sending a gleam of moisture to his forehead. His dark hair falls forward, as if ruffled by the wind. He wears jeans and a white shirt with the sleeves folded midway up the forearm, no tie. There are tiny spots of oil paint on his fingers, and when he first walked in I thought he looked like a small boy with a wonderful secret he was bursting to tell. Now, however, his demeanour is more serious. He is wondering how to say something without hurting me; this I know from our many years as friends.

"What is it?" I ask.

He sets down the tea and clears his throat. "You're doing a wonderful job with the house, Jo. All this new paint, the furniture . . . it's not that." His gaze fixes on the rug before the fireplace. The skin on his forearms prickles. "It's just that I don't understand why you wouldn't want to sell."

"But if I give up Pennoryn now—if I sell it—it will be as if David has won, somehow."

He frowns. "Won what? The man is *dead,* Jo. You have nothing to gain, win, or lose from him now."

I seem unable to form words that would help him understand. "I don't know how to put it. It's a feeling I have that I need to be here, to put things together."

"The past, you mean?"

"Precisely. I have to know why I did certain things. Why I put up with certain things."

"But once we're married and living at my cottage it will be a whole new life for you, a new beginning. You can forget all that."

"No. Things are coming back, Michael. I keep shoving them away, but I know they won't stay gone forever. Sooner or later I'll remember that night. And I must be here when that happens."

He looks away. I study his face, but cannot read it; I see only the clenched jaw, the cheek muscles working. Without having planned it, I say, "Michael, Charlotte and I were talking the other day. She—she thinks it must have been someone who cared about me. Whoever did it, that is. Someone who cared personally . . . because, you know, of the way I was covered with that blanket."

He stares into my eyes. In times past I have felt I could read all of Michael's thoughts in his eyes. At the moment, they are a blank screen. A chill sweeps over me. I have always been afraid of confrontation with any man, and this is not even a confrontation, but more a query. Yet it shakes me.

"There's a . . . a police inspector asking questions again," I say.

A startled expression crosses his face. "A police inspector?"

"Yes," I say lightly, laughing a bit. "Apparently, he finds that business of the blanket to be rather . . . intriguing."

"Does he now?" Michael's lips curve into a slight grimace. "I seem to remember the newspapers making something of that at the time. A 'gentleman burglar,' I believe they called it."

"Yes. That's what the inspector said."

He stands and walks to the fireplace, leaning on the mantel and staring in. "Well, stranger things have happened. The rapist who says 'please' and 'thank you,' the burglar who knocks, asks permission to enter, then leaves things in perfect order."

"Except that I've been home quite a while now and I've not found any evidence of a burglary. There's not a thing missing."

His gaze swings back to me. "Nothing at all?"

"Well, actually," I say, remembering, "there is the stone hare you gave me shortly after David and I were married. It's not in the garden, and we haven't found it anywhere on the grounds. Do you, uh, do you have any ideas about that?"

"About who might have taken it, you mean?"

"Yes."

"No . . . I haven't a clue."

"Or about any of it? Personally, I've been thinking it's possible that someone I know came upon the scene and didn't want to get involved. It would make perfect sense to me that if she . . . or he . . . was a friend, and there I was half-dressed that way, they might have covered me with that blanket out of a sense of decency. Don't you think?"

Again that stare I'm unable to read. Michael shakes his head. "I don't know, Jo. I simply don't know."

"Michael . . ." This is more difficult, but I feel I must say it. "Charlotte suggested it might be you who covered me that way."

"I?" He blinks, and I feel cold, detached, as if surrounded by a cottony cloud, the way I used to feel when questioning David about where he had been, or what he had done in London. As if I have no right to be asking these things.

Further, I can see Michael is angry—just as David always was. Immediately I back off. I must smooth things over, make everything right again. It is one thing for me to be uneasy, but to make Michael feel that way is wrong. *There are times when you must honour your own feelings,* Dr. Shahi would say, and I know this is one of those times, for I can see him, hear him, uttering the words. But I cannot stop myself from jumping in with a disarming laugh. "I told Charlotte that was crazy! Where on earth does she get these ideas? I told her that if it had happened that way, you'd have told me from the first."

Standing, I gather up the tea tray. Giving Michael a smile, I head for the kitchen, calling back to him, "Let's just forget all this. I can't wait to see what you've planned for today." Still chattering on, I see he's followed and is standing in the doorway. His gaze is brooding, his arms folded.

"Jo?"

I pause with my hand on the water faucet. "Yes?"

"You were right. I *would* have told you from the first . . . if it had happened that way."

"I know that, Michael. Isn't that what I said?"

He comes and places a hand on my arm. "But do you believe it?"

My voice is far too brittle. "Of course! I never believed otherwise."

His frown holds for another moment, and I see that anger is working behind his eyes, anger that ends in a twist of the lips. "Do you *believe* it?" he insists. *"Tell me."* His hand tightens.

"Michael, you're scaring me." I pull away and rub my arm. The frown fades instantly.

"God, I'm so sorry!" Michael's tone is filled with remorse. "Let me see that." He takes my arm gently, and there is no imprint. It is more his anger that hurt. "You're all right?"

I nod.

His fingers soothe my skin. "I really am damned sorry. Jo, I don't mean to shift the blame, but it's this thing with Charlotte, these suspicions she's filling your mind with. Can't you see the harm it's doing?"

"Yes," I say truthfully. "I do see it, and I've told her to stop. But I'm not going to lose her friendship, Michael. Charlotte and I will work it out, and after we're married she'll be part of our lives. You have to understand that."

He sighs. "Believe me, I do. I only wish you understood—"

"What?"

"Oh, I'm asking too much, I suppose. I've got you back, and we're going to be married . . . Nearly everything is perfect, now, isn't it?"

"Nearly everything?" I send him a smile.

"Well, I've been dealing with a few business problems. But they'll soon be sorted out."

"Problems?"

"Nothing a hundred thousand pounds wouldn't cure," he says, smiling. "And it's nothing for you to worry about."

"But that's a lot of money, Michael! Why so much?"

"It's for the gallery in London," he says, picking up a towel. "I've put in a bid to buy the place, but it needs quite a bit of work. New heating, plumbing, and the like. But we don't need to talk about that today. You wash, I'll dry?"

I turn the hot water on and reach for soap. "It is open

now, though? This is the one where you're preparing for a showing?"

"Yes. It's been operating under another owner. But it's old, and he hasn't kept things up. Listen here, now," he says in a mock grumbling tone. "I thought you wanted to hear about my plans for today."

"I do. But I want to share the bad as well as the good. If you're having financial problems . . ."

He leans over and kisses my cheek. "There'll be plenty of time for talk about that after we're married, my love. And this isn't your problem. I don't want you worrying about it, even for a minute."

I rinse a delicate teacup and hand it to him. "All right," I say, remembering Charlotte's insinuation that Michael was after my money. I only wish she could know how wrong she was.

"As for today . . . remember that jeweller on Two Moon Street?" Michael says. "The one with the hand-crafted settings and all those wonderful gemstones?"

"Yes, Weatherby's! We used to walk by there after school, and sometimes we went in and he let us try the rings on. All those wonderful rubies, sapphires, emeralds . . ." I laugh. "Or so we thought."

"And later we learned they weren't precious gems at all, but relatively inexpensive gemstones—"

"Which is why he let us play with them as if they were glass."

"Piles of them." Michael laughs.

"One day, we even pretended we were getting married, and he gave me an old scrap of lace from his living room in the back to wear as a veil. Mr. Weatherby was the minister, and for music we had his old electric teakettle singing away in the background. It was shaped like a cat."

Michael touches my hair. "I wondered if you'd remember."

How could I forget? It was one of the happiest days of my childhood. Michael always did that for me; he didn't just get me away from the house. He came up with things that made me forget.

He turns me to him. My left hand is holding a soapy cup,

which he takes from me and returns to the sink. "Jo, we don't have to go there. I can afford now to get you any kind of ring you want. We can go up to London and I'll buy you the biggest diamond we can find."

"No! Oh, no, let's not. I want to go to Weatherby's, it's a wonderful idea."

He smiles. "I'm happy you agree. And then I thought we might have our picnic afterwards at Lost Inn."

"Lost Inn . . ." My soapy arms go around his neck and I give him a hug. His lips touch my forehead, and I am blissfully happy. "Let's go," I say. "Let's go right now."

He smiles and takes my hand, kissing the palm. Laughing, I try to pull away, for it tickles, but he won't let go. There are kisses raining all over my hand and up my arm, all the way to the car.

The fog lifts as we drive south in the Range Rover; a warm breeze blows my hair. Entering Mevagissey, Michael parks in front of Weatherby's, which is in the same lane as The Blue Swan, but farther down. He comes round to hold the door for me. "You know, you don't have to do this sort of thing for me," I say. "I'm quite grownup and capable."

"I like doing things for you," he says. "And this is only the beginning."

Entering Weatherby's, it is hard to believe it's been fifteen years since I've come in here. I feel as if I'm in a wondrous sort of time warp, so little has changed. The brass bell over the door still tinkles to alert Mr. Weatherby that someone has entered his shop. Along the left as we step inside are the shelves with handmade pillar candles, and on either side, posters with astrological prints of the sun, moon, and stars. Below them are long glass counters with the same jars and bowls filled with semi-precious stones of every colour, like so much hard candy in a confectioner's store. They appear to be the same gems I remember from my childhood, although surely Mr. Weatherby has sold his stock and replaced it many times over since my childhood.

On the right is another display counter with rings, bracelets, pendants, brooches. Some are plain silver or gold, others are studded with rose quartz, amethyst, malachite, tourmaline, peridot. I see that something new has been added—a moving display of crystals. They sit on blue velvet: tiny little cats, elephants, butterflies, even clowns fashioned of cut glass. The light above them makes them shimmer as if alive.

As we wait for Mr. Weatherby to come from the back, my eye is drawn to a crystal that looks like the Emerald City from *The Wizard of Oz*. Slender glass spires an inch to two inches in height are clustered together on a base that changes colour from blue to green, then mauve to gold, as the moving display shelf turns in a circle beneath the light. I remember how excited I was one day to learn that *The Wizard of Oz* was to show in a nearby town. It had been released in England long before then, of course, but only when I was six did I become aware of the film and what it was. Several of the girls from school had been talking about it, and two who were best friends were going together. Life was not pleasant for me at home, but it had not yet turned thoroughly evil, so I had a child's faith that anything was possible—even that I might get to see, somehow, *The Wizard of Oz*.

I knew it would be no use to ask my mum to take me. Or my dad. And though I knew Michael from school in those days, we were not yet close, or for that matter old enough to go alone. But my brother Ian was fourteen, and he had a date with a girl from the village. He was taking her to see the film that night, and I begged to go along. When that didn't work, I bribed. "I'll clean your boots every single night for a week if you'll let me go," I pleaded. Ian had frowned. "You think I want a little twit like you gettin' in the way? Get on now with ya. Get away."

Joseph had come to my rescue. "I'll take you. I don't mind." Ian had given him a look as if he were addled. "Y'd better not be sittin' anywhere near me, then. You think I want 'er comin' home and tellin' Mum and Dad what I do with m'birds?"

"C'mon, Josie," Joseph had said, taking my hand and using his pet name for me. "Josie and Joseph," that's what he called us that day, "a team." We went to see *The Wizard of Oz,* and I will never forget the beauty of that day or that movie as long as I live.

That is why it is so hard to forget that Joseph, along with Ian and Denny, raped me. I had thought he would always be on my side. He was the brother who read me bedtime stories, who walked me to my first day of school. His betrayal, therefore, seemed worse than all the rest.

I feel Michael's presence behind me. "Have you seen a ring you like?" he asks, for the rings are in the case below the crystals.

"I haven't really been looking," I admit. "More woolgathering." I realize I am still holding the crystal. Reluctantly, I put it back on its revolving shelf.

Michael slips an arm around me and gives me a gentle kiss on the temple. "Someone wants to say hello."

With my arm around his waist I turn and see that Mr. Weatherby has come from the back. His face is softened by sunlight drifting through the stained glass window over the front door. Nevertheless, he looks much older. The beard is pure white, there is a larger paunch above his belt. He wears a white shirt now, with short sleeves for summer—but I remember that in winter he often wore red flannel, and resembled St. Nick.

"The little bride," he says, holding out his hands, which are rough and rather thick for a jeweller. He beams from Michael to me. "Do you remember? The two of you, married right here in my shop."

I smile. "We remember. That's why we're here."

"We're going to do it for real now," Michael adds.

Mr. Weatherby is looking very pleased. After much searching through his display cases, I have made my choice. "I could be wrong," he says, "but I do believe this to be the same type of stone . . . and perhaps even a similar setting to the ring you wore in your make-believe wedding all those years ago."

Holding my hand up I admire the amethyst nestled in a silver setting that is so intricate, it would seem to be antique. On either side of the stone are gossamer vines, and along them, tiny rosebuds. It is not expensive as rings go,

but as a child I chose a setting like this because I longed
for a rose garden—for anything, really, that would brighten
things up about the house, make it seem more normal,
more like those of my friends.

"It is almost exactly the same," I say. "It's perfect. Isn't
it, Michael?"

"Yes," he agrees, holding me close, a smile in his eyes.
"For an engagement ring it's perfect. But are you sure you
wouldn't like a wedding ring as well?"

"Absolutely not. This is what I had before. It's all I
want." I turn to Mr. Weatherby. "It can be both, can't it?"

"Indeed it can," he says, smiling. "It can be anything you
want."

Michael extends his hand. "May I see it, please?" And
when I hold it up for his inspection he shakes his head.
"No, take it off."

Bewildered, I remove the ring and give it to him. "Could
you engrave it, please, Mr. Weatherby?" he says. "I hope
you still do that."

"Most certainly I do. What would you like?"

"Why don't we make it a surprise?" Michael turns to me
with a smile. "*If* you wouldn't mind . . ." He gives me a
light push towards the front of the store.

"Oh, you want me to lose myself now, do you?"

"Just for a bit."

"Hmmm. Will the front of the shop do it, then? Or am I
supposed to go off into the street?"

"Just go," he says, laughing. "And stop giving me a bad
time."

"Well, I never. And on my engagement day, too."

But I am feeling very loved, and the feeling is good.

Lost Inn is a good thirty minutes from Mevagissey, but the
drive is enjoyable. Heading south there are rocky cliffs and
coves to the left, where pirates once landed their ships; to
the right a stream winds through gorse and bracken. The
air is clear and crisp, with a warm breeze blowing off the
Channel now that the fog has lifted. Michael thoughtfully
sets a moderate pace so that I can see all the many birds
along the way. He knows I must comment excitedly upon

every one or burst, and he smiles patiently. The Range Rover's windows are down, and my feet are propped against the dashboard. I've rolled up my trousers, so that the sun is on my bare legs.

"What are you thinking?" Michael asks, turning to me and smiling. I shake my head and don't answer. What I am thinking is that I am on pins and needles, and wonder if he will *ever* get round to giving me my ring. There is a small package in his shirt pocket, and when he held the car door for me I saw that it was wrapped in pink tissue with tiny silver stars. I can't wait to see how he's had it engraved, but when I asked him about it five miles back he simply grinned and looked mysterious.

Well, let him tease me with it, then. It is a gentle teasing, much like that of our childhood, and I've got him myself a few times in the past.

I am also thinking that all in all, life could not be better. I have beside me a man who has been my friend since the day we met. He stood by me through the terrible years of my childhood, and even later when I married someone else. This man beside me is sweet and gentle, and yes, romantic. He thinks of my comfort, my well-being. Michael will never hurt me.

If there is a tiny niggle of fear that I'm putting too bright a sheen on things, I tell myself it is only pre-wedding jitters. The worst is behind me now. The best is yet to be.

I reach for Michael's hand. "I love you so much," I say in my heart, though saying the words aloud is more than I can manage just yet. The important thing is that I have never meant them in quite this way before.

As we near Lost Inn, the road becomes thick with traffic, and we're forced to slow down. I dip into the picnic sack for an apple. "Would you like something?" I ask.

Michael shakes his head. "We'll be there soon, don't you think? We can have our lunch straight away."

I bite into the apple. "Can't help it. I'm hungry now."

"Well, I suppose that's a good healthy sign, isn't it?"

"If you want a fat bride. All I do is eat these days."

"Not to worry. We'll get Old Robert to cart you down

the aisle in his wheelbarrow." Michael grins. "We'll have a hedgerow for an altar and we'll fill it with birds—"

My mouth freezes in mid-bite. "Oh my God! Michael, *no!*"

He gives me a look. "Jo, I was teasing."

"You don't understand! I haven't reserved a church!"

He lifts a brow. "We've got no church?"

"Well, not yet, anyway. I've had so many things to do, so much to think about. And you know how it is this time of year, everyone getting married. We'll never be able to reserve one now."

Michael removes his hands from the wheel and throws them up in a fatalistic gesture. "Well, then, that's it. The wedding's off."

I smack his arm lightly. "Don't even tease about that. And watch what you're doing." We have come up rather quickly upon a large motor coach.

He takes the wheel, brakes, and sighs. "Shortest engagement I've ever had. And won't Mr. Weatherby be disappointed."

I fall silent at his words. Then it comes to me: "Michael, that's it! That's what we'll do."

"Cancel the wedding?" He looks to see if I'm serious.

"Don't be silly. I mean, that's where we'll be married—at Weatherby's."

"Now *you're* joking."

"Not at all. You know he'd love it."

"Possibly, but don't you think it might be a bit crowded there?"

"Well, I don't exactly have a three-hundred person guest list. Even Charlotte is balking. Who knows? I may not have anyone there at all." I munch on the apple, thinking through it. I could bring flowers from the garden at home, and we could find, I am sure, an appropriate music tape to replace the old singing teakettle. As for candles, there are plenty to be purchased around Mr. Weatherby's shop.

"What could be more perfect than being married there for real?" I say.

"Hmmm." Michael looks thoughtfully at the road ahead. A smile plays around his lips, and it is clear he doesn't need much persuading. "I have no one, really, that I care that much about—not now, with my mum gone. I would like to invite Annette. And Charles from the Harbourside Gallery. Perhaps one friend—Gregg King, from London. Have I ever mentioned him?"

"A stage actor, isn't he? You wrote about him in a post-card you sent me in hospital. Mrs. Rimes said she knew all about him." I slant a smile at Michael. " 'Right handsome,' is what she said."

He smiles and takes my hand. "Don't you be getting any ideas. You're mine now, and I'm not letting you go."

I snuggle against his arm. "Tell me more about this friend of yours."

"Gregg's in one of this season's biggest hits—*Death Spiral.* I met him when he came down to look at my work in progress. He's one of my best customers, and a good friend."

"Well, then, he must come. And it might be a good idea to find a *real* minister this time."

"I can ask Dr. Hardesty at the Presbyterian church. He comes by the gallery rather often. A nice chap."

"And I'll talk to Mr. Weatherby."

Michael tosses me a glance. "Oh, no, you don't. You forgot the church. I don't trust you with Mr. Weatherby."

I take one last bite of the apple. "Watch the road," I say.

It is a perfect day. The sun is shining, it is warm on my skin. My nose, in fact, feels pink. To our right as we drive south the gulls soar over the cliff upon which Lost Inn stands. I see its rooftop over the next hill, and it seems a symbol—that a new life is just over the rise.

"Your nose is sunburned," Michael says, touching it lightly.

We have spread a blanket on the ground and sit on a hill with our picnic lunch, looking across a valley that is half sand, half field, to Lost Inn. This is not the original Lost Inn, but one built on the site of the original. Fifty-odd years ago a hurricane roared up the Channel and caused a shifting of sands along the coast. When the storm was gone an old farmstead was found standing here, unearthed from the roof right down to the lintels, and as perfectly preserved as the remains of Pompeii. Soon there were people coming to see it from miles around, and it gained the name Lost Inn. Unfortunately, the following year another storm swept through and covered the farmstead up again. It disappeared as surely as it had appeared.

In recent times, this new inn was built approximately one hundred yards from the site of the old. It is said to be a near replica, the plans based upon historic photographs. Often, as a child, I would sit on this hill and wonder if some day another storm might sweep through, and then there would be two Lost Inns, the new and the old.

"I remember you telling me about this place when we were kids," Michael says. "And how you loved it. But we never came here together. Who did you come with?"

"Myself."

"All this way? Surely you didn't walk."

"No. You remember Mrs. Litchfield, who drove the school bus when we were, oh, around twelve, thirteen? Sometimes she drove a charter coach down here for extra pay, and she'd let me come along free for weeding her garden."

Michael smiles and shakes his head. "Why didn't I ever know this?"

I shrug. "I think I might have wanted something that was all mine. It made it more . . . oh, magical that way."

In truth, it wasn't the inn itself I'd always been attracted to, but rather the ancient Roman stones that had been upturned in the fields nearby. One stone stands on end and has a hole in the middle, like Mên-an-Tol. Old Cornish superstition has it that if one comes upon such a stone, it's best to crawl through it nine times against the sun. This is said to ward off bad luck and disease.

David laughed at my superstitious need to do this, the one time we visited the inn together. "We make our own luck," he said, and while intellectually I believed he was right, some ancient blood knowledge in me made me crawl through those stones against the sun. David walked off and stood arms crossed with his back to me, pretending not to know me.

Of course, David is now dead.

* * *

"Go on, lady, do it!" the boy is yelling. He stands next to the stone with the hole in it, chewing gum. The knees of his jeans are grass-stained, and his face is too sharp and hungry for a boy of fifteen or so. There is a nasty-looking scab at the corner of his mouth.

Michael has gone inside the inn to look for ice cream, and I am here alone with the boy, smiling but shaking my head. The boy wants me to go through the hole with the sun at my back, and I am saying no, I will not do it. It is bad luck. But he is young, and he likes to tease, to dare. His parents, I think, must have walked off and left him here with nothing better to do but hound tourists.

I turn, looking for Michael. He's nowhere in sight. I wonder if I should go and find him. It's been over fifteen minutes since he left.

"You don't believe all those old stories, do you, lady?" the boy taunts me again. He moves closer and the sun shifts, his face becomes sharper. "You don't believe in bad luck, do you?"

A chill moves down my spine. I would like to look away, but I am mesmerised. "Of course not," I lie.

"Because if you believe in bad luck, it'll fly right at you. That's what my mum says. Like a bird, lady . . . it'll eat your hand."

I am feeling tension between my shoulders, and I laugh uneasily. "Birds eat *from* your hand."

The boy shakes his head back and forth solemnly. "Not if you're afraid."

I stare at the boy, and there is a long silence. Then suddenly a gull swoops, and for a moment it seems as if it might fly right into the lad's face. "Yipes!" he hollers, covering his head with his arms. He squats quickly, so that the bird zooms over his head. The boy waits a moment, then stands cautiously, shading his eyes to watch the gull leave. He is laughing now, boyishly, good-naturedly. And I wonder why I thought his face sharp. He looks almost angelic now, the cheeks round and the eyes bright blue and innocent. *Nearly hoist by me own petard,* they seem to say as they meet mine. I laugh, too, and it seems a joke now between us—his little act, and my all-too-naive response.

"Do they pay you to stand here and frighten tourists?" I ask.

He shrugs and looks at his feet, twisting a toe in the ground.

"Well, just so you know, I'm not in the least afraid," I say, and still laughing I turn and march the fifteen paces or so to the round stone. He is right about one thing: fear is like a bird that bites. And it is high time I began to put childhood fears behind me. Closing my eyes, I pass through the stone—not against the sun as superstition would have it, but with it at my back.

I have never done this before, not in my life. In my mind I hear the old Cornish farmers telling their dire tales about these stones when I was a child, and it takes me by surprise: I am frightened. I wait for thunderbolts to strike, locusts to swarm from the sky, a plague to befall.

Nothing.

Opening my eyes, then, I laugh, throw up my arms and say, "So there!"

But it is Michael's concerned face that is just before me, not the boy's. "Jo, what on earth are you doing?"

He is holding two vanilla ice cream cones, and I laugh and take one from him, licking it gratefully, as it feels very hot now with the sun on my back. "Proving that I'm not easily intimidated," I say. "Isn't it about time?"

"Well, you don't have to prove anything to me."

"No, to that lad over there. Would you believe he deliberately tried to frighten me?"

Looking round, I gesture in the boy's direction. But he isn't there. "Now where on earth did he go?"

Michael shakes his head. "There wasn't anyone else here. Just you."

"Before I went through the stone, I mean. I was talking to him. A boy, about fifteen or so."

"Jo, I saw you going through the stone when I was crossing the field. I must say it gave me a turn. But there wasn't any boy here. I'd have seen him."

"But that's crazy. I tell you, he was *here.*"

It may be only my imagination that the sun goes behind a cloud then. I do know that my skin turns cold. I stand hugging myself, and the vanilla cone drips onto my arm, but I barely notice. My eyes scan the entire field, from hill to inn. Michael is right; there is no boy.

We return to our picnic spot on the hill, and for a long time we sit quietly, the blessed sun once more on our faces. Mid-afternoon has arrived, and the tourists are in full flourish at Lost Inn. Below us are hordes of people in shorts and sun hats. They carry heavy tote bags or backpacks, as if unable to leave home without bringing part of it with them. Several Indian women wear saris in shades of turquoise, pink, and gold. Little children run through the hole in the rock playing tag, unaware of the superstitions of Cornwall or any threat of bad luck. They are happy, and this will be a good memory for them; the chance of their little games bringing bad luck, I would think, are nil.

The boy, wherever he went, was right about one thing: it is what we believe that gets us in the end. Believe in ill luck and it comes running at one, screaming like a banshee. Believe in good, and, well, it is here.

I lean back against Michael's chest, and his arms come around me. "I had feelings for you when we were only children," he says. "Did you know that?"

"No."

"It was just that after what happened . . . you know, that day on the cliff with your brothers. I felt it was wrong to even touch you. I thought you might become afraid of me."

"But I had feelings for you, too. I just didn't think you cared about me that way. You had all those girlfriends, remember, when we were in high school?" I turn to him and smile. "They were all over you, my boy."

He lifts my face and kisses me on the forehead. "They didn't mean anything. I was young, the hormones were running. And I was going crazy, trying to stay away from you." He sighs. "My poor sweet Jo, what have we done with our lives? So much time wasted."

I snuggle into his arms. "It's over now. Let's just enjoy what we have."

"Speaking of which . . ." Michael shifts and reaches into his shirt pocket. He draws out the small package that I have wondered about since Weatherby's. He hands me the package, perhaps three inches by four and wrapped in that soft pink tissue paper, dotted with silver stars.

"An engagement gift," he says.

"Michael! Not my ring?"

He shakes his head. "Something else."

Pleasure brings heat to my face. "But I didn't get you anything."

"*You* are my gift," he says gallantly.

"Well, not nearly as prettily wrapped, I'd say." I loosen the silver string. The tissue comes undone, and my voice catches in my throat. Into the palm of my hand tumbles the Emerald City crystal, raining sunlight in every hue. Tears spring to my eyes. "How did you know?"

"I can't take my eyes off you," he says. "I know more than you think."

My lips gently touch his cheek, and it is more than a thank-you for a crystal. It is a thank-you for love.

"Now for the ring." He reaches into his back pocket, where I have not seen it, and pulls out a smaller piece of tissue. I unwrap it excitedly and hold it up to the light, reading the engraving: *Forever, my love—my Jo.*

"It's beautiful," I whisper. "So beautiful." The amethyst twinkles in the sun, and the silver band of entwined roses is polished now to a sheen. I give the ring to Michael and lift my hand so that he can place it on my finger. When he is finished I take his hand and kiss the back of it softly, then the palm, lingering. Michael's eyes darken, his breath catches. "You'd better not do that here in public, Jo."

I touch his lips. "Why don't we leave, then? Why don't we go where we can be alone?"

He holds me slightly off, searching my eyes. "Are you sure?"

"Yes," I say, although I am trembling right down to my knees. "We've waited long enough. I'm sure."

* * *

I cannot believe this is happening at last. A kaleidoscope of memories passes before me: Michael and I taking picnic baskets to Hitler's Walk in summer, Michael and I watching the fishing boats come back as the sun sets, Michael and I, Michael and I . . . always the two of us, so many years. Glances cast at each other as we grew older, a flare of desire before it is quickly hidden. Michael packing for Paris, while I sit in my bedroom window looking out over the quay, crying. And now Michael is here, and he whispers in my ear, "I love you, Jo," and the kaleidoscope comes round; I'm back to childhood again, watching Michael fashion a ring of sea grass, seeing him place it on my finger that day on the cliffs. "I won't let them hurt you anymore," he is saying. "I promise you, Jo."

We don't go back to Pennoryn; the drive is too long. We go to Michael's cottage instead. By the time we are there, we are both so aroused with the waiting, we are barely inside the kitchen door before we are at each other. Michael's hands are on my face, my neck, my hair. Mine tug at his shirt. We fumble a bit, for it is all so new to us, this ancient dance that lovers everywhere have known, and we are touching each other in places that were never allowed. But we are friends, we can trust each other, and through the fumbling a gentle passion flares. My eyes tear, for I can savour him now, I can even caress that tiny scar on his ribs that I've only seen on hot summer days when he's shirtless. I can kiss it, and I am rich, I have treasures beyond compare. Our lips come together and I am astounded at how it feels—so sweet, so warm—for I have always wondered, and now here it is.

But it is bittersweet, this love; my heart aches for all the lost years. Michael looks at me, his breath unsteady, eyes dark, and I nod. I'm all right, it's okay. His mouth comes down on mine hungrily, and his hands slide beneath my shirt and round to my breasts. I feel that exquisite swelling and warming of blood. My arms tighten, my breath quickens. "Yes," I say softly, this feels as it should. My hands tug at his belt, and I am saying words, sounds of love, *please, yes,* and his hand is moving down.

And then there is a sharp, wicked memory, stabbing like

knives at my heart. I see David's face, his head thrown
back, laughing. *"You don't know a thing about making love,
do you? Honestly, Joanna, who would put up with you but
me?"*

The room tilts. My fingers that were one minute reaching for Michael, begin to push. I am cold, like ice. My legs
shake so hard I can barely stand. "Michael, wait . . .
please, wait."

He pulls back, breathing heavily, his focus unsteady.
This is a terrible thing to do, stopping a man like this. For a
moment I wonder if he will strike me. But then I remember: this is Michael.

"What's wrong?" His voice is stricken. "Jo, what is it?"

Tears stream down my face. He tries to put his arms
around me.

"No, don't! I'm sorry, I just can't."

It comes out baldly, just like that. *I can't.*

Michael stands before me, silent. Then his face turns a
dull angry red, and he swings away, slamming his fist
against the wall. "Dammit! Dammit all to hell, Jo!"

I am shocked by his fury. Hesitantly, I put out my hand
to touch his shoulder. He shrugs it off, pivoting back.

"It's David, isn't it?" His eyes fix upon me, destroying
any hope I might have to put him off with a lie.

"I knew it!" He grips my shoulders and shakes me.
"You've got to get out of that house, Jo. Do you hear me?
You've got to get out!"

I wrench away. *"Don't!* Don't touch me like that! And
don't ever raise your voice to me like that again!"

There is more power behind my words than I've in-
tended, and I have shocked myself that I've spoken this
way to anyone, much less Michael.

He stares for what seems a very long time. His hands
open and close, and I can see the frustration, the rage.
Perhaps he *would* like to strike me; he is, after all, a man.

Finally he says quietly, "I apologise."

Michael drives me home. These are the longest twenty
minutes of my recent life, and into the silence I insert tiny
little bursts of fear.

"It's just . . . everything's happening so fast," I say. "I don't feel . . . ready."

Michael's voice is even, his eyes are fixed on the road. But his hands grip the wheel, and I know he is fighting for control. "We've known each other twenty-five years, Jo."

"But not this way."

"No . . . not this way."

"And it's not about David, really it's not. I just think . . . well, it would be ever so much more romantic, wouldn't it, if we were to wait? It's only two weeks."

He sighs. "It's not the waiting, Jo."

It's more. We both know it.

At Pennoryn he leaves me at my door; he doesn't come in. "Are you sure?" I say, the fear escalating. "I'll make coffee to keep you awake for the journey back."

"I don't think so. Thanks, Jo." He leans forward and kisses me, but on the forehead. He seems distracted.

I stand on the driveway in the dark and watch his car disappear down the road.

CHAPTER 13

All that night I walk the floor, from bedroom to living room and back again. I don't bother to switch on lights. They are not essential to the flogging of my soul: *I have lost him. He is a grown man, disgusted with my adolescent fears. I won't ever hear from him again.*

Going from friends to lovers, so much has changed. There are so many new tensions in the air.

Now and again I see my image reflected in the dark windows as I pace, and I fancy I see David there. He is just behind me, laughing. "You're damaged goods, you know. Not a true emotion in you. You'll never be right for anyone now."

"Get out of my life!" I yell at that taunting image. "Get out of my life, or I'll kill you!"

My words shock me. I do not know myself at all these days. Perhaps I never did.

I picture Michael lying in his bed in Mevagissey alone, and wonder what he is thinking. I should telephone him, I should apologise. I should say all those things that lovers say: *I'm sorry I spoiled everything, it was all my fault, please forgive.*

But I am afraid.

At five, when the horizon turns pink, I crawl between the sheets, exhausted. At half past seven the phone rings by my bed. I struggle to come awake, and reach for it, knocking it to the floor. "Hullo," I say groggily, pulling it to my ear.

"Good morning." It is Michael. His tone is normal, upbeat, not angry. My heart leaps, just as they say in books.

"I . . . good morning."

"How are you?"

I rub my eyes and blink. "All right, I think. Better."

"Jo, I'm sorry about last night. It was my fault. I rushed you, and I was terribly insensitive. Can you forgive me?"

A wave of relief washes over me, so immense it leaves me weak. "But Michael, I'm the one who ruined everything. Can you forgive me?"

He laughs softly. "I love you."

I sink back against the pillows. *Thank you, God, thank you.* "I . . . I'll be a good wife to you, Michael. I'll do everything in my power to make you happy."

"Just be you, Jo. That's all I'll ever ask."

I swallow. "But what if that's too much? There are moments lately when I don't know who I am."

"You'll be all right. You've been working too hard, that's all. And I shouldn't have pushed you to marry me so soon. I understand if you need more time."

I slide to the edge of the bed. "No. No, that's not it at all. I want us to be married when we planned." *Oh, God, don't let him break it off. I'll try really hard to make things right.* "Michael, I was up thinking about this in the night. What if we have a smallish garden party here on the weekend? Just you and me, Charlotte and Henry—and if you'd like, your friend Gregg. That way we'd have our entire wedding party here." *And with all those people about, there won't be time to think.*

"Well, I like the idea of a garden party," Michael says, then puts on a groan. "But *must* you invite Charlotte?"

"Behave. I just thought that if we all got together here at Pennoryn, we could have a good talk, and you and Charlotte can get to know one another better."

"I really do know all I need to know of Charlotte," Michael says glumly. But I believe he is only making noises, and will come round.

"It's just that I do so much want her to be my matron of honor. And how can I get her to agree, if the two of you aren't even talking? Will you do this for me? Please? You are so very good at handling people."

Obviously, I am remembering from married life that a bit of sugar with the bitter never hurts.

Michael's voice tells me he is smiling. He's on to me. And he won't give in all too easily. "Must I?" he says with a sigh.

"You must." I laugh, feeling better about everything now. "And I will make your friend welcome, as well."

"Hmmm. Well, all right, then. But you won't be going to a lot of trouble for this party, will you? I don't much like the idea of you wearing yourself out even more."

"I don't think there's that much to do. Old Robert and I have already got things in rather good shape, don't you think?"

"Food, though. How about if I come over early and take that off your hands?"

Since I have never been known as a good cook—my most notable attribute being that I've at least never poisoned anyone—I heartily agree.

"Anything else?" Michael asks.

"Well, you should probably be the one to call your friend."

"Right. I've already written it down. Are you thinking about Sunday for this?"

"Yes. Around two?"

"I'll call Gregg tonight, then. Right now I should be shoving off. I've got to be in London about that showing. Talk to you later?"

"Yes."

"I love you, Jo."

I am so lucky. "Love you."

CHAPTER 14

By Saturday morning I am forced to admit that my "little garden party" has become more than I'd bargained for. While I'd thought things were in good shape outside, I keep finding weeds to pull, grass that needs trimming. And one minute I'm after Old Robert to dig a hole somewhere, while the next I'm finding things to be repaired.

It seems I'm looking around the place with unveiled eyes, now that people are to come. *What will Charlotte think if she sees that window trimming I've not yet painted?* I wonder. *And Michael's friend—it will be his first impression of me. Therefore, both I and the house must look good.*

Then there's Henry. Surely the roses must be sprayed; if there are aphids when Henry comes—not that he'd criticise, he's much too kind for that—he might worry over the roses rather than relaxing with us at lunch.

When I voiced some of this to Michael the night before on the phone, he said, "Jo, relax. You're working yourself up too much over this. You'll be a wreck by Sunday."

And I know he's right. So this morning instead of going straight out to spray the roses, I take a cup of coffee outside and sit on the porch steps in the sun, looking out over the garden, the meadow, and the low hills beyond. My thought is to relax this way, to gather strength for the one chore I've been avoiding like the plague all week long.

Sipping my coffee, I watch the birds plucking at berries in the hedgerow and listen to them nattering away at the feeders, all so caught up with the serious business of living.

Now that they've decided I won't bite, they are down here all the time. As the sun rises each morning I am dashing about, replacing seed, nuts, and fruit. My birds are well fed —even fat, some of them—and they've got plenty of water for bathing. Yet they search out food like there's no tomorrow, dashing hither and thither as if at any moment some terrible fate might befall and grab every smidgeon of berry, nut, or seed away.

Robert, in all his ancient wisdom, was right about them. Their problem is not that they don't have enough. Their problem is that they don't trust it.

Sitting here sipping my tea, I acknowledge that as my problem, too. I know that I am fortunate to have this land, this home. I know I am fortunate even to be alive. And I know that life has been good in giving me Michael. I've only been wary of trusting it; of trusting him.

With this knowledge I begin to feel more at peace. It is a good feeling, one that gives me a sense of inner strength. It is time now for that chore I have been fearing: I must phone Dr. Shahi.

In the living room I pace back and forth with the phone. "I know I should have phoned yesterday," I say after the preliminaries. "I kept meaning to, then forgetting. There's just been so much . . . Dr. Shahi, I'm getting married."

His tone, as I have expected, is one of shock. "Married? So soon? To whom?"

"To Michael. My friend, Michael Lamb."

There is a moment of silence. "Joanna, I'm sorry, but I'm afraid this is far too soon."

My argument is all prepared, just as my answers to the examiner's questions were prepared. The last thing I need right now is for them to decide this is insane, and yank me back inside.

"It's not as if I've just met Michael," I say reasonably. "I've known him all my life. And it's helping me, being with him. I'm feeling better every day."

"Please understand, Joanna. It's not that I'm doubting that. But I'd like to see you recover fully first. In a year's time you may feel differently about many things."

"Not Michael," I say firmly. "I've loved Michael forever, Doctor Shahi. I always will."

"Even so—"

My voice lifts with sudden inspiration. "In fact, I've been feeling so much better, I've even planted an herb garden!"

"Really?" he responds with interest to my bald-faced lie. Dr. Shahi is a great herbal remedy champion. In his office at Whitehurst he has boxes of herbs growing in all the windows.

"Yes, and the valerian root is just about ready to harvest. It's wonderfully calming to the nerves, you know."

"Oh, valerian is marvelous," Dr. Shahi says enthusiastically. "So many applications. Nerves, insomnia, even uterine cramps. Excellent for baby colic, as well."

I laugh. "Now that I didn't know. I'll have to remember when the time comes."

"Well, I must say it sounds as if you're doing well, Joanna. It's always encouraging when a patient assists in her own healing. You are getting out, taking walks, exercising?"

"Absolutely. I'm working in the garden for exercise, too. I've weeded around the entire house."

"Wonderful. And you're eating well?"

"Fresh green salads, plenty of grains. Not very much red meat. I don't seem to do well on that these days." Dr. Shahi is a vegetarian.

"Hmmm. Well, that, of course, could be a good sign. Once the body is cleansed of toxins, it doesn't ordinarily want toxic foods."

"Yes, that's what I thought." I wait.

"In fact, I'd say you must be doing splendidly. I suppose there's only one thing left, then."

I smile, expecting his blessing. We'll be done with it, Michael and I will be married, and everything will be fine.

"I'd like to see you," Dr. Shahi says. "You and Michael together."

"But—"

"In fact, it's not a very long drive, and I should very much like to see Pennoryn, after all you've told me about it. Can you spare me a moment next week? I wouldn't want to intrude."

"I . . ." I am trapped. What can I say? "I'll have to check with Michael about his schedule. What day did you say?"

"Monday, perhaps? I can be flexible, however."

I fancy he can hear my thoughts churning through the line. I wet my lips. "All right. I'll ask Michael. But he's up in London a lot these days, setting up a showing. I'm not sure—"

"Joanna, try to impress upon him the importance of this. And I am sorry about the intrusion. But you've been my patient for a very long time. I am naturally concerned about you. And I do have to report to the board about your progress. Anything so important as a marriage, this soon after your release . . . You understand."

Oh, bloody hell.

"Monday, then?" Dr. Shahi presses.

"Actually," I say, barely containing my anger, "why not come tomorrow, two-ish. Michael and I are having friends in."

"Tomorrow?" I hear him flipping pages on his calendar. "I'd like that, Joanna. But do be sure to set aside time for us to talk alone."

"Certainly."

"I'll see you then."

"Mmmm."

He hangs up and I slam the phone down and stomp to the kitchen. Yanking a pasty chock full of lard and red meat from the fridge, I eat it cold, standing there.

Damn. I'd forgotten how tricky Dr. Shahi could be.

"I'd like two sprigs of mint, one rosemary, one dill, some burdock—and that valerian over there," I say crisply to Mr. Abbott.

"Lavender's on special this week," he says.

"Right. Some of that, too." I can't believe I am having to do this. Now I must plant an herb garden between now and tomorrow, as if I didn't have enough to do.

"And how is Old Robert doing for you?" he asks as he hands me my change.

"He's very good," I say.

"Not any trouble to you, is he?"

"Trouble? No, of course not. Why would he be?"

Mr. Abbott shrugs. "No reason. He's always been a good worker, but then it doesn't hurt to ask."

"In fact, he's very helpful," I say. "I like Robert."

I may be the only person in the village who has ever actually liked Old Robert—or at least admitted to it. Mr. Abbott nods but can't hide his surprise.

Ah, well, she's loony, too, I can almost hear him thinking.

I am on my knees planting herbs when Henry comes to call. I hear the old familiar purr of his antique Morris and stand, shading my eyes. Henry pulls to a stop in the drive and climbs out. He moves arthritically—cautious, I can see, about pain. Piece by piece he disembarks, pausing now and then as if over a puzzle. *Right leg first? No, that will hurt. Try leaning on the door with the arm.*

Time has not been gentle with Henry. I am struck once more by how much he has aged in this past year. It is like this with some people, I know, as if some giant force of will has held things in place until, almost overnight it seems, that will deflates. Like a balloon without air, the frame shrivels, and whatever's been puffing it out is gone.

"Joanna!" Henry calls out to me when the puzzle's done and all apiece, and I smile and wave.

"Hullo, Henry! How nice. But I hadn't expected to see you today. You and Charlotte are coming to my party tomorrow, aren't you?" I'm anxious for a moment that he's come to cancel.

"Oh, indeed, we'll be here," he answers, coming towards me in old sweater and rumpled khaki pants with grass stains at the knees. He too has been out weeding in the glorious weather, it seems. I wipe my hands on my grubby jeans and hold one out to take his.

"Charlotte's having her hair done in town," Henry continues. "I thought I'd just drop by meanwhile and see how you're doing." He hesitates, looking uncertain suddenly.

"It's all right? I simply slipped away, and didn't think to call, but of course if you're busy . . ."

"Nonsense!" I laugh, glancing around. "As you can see, I've got my hands full here. But I'm always glad to see you, Henry."

"You've been working hard, haven't you?" he says admiringly. "The peonies are new, and these primroses . . . not the old ones, are they?"

"No, they died off. It's not quite the right time of year for them, I know, but I thought I'd plant some new and see what happens. We've planted almost everything new. Old Robert and I, that is."

"Old Robert? From the village? He's helping you out, is he?"

"I can't tell you how much. He's working down by the pond today. Henry, would you like some tea?"

"Oh, no, dear, I don't mean to interrupt your work."

"Do interrupt me, Henry. Please. I'm getting so I dream I'm digging in dirt."

He smiles along with me. "Well, then, a spot of tea would be delightful."

We sit in the garden on the bench, where Old Robert and I had lunch the other day. Between us is a tray with a teapot, two cups, and a plate of scones. In tiny blue bowls I've put clotted cream and strawberries, remembering that this is Henry's favourite treat. Now and then a bee comes down to inspect the fare, but they are either very friendly or very lazy today, it seems. They circle slowly, then disappear. Perhaps it's the unusual heat. Even I am beginning to relax, between the hot tea, the food, and Henry's easy companionship.

"How are your roses this year?" he asks. There is a spot of cream on his chin, and he dabs at it with his thumb.

"Better now. They were straggly and full of holes when I first got home, but we've been spraying and feeding, and Robert did a masterful job with the pruning. Would you like to see them?"

"Very much so."

"We can go round there when we're finished. Henry, do

you remember the little stone hare that was in the prim-rose garden?"

He squints. "Hare? Yes, I believe I do."

"It was a gift from Michael. I haven't been able to find it anywhere. Doesn't it seem odd that it's gone?"

"You've not found it about?"

"No. I've had Robert looking, as well."

"Hmmm. Hares, of course, are not all that beloved in these parts. According to superstition, they've always been abhorred."

"Really?"

"Oh, my yes. In ancient times—and not-so-ancient as well—it was thought that the spirits of the dead, even witches, resided in hares. And to even speak of a hare to a fisherman could spoil the catch of the day."

"Now that you mention it, I remember a picture in a storybook when I was young. A white hare, with burning eyes. He was surrounded by a group of villagers, his teeth bared, and they all looked paralyzed with fear."

"Ah, yes. Anyone injured before dying was thought to take the form of such a beast. Even dogs ran from it, howl-ing."

I give a mock shudder. "Well, my hare was perfectly safe to be around, and I miss him. I'd like him back."

Henry smiles. "There have been vandals about the coun-tryside lately, of course. It's not quite as peaceful here as it once . . ." His voice trails off, and then he looks at me, red-faced.

I swallow my bite of scone. "That's all right, Henry, you don't have to avoid reminding me that a murder took place right here at Pennoryn. In fact I've been wanting to talk to someone sensible about it."

Still, he seems uncomfortable.

"It's only that I haven't remembered another thing about that night," I say. "I hope that you . . ."

"Yes . . . mmmm, well . . . what do the doctors think?"

"They believe my memory will most likely come back in time. Whether in bits and pieces or all at once, who's to know? Henry, I don't think I've ever thanked you sufficiently for that night . . . you and Charlotte, for finding me and getting me to the hospital."

His embarrassment deepens and he looks away. "No, no, not at all. Please, Joanna. We did very little."

"But you may have saved my life, arriving when you did. You probably frightened off whoever it was."

"Oh, on the contrary, I would think the perpetrator was long gone. And I doubt he ever meant to hurt you—" He breaks off, looking down at his hands. "You . . . you had no injuries, after all . . . only that bump." Henry clears his throat, as if a bit of crumb has stuck in it. "That . . . that must tell you something."

"I don't understand."

His face is pink to his few remaining roots now. "Well . . ." he says, fumbling with his teacup, ". . . only that the perpetrator might have been someone . . . someone who cared about you."

It comes upon me slowly. "You mean Michael. You think he did it? *Et tu,* Henry?"

He looks startled, but doesn't answer.

"Henry, I'm sorry, but you cannot possibly know how tired I am of all these innuendos!"

"Please, Joanna, don't get excited."

But it's too late. I set my cup and saucer on the bench with an angry clatter. "Is that why you've really come today? Did Charlotte send you here to convince me to give up Michael? To tell me he may even be a *murderer?*"

"Please, Joanna, please."

He keeps repeating that word *please,* reaching out awkwardly to pat my shoulder, his hand trembling with distress. And finally I am able to see through the red haze of anger. I see Henry come into focus, the gentle grey eyes, the kindness—a good man, one who has always wanted only to be my friend. I understand that what he sees is not what I see, and finally that is all right.

We stand looking at the roses. One very large red blossom has popped out only today, encouraged, no doubt, by the heat. Henry is still obviously ill at ease from earlier, but he rises to the occasion, admiring the blossom's shape and scent. "*Périlleux*, is it not?" he asks.

"The name of the rose? I'm afraid I wouldn't know," I have to admit. "I'm not as up on the names as you."

"I believe that's it," Henry says. "*Dangerous*, as only seemingly perfect things can be."

"Why do you say that?"

"Oh . . ." he answers rather sadly, "perhaps, being seventy, there's more time to think. But it seems to me that perfection, or the appearance of it, draws one in so easily. We seldom see the pitfalls till it's far too late."

I smile. "You know, Henry, I remember when David and I first built this house. I stood on top of that hill there looking down at Pennoryn, and thought how perfect it was. The evening sun had turned the windows to flame, and there was smoke spiraling from the chimney. The gardens weren't in yet, but we'd left nearly all the natural shrubs and trees. As I watched, a bright red bird perched just above the door, as if to say he knew there would be life here soon. *Perfect*, is what I thought. *Absolutely perfect. And David did this for me.*"

Henry frowns. "I do seem to remember you worked with the contractors as well."

"Yes, a bit. But David did the lion's share of the physical work. Building this house was his pet project, you know."

He looks at me worriedly. "And how do you feel about Pennoryn now?"

I smile. "There is a bird, Henry, a male bird, who builds a beautiful nest to attract females to him. But it's a fake nest, a ruse, and once the female arrives, she finds she must build her own. I feel a bit like that female bird."

He takes my arm and we walk towards the front of the house. "I'd say you are getting well, Joanna."

"Oh, I have my moments. I'm reasonably grown up and well one moment, then insecure as can be the next. But I do believe I'm getting there."

He pats my arm. "I am sorry about earlier. But truly, you did misunderstand me. I must tell you, my dear, I don't agree with Charlotte about your upcoming marriage. I think that whatever difficulties may present themselves—

and certainly they will, they always do—you will work it out in the long run. You are a very wise woman, Joanna."

I stare at him, surprised. "Why, thank you, Henry. I had no idea you felt that way. Particularly about Michael."

"Yes, well, we do tend to lump married couples together as if they have only one thought between them, do we not?"

I give his arm a hug. "I suppose you're right. Especially when those couples are as happy and as perfect together as you and Charlotte. Oh, sorry . . ." I stop walking and smile. "I forgot. We had just decided there are dangers in perfection, hadn't we?"

Henry looks blank. For long moments he simply stares. "Dangers in perfection?" he murmurs finally. "Is that what we said? Oh, yes. Well, the appearance of it draws one in so easily. We seldom see the pitfalls till it's far too late."

My smile falters. Not only does he seem to have forgotten what we talked about only moments ago, but Henry is repeating himself, word for word, and he doesn't seem to realise it. I wonder if I should say anything. But we are at the Morris, and he grips my hand. "I must be off, my dear. I've enjoyed our little visit."

"Henry, you and Charlotte, you are still coming to my garden party tomorrow, aren't you? Charlotte never called to cancel."

He looks confused. "Garden party? Tomorrow, is it now?"

"Yes, Henry," I say gently.

"Well, of course we'll be here, then. Absolutely. We'll be here with the proverbial bells on."

"I'm glad. Two o'clock, then?" I give him a hug, and he smiles.

"Right you are. Two o'clock. Thank you, my dear, for the talk. Now I really must go and collect my lovely wife. I do believe it must be time for tea."

He is fumbling with the car door, and he looks very old and tired. I cannot bring myself to say, *But Henry, we just had tea.* Instead I hold the door as he eases himself in. The arthritis makes it difficult, and I help, which I can see embarrasses him a bit.

"Thank you for coming, Henry. I do love you, you know." I give him another light hug through the window, and he smiles, but then winces when I accidentally squeeze his arm.

As I watch him drive away, I am filled with sorrow. My old friend's mind is not what it was. No wonder Charlotte has been concerned for her husband.

And if I can relate to anything, it is the pain of not being able to remember, clearly, what has gone on.

CHAPTER 15

Showering the next morning, I remind myself that I must get Charlotte aside sometime during the party and ask her about Henry. If his forgetting was an isolated incident, that is one thing. But if it's more serious, perhaps we can put our heads together and come up with some way to help him. Then I am swept up in last-minute chores, and as I shower and dress I am more nervous about this party today than ever. In particular, I don't feel ready for Dr. Shahi to meet Michael. I hope he doesn't probe too much. Not that Michael has anything to hide, but a doctor rummaging about in one's mind can be so irritating.

Nor do I feel quite up to meeting Michael's friend Gregg, but only because he is an unknown quantity—someone I will have to treat carefully, like a new silk dress rather than an old bent shoe.

It comes to me that I have never liked the tensions associated with meeting new people, and then of course it seems clear that this is why I have so few friends. It has always been easier being with Charlotte, despite our difficulties, than venturing out with someone new.

Nervously, then, I dash about the house like a hungry bird, pecking excitedly here and there, making sure no pillow, no dish, has been untended. Michael has come bearing trays of hors d'oeuvres that he's made at home the night before. I can hear him in the kitchen rattling pots around, and the smell of garlic wafting from there is divine.

As for the gardens, I never did finish, what with all that

foolish business with the herbs. Their little plot is pristine, however—not a weed in sight as of an hour ago. It occurs to me that this is not good; only a new garden has no weeds. If it had been planted weeks ago, as I told Dr. Shahi, there would surely be a weed or two cropping up somewhere.

For a brief moment I entertain the thought that I should go out, take a handful of Robert's newly plucked weeds, and plop them down into the herb garden—arranging them all quite randomly, of course.

That this is truly insane reaches me before I am fool enough to do it.

Michael appears at the kitchen door. "I'm finished with the food, but I warn you, the scullery's a mess." He removes my pink apron, but not before I get to see how cute he looks with it on.

"Wonderful. How do you think everything looks? The rest of it, I mean."

He pops a tiny tart into my mouth. "Here, try this."

"Mmmm, I do so love garlic. Potatoes, peas . . . and lamb as well, right?"

"That, and my famous secret ingredient."

"You'll share it when we're married, though, I hope."

"We'll see." He touches my mouth with a fingertip and comes away with crumbs. Impulsively, I lick them away. "Mmmm, this must be your secret sauce."

"You're very bad," he says, laughing.

"So how does it all look?" I wave an arm about.

"Jo, even the Queen Mum couldn't complain. But don't you think you're going a bit overboard here? None of the people you've invited will expect things to be perfect. Everyone knows you're just out of hospital."

I spot a pillow I haven't plumped, and cross over to it, knocking it against my hand. "That's just it. I don't want them to think I'm not up to things."

"But everyday life is all anyone could expect of you—*if* that. You've been almost maniacal about this party for a week."

I cast a glance at him. "Maniacal?" I stretch my lips and eyes and make a face like a crazed monster.

He laughs. "You know what I mean."

I throw the pillow at him. It smacks him in the face.

When his look of astonishment passes, he leans over to the sofa, grabs up two pillows, and takes aim. "So you want a fight, do you?"

They bounce from my chest and arms, and I throw up my hands, laughing. "No! Stop, you'll mess everything up!"

"I'll mess *you* up," he says, scooping me into his arms and planting a kiss on my lips. He is sweaty, and smells of sage, onion, thyme. As we tumble onto the sofa I think briefly that we're getting it dirty, and that pillows are being knocked askew, and if we aren't careful, we may even knock the lamp over with our feet. Then I don't think about that anymore.

I sit before my bedroom mirror and try to collect myself. My initial jitters are subsiding, but only just. My makeup is smeared a bit from that playful romp on the sofa, and I am hurrying to repair it. Michael, of course, insisted I looked fine. No—*lovely* is what he said. And I am grateful for that, because I do think he means it.

The catch, for me, is that I once thought David meant it as well. So I began to relax, not always putting makeup on if we weren't going anywhere, and oft-times pulling my hair back in an elastic band, rather than letting it fall free. I've always worn it long, as I like long hair, but it irritates me when I'm trying to work and it swings about my face.

Then one day I was cleaning David's office, while he was in town posting his manuscript off to a publisher. He hadn't let me read it, and I was curious. I expected to find a copy on David's desk, and thought it might not matter if I took just the smallest peek. But his copy wasn't there.

Rooting about in my husband's desk drawers was something I never did. Having had little privacy as a child, I tended to respect the need for it in others. But as I said, I was curious. David had been working on his book for months, and all he would say is, "I think it has a bit of a literary bent."

That seemed rather obscure to me. What did it mean? Was he writing a sequel to *War and Peace*—or a Holmesian-type mystery that I might one day see on the BBC? I could, I thought, simply pull out a drawer, and if it was there . . .

A copy of David's manuscript may in fact have been in one of those drawers. I never did find out. I began with the top drawer on the right. There were pens, pencils, paper clips. The next one down had typing paper and carbons, all neatly layered and separated by wooden slats. A stapler. A three-hole punch.

In the bottom drawer there were magazines. A stack of them several inches high. I pulled one out, surprised, as I didn't think David to be a magazine reader. But this was no ordinary fare. On the cover were a man and two women, naked, in the act of intercourse and sodomy. I felt heat rise to my face. Yet I couldn't restrain myself; I flipped through the pages. There was more. Not art, but hard-core pornography. "Candid" shots of mostly middle-aged men and very young, nubile women, in a variety of sexual acts.

The women, I thought, must be teenagers; there was not a spot of cellulite, not an ounce of fat. While the men were untouched in the photographs—some of them portly, wrinkled, sagging—the women were heavily made up, their long hair glossy, falling artfully between breasts and thighs, caressing genitals and nipples. They were clearly "tending" to the men's needs—in ways I had never even imagined. There were chains, handcuffs, instruments of torture.

With a growing sense of unreality, I pulled out another magazine, and another. The same. The dates on the covers spanned a couple of years, right up to that present day. There was no mailing address, and I couldn't think that David had found them anywhere in the village. I knew he must have brought them down from London.

He's been researching a book, I thought, *and he felt he had to hide these from me. He didn't think I'd approve.*

Well, he was right. And yes, I know the arguments that even psychologists make. They say there's nothing wrong with men looking at these things, that it's normal, that it doesn't mean they don't love their wives. We're supposed to be glad they're red-blooded, masculine.

I don't give a damn what they say. After I saw those magazines I would lie in bed alone and wonder what David was doing in there. Reflecting on those bodies page by page, finding what he wanted in them, rather than with me? I could never even bring myself to ask him about them, afraid that once he knew I had seen them, it would open a Pandora's box I would rather stay closed. If David knew I'd seen those books—that I knew such things existed —would he ask me to do them?

From then on, when I knew David was in his office at night, such thoughts would torment me. Giving up on sleep, I would climb out of bed and sit here before this mirror, staring at my reflection—and I would hate myself. *Not enough*, I would think. *Not pretty enough, good enough, sensual enough.*

Sitting here now, staring into this same mirror, I replace my smeared makeup with utmost care. Turning this way and that, I look for signs of flaws: a puffiness beneath the chin? Is it not quite as sharp as before? Are there new lines at either side of the eye?

And this tiny mole—quickly, now, plaster it over. Pluck that stray brow.

It is a sad, panicky thing, this need to erase or hide every fault. Yet I cannot seem to stop, even now. For though Michael has said that he loves me as I am—imperfect, unfinished—I wonder if he is not simply being kind.

We gather in the garden at a large wrought-iron-and-glass table Charlotte has donated for the day. It is lovely, as she has set pots of bright yellow marigolds beneath, around its post. My only complaint, were I to complain about anything on this lovely day, and of course I should not, is that we can see each other's legs through the glass—like speakers at a dinner, the cloth having hiked up.

Not that this matters to the men—only to Charlotte and me, and really only to me. Charlotte seems confident and composed in her flowing silk dress that is the same sea-green colour as her eyes—though one would never know, as she wears sunglasses and never removes them. She wears a picture hat, too, and looks for all the world like a young Marlene Dietrich, portraying a glamourous Russian spy.

I, on the other hand, twitch and wiggle like a farmgirl, always checking to see that the hem of my knee-length white skirt is down.

"You've a beautiful place here," Gregg King is saying. "I've always wanted to live in the country." He has a ruddy, rather nice but ordinary-looking face, and his chestnut hair gleams under the bright sunlight. I wonder if he uses pomade.

But of course he would; an actor certainly wants to look his best. And I don't mean to be unkind; I like Michael's friend. It is only that I find myself looking from one person to another and analyzing, studying. I seem to go inside this way quite often since coming home. I cannot let things be.

"I suppose most city people think they'd like to live in the country at one time or another," I answer, thinking of David. "It's very quiet here, though. No bustle of traffic or people."

"Do you get lonely at all?" Gregg asks. "That's the one thing that might put me off a bit."

"Well, with a good car, you're not too far from London, of course," Henry says.

Gregg makes a face, having just driven down from there. "Took me a bit over four hours, with the weekend traffic."

"Oh, I hadn't thought of that," I say apologetically. "The traffic, I mean. You really must stay over." I glance at Michael, wondering if he'll extend the invitation, as I don't know just where precisely I'd put his friend.

"Thanks very much," Gregg says. "I appreciate that. But Michael's already offered, and I'm afraid I've had to turn him down. I must be in London early, so I'd best be on my way tonight before it's too late. Another time?"

"Absolutely," I say.

Dr. Shahi glances at me, checking, most likely, to see how I'm holding up with all this social chatter. He is dressed in a neat dark suit, and his polished black shoes look rather quaint beside the sport shoes of the other men. I give him a smile, and he smiles back.

Charlotte's head turns our way. The hat brim dips as she

lifts her wine glass and takes a sip. "Dr. Shahi, I've been wondering. When one simply 'goes away' in their mind—as Joanna did, say—what does one think about? Or is there simply a blank screen?"

Several pairs of disconcerted eyes turn her way, then mine—among them Michael's and Henry's. They seem worried this talk might upset me.

Charlotte gives a light laugh. "I'm just so fascinated by this business of lost memory. In general, that is. You don't mind, do you, Joanna?"

I do not. In fact, I am as interested in Dr. Shahi's answer as she. "No, of course not. Please go on, Dr. Shahi."

He lays down his fork and touches his serviette to his mouth. "I cannot say we know a great deal about catatonia," he says, carefully placing the serviette by his plate. "There is some evidence to suggest it is much like being in coma. Some patients tell stories of having heard conversations that actually occurred in their rooms—between doctor and nurse, say, or relatives. Then again, there are reports of patients imagining entire scenarios."

"Really?" Charlotte leans forward. "Real scenarios, things that have actually happened in their lives, or things they've made up?"

"Both. As in dreams, the imagination, or psyche, seems to be working through problems as the body lies passive, healing."

"Amazing. And other kinds of memory loss?" she says, smiling artlessly. "People who simply forget. Say they remember an incident later. Will they necessarily remember it just the way it happened? Or might they imagine something?"

"Well, there are many kinds of forgetting. There's the alcoholic blackout. People seldom recall things at all. Then there's trauma-induced amnesia. When people remember after this sort of thing, they generally do have near-total recall. The kind of forgetting that comes with aging or Alzheimer's, however, is another situation entirely. When a patient is having one of these episodes, past memories are often accessed as if they were occurring at that moment. A man may think he is still married to a woman who actually died forty years ago, for instance. Then, when he comes out of it, he'll forget entirely that he thought that. He won't even remember the episode."

Charlotte says tightly, "And is there nothing that can be done to help someone like that remember?"

"There is a great deal of research taking place with Alzheimer's," Dr. Shahi answers. "Particularly as to the changes in personality that often take place—"

I glance at Henry, and see that he is staring at his plate, and his face is flushed.

"You know, on second thought," I say, breaking in and smiling at the table at large, "why don't we talk about something else? This is supposed to be a party."

Both Michael and Dr. Shahi look at me and then nod slightly, agreeing. Gregg, obviously wanting to be a good guest, takes my cue and tries innocently to lighten the conversation.

"I've been reading something," he says brightly, "that's nearly the opposite to this. Rather than helping people to remember old memories, it seems a lot of therapists are teaching them to reconstruct them to their liking. A person abused in childhood, say, may visualise the abuser as not being an abuser after all, but someone kind and good. I've been particularly interested, as I've just got a part in a play about a serial killer who was horribly abused as a child by his stepfather. I can't help wondering if people can do this with all their unpleasant memories—a broken love affair, for instance, or a lost job. Can we really get over these things more easily by imagining they turned out differently?"

"Well," Dr. Shahi says, "this technique is still being studied. I have, however, used it in my own practice at times. I've found it can help a patient to recall certain painful scenes in his life and reconstruct them—order up a better memory for himself, so to speak."

Michael leans forward and says curiously, "This new memory, however, is made up? It's not real."

Dr. Shahi smiles. "Well, as to that . . . what is real?"

Michael looks thoughtful.

"Perhaps it is best understood this way," Dr. Shahi continues. "The mind sends a new 'memory' to the cell. The cell reads this new memory and accepts it as fact. Much as a computer, say, accepts a revision. You take out the old word and put in the new. The computer does not care. It does not say, 'Oh, a new word—how nice!' Or, 'Oh, a new word—how bad.' It simply accepts. And from then on, the new word is the one that exists. For anyone reading it or using it, that word is as real as any other."

"Are you saying the mind, then, is no more than a computer?" Gregg asks.

"I would argue with your phrase *no more*. But yes, I do believe the mind works much like a computer. And to continue the metaphor, I believe as well that it is up to the operator, the individual, to plug in the most helpful data for his or her own healing."

There is a small, thoughtful silence. Finally, Charlotte laughs uneasily and says, "My, my, this is all so terribly complicated, isn't it? Far too much for me!" I notice her wine glass is empty, and she is reaching for the bottle in the center of the table. It too is empty, and her mouth tightens, though of course I cannot see her eyes.

I stand. "I've picked some lovely chamomile for tea. And mint. Would anyone like some?"

Dr. Shahi answers immediately. He too stands, pressing his hands together in a prayer-like gesture that I've come to know means "peace to all." He smiles at me. "Tea would be delightful. And, Joanna, I haven't forgotten that you promised to show me your garden."

"Yes," I say gratefully. "Let's go now. And we'll stop in the kitchen afterwards for the tea. Michael, you'll entertain our guests till we get back?"

"Of course." He stands and leans towards me, kissing my cheek. "Take your time. We'll be fine."

We follow the path round the house to the kitchen garden, through roses that are so rich now with scent I begin to feel a bit dizzy. Or is it all that business with Charlotte and Henry? I do feel shaken.

Dear God, I must talk to Charlotte and find out how far his forgetting has gone and what they're doing about it. I am also anxious to offer my support. It is important in times of trouble to have someone to talk to, and Charlotte has been bearing the brunt, no doubt, alone.

Meanwhile, I am having to convince my doctor that his fears about my marriage to Michael are needless.

". . . and over here," I prattle on and on—having ticked off each variety of rose, no less it's botanical history, "is my herb garden. I've tried to apply everything I learned from you." The herbs are surrounded by a low border of violas. "I remember you told me to mix in a few edible flowers. I'm using the violas in salads."

"Lovely," Dr. Shahi says. He hitches up his trouser pants and stoops down to feel the soil, holding a clump in his hand as if weighing it. He makes no comment, but I am almost certain he is noticing the freshness of upturned earth. He stands and smiles. "I see you have rosemary, marjoram, Italian parsley . . ."

"And over here, chamomile, lavender, mint . . ."

"All of which may be used in healing as well as cooking," he observes, wiping his hands on a clean white handkerchief.

"I know." I flash him a smile, remembering the way he would take me over to his herb boxes during my treatment sessions, and have me pick one that "felt right" to me. I would hold it during our session, now and then sniffing its redolent scent, and somehow that seemed to be healing. *If you listen,* he told me, *the herbs themselves will tell you which of them your body needs at a given time.* I was never certain I fully believed this, but I was more than willing to learn. I would do anything to get well, to get out of there.

In truth, I found planting this garden—even with so little time, and all the panic—healing. It turned out to be a blessing in disguise.

"You've been very busy with all this," Dr. Shahi notes.

"I wanted everything to be perfect, I suppose, for today."

"You aren't doing too much? You have help?"

"Yes, a man who was recommended by the nursery. He's done most of the digging and hauling. I've had the better half, planting things and trimming."

"Still, when you showed us about the inside of the house, so much new paint and wallpaper . . . Joanna, you look a bit all-in. I'm concerned you're overdoing it."

He doesn't say "obsessed." But I see it in his eyes.

"Not at all. Old Robert helped me inside as well. We even tossed out everything in David's study. It's a sewing room now." *Robert* tossed out everything, actually. I couldn't bring myself to go near David's room.

"And your friend . . . Charlotte," he says.

"Yes?"

"I'm concerned. Is she still your only close friend here?"

"Yes. Aside from Michael, that is."

"Joanna, don't you think it might be wise to, oh, broaden your horizons a bit?"

"Are you saying you don't like Charlotte?"

"Not at all. It's not a question of like or dislike, as I've not had the opportunity to really get to know her. It's only that she seems rather . . . intense."

"I know. You're right, of course. I think she's worried about some personal matters just now."

"And might those personal matters have something to do with her husband?"

"You caught that, then? Yes, I believe so. I've only just recently discovered that Henry's memory is failing."

"The thing is, I'm concerned that the people you thought would give you support here at home are proving to have too much on their plate."

"But there's Michael," I say quickly. Impulsively, I turn and grasp his hand. "Do you like him? Oh, please tell me that you do!"

Dr. Shahi smiles. "I do. He seems to genuinely care for you. But that doesn't necessarily mean you are ready for a relationship, Joanna."

My heart begins an irregular flutter. "What are you saying? That you won't recommend our marriage?"

"Not precisely. I am saying that I would advise you to wait a year at the very least. Give yourself time to remember everything." There is a pause. "You haven't, have you?"

I drop his hand and stoop to root out a miniscule weed

that has popped up, after all, amongst the herbs. "Remembered the way David died? No. I think . . ."

I can't tell him what I think—that for whatever reason, the manner of David's dying has become a nasty slug beneath a rock that I cannot steel myself to upturn.

"I think I should simply accept the police theory of a vagrant," I say, "and get on with things. You were right—I was obsessed with David. I see that now."

"Even so, Joanna. To be ready for marriage again, there are things I think you need to understand. Things about yourself, and your childhood."

My face pales; I can feel the blood rush from it. "My childhood?" I have never told Dr. Shahi about that. "Did Charlotte . . . ?" I feel laid bare, as if people are gathering behind my back to talk about me, undressing my very soul.

"Did she tell me about your childhood when they brought you in?" Dr. Shahi says. "No. I've only suspected, from our talks. And I am sorry to bring up such unpleasantness on this otherwise lovely day. But I do feel certain there are things that must be brought into the open and worked through."

I reach a hand out to the wooden bench and sit, feeling tired now. "What sort of things?"

What clues might I have given away? Is there an imprint on one for all time, some certain set to the wrinkles on one's forehead, for instance, something everyone can see?

Dr. Shahi sits beside me. "I can't know the details, of course. But there must be something wrong in your family. Else why did they never, in eight months, turn out to visit you?"

"Even so . . ."

"It also took you rather a long time to relax with me, to tell me anything at all. Even then, you wouldn't talk about your family. Your mother, a bit. Nothing at all about your father or brothers. I'm trained to watch for these signs."

I stare at the ground, unseeing. "But you never said anything."

"I felt it best to let you bring the matter up. If these memories are forced out into the open, they often become tainted. You might think you remember something, for example, but you'd only be trying to please me, coming up with whatever you thought I was looking for, you see. It's part of the pattern."

"Pattern?"

"Accepting abuse—or striving to please in order to prevent it—tends to become a pattern in an abused person's life."

I think about that. "My husband . . ."

"He was abusive?"

"It's odd. I don't believe I saw it that way, until recently."

"Since you've been home from hospital?"

"Yes. I've been remembering things he would blame me for, like interrupting his work, even when it was necessary. Or things he would say that hurt me. And I took it. I thought, well, Joanna, you don't know how to be a good wife, that's all. You'll have to do better."

"And your childhood, can you talk about it now?"

My face grows hot with shame. But I force the words out, as I can see he's right; things must be faced. And who better to face them with? "My brothers . . ." I begin haltingly, ". . . they raped me . . . from the time I was ten until I was thirteen. I suppose one might say the whole family was in on it. My father watched, he applauded. My mother . . . she pretended not to know."

Dr. Shahi sits quietly, not speaking, and from this I know he is with me, that he is shocked for me, and feels my pain. I turn my head away to hide tears I would rather he did not see.

At last he releases a long sigh. "Joanna, it is a wonder you survived. The human spirit is indeed a miraculous thing. And now you have come to a bridge, I believe. You can cross that bridge into healing or you can stay where you are. If you do that, you might even backtrack. The choice is yours, of course. However, if you decide to heal, I'll do all in my power to help you."

"But I . . . I just think I've already crossed that bridge. I feel I'm getting better every day."

"That may be true. But can you honestly say you are completely healed?"

I think of all the crazy things I've done these past weeks —the last-minute dash to grow an herb garden not the least of them—and I am forced to admit I am not.

"What exactly are you saying? What is it you want me to do?"

"I think we should begin with your coming to see me at Whitehurst at least twice a week, perhaps three if it seems we need that at first. And this time, I would want you to bring everything in the past out into the open, all that you remember as abuse. Once we've carted it all out, so to speak, we can examine it in the light of day and see how best to proceed."

"To reconstruct it, you mean? That thing you were talking about earlier?"

"We might do that. We have to see what is best for you. Will you come out to Whitehurst?"

"I . . . yes."

Dr. Shahi smiles. "Excellent. And meanwhile, Joanna, I strongly recommend that you put off marriage for now."

"Put off—oh, but I can't do that, it's all planned!"

"A small delay only. Until we examine that pattern I spoke of earlier. Joanna, with your background of abuse, it does not surprise me at all that you went straight from your parents' home, in a manner of speaking, to an abusive husband."

"But it's different now! Michael is different!"

"You may very well be right about that. I pray you are. Often, however, people are drawn to us when they know they can abuse us, or even simply take advantage of us. It may not be anything they deliberately think, but at some deep level they are drawn because our illness can fill their own needs."

I stand and begin to pace. This is not going the way I'd planned it at all. Irritably, I push my hair from my neck; it is much too long for this heat. I have a sudden angry urge to chop it all off.

"I understand what you're saying, Dr. Shahi. But *you* don't understand. Michael is the one who saved me from a gang rape by my brothers and their friends on my thirteenth birthday. He saw to it they never touched me after that. Michael is different. He would never hurt me."

"I am not saying he would. I simply think you should go slowly now. Rethink all of your relationships, how each person relates to you, and you to them."

My voice rises angrily, yet there is a small, frightened quaver. "Are you saying you won't recommend my marriage to the examiners?"

He spreads his hands. "There is no actual law, of course, by which I or the board could stop you. You may still be healing, but you are not, after all, mentally ill, or incompetent. And while the examiners may seem intimidating, they are there for your good, nothing more. My reports to them are solely to monitor my work as a physician. A check on me, so to speak."

I am stunned. "But I didn't know that. When I was in hospital, they seemed to have so much power over me. *'Yes, you can go home'*, and *'No, you can't.'* I even thought they, and you, could make me come back if I didn't—"

I am about to say, "If I didn't behave," when I hear the words in my head and understand their origin. *I must be good, must do as I'm told—or suffer pain.*

I look at Dr. Shahi, and he nods. "If you had come straight out and asked me, instead of playing games with the examiners and me, you would have known this, Joanna. These are the kinds of things we need to work through, you see."

We go inside, Dr. Shahi to use the telephone, I for the tea. I've put the kettle on and am thinking through our conversation—growing more aggravated by the minute—when Dr. Shahi returns to the kitchen. "Have you made a decision?" he asks. "Will you wait to be married?"

I put slices of saffron cake on the tea tray, lining them up deliberately so that the edges are an even quarter inch apart. I shake my head. "No. I know you think that would be best." I flash him a sour look. "You can put that in your report, if you like. Tell them I listened to your recommendation, but rejected it."

"I see. Are you angry with me?"

I wipe my hands on a towel and sigh. "No. No, not really. But I've waited all my life for Michael, don't you see? It feels right to me." Slyly, for I am not through yet with playing games, I add, "I seem to remember you saying that people should listen more to their own instincts, and less to so-called experts."

My doctor sighs. "Sometimes that backfires on me. Are you firm in this? I cannot talk you out of it?"

"No."

"But you will at least begin therapy right away? You won't put it off?"

"I'll call tomorrow and set it up."

"Well, then . . . I suppose I must settle for that."

But he looks so unhappy, I am prompted to say, "Why don't you come to the wedding? It's to be a small affair, in a little shop in Mevagissey."

"A shop?" If I thought he looked doubtful before, that was nothing compared to now.

I laugh. "It's not a crazy idea. Weatherby's has very good memories for Michael and me."

"Well, that's something." Again, he sighs.

"Yes. I won't have to reconstruct those."

Dr. Shahi smiles. "Are you handling all the wedding preparations alone?"

I brush a tired hand through my hair. "For the most part. Michael's been busy setting up his paintings at a gallery in London, and I don't know what else he's got scheduled. As for me, I still must shop for clothes, have my hair and nails done . . . the usual things."

He studies my face. "Joanna, I would feel much better about all this if you'd have a complete physical sometime in the next few days."

"Oh, but that isn't necessary at all! I'm only tired right now from the party."

"Even so, it's stressful, beginning a new marriage. And the days before can do one in. Won't you do this for me, please?"

I narrow my eyes. "So you can write it in your report?"

He laughs. "Yes. So I can write it in my report."

He is being so nice about everything there doesn't seem any way out of it. I finally agree to call Dr. Woolery, Charlotte and Henry's physician, the next day. Perhaps he can fit me in.

Dr. Shahi has rejoined the rest of the guests, and I am on my way back into the garden with the heavy tea tray when I hear Michael's voice from behind the hedgerow. I wander over there, thinking to ask him for help with the tray. Rounding the corner, I find him deep in conversation with Gregg. They are so caught up, in fact, they neither see nor hear me.

I stand twenty feet away, half hidden by a small copse of trees, watching—not to eavesdrop, but because I enjoy so much watching Michael when he is talking. I love his energy, and the way his eyes light up, his every tone and gesture. There is so much life in Michael, and I feel that somehow it rubs off on me.

I cannot hear their words, and I don't even strain to listen. But then Gregg's voice rises. "Good Lord, Michael. When you said you were marrying someone named Joanna Carr, I didn't know you meant David Carr's widow!"

I give a small start of surprise. Michael's friend knew my husband? Where? In London? I am about to step forward and ask when Michael says, "I don't want you saying anything about that to Joanna. She doesn't remember any of it, and for now it's best left that way."

I freeze in my steps.

"I just don't understand," Gregg says. "The way he behaved at the Red Unicorn, you'd have thought he was married to the Mud Hen herself."

"David Carr was an ass." Michael's voice rises. "He deserved what he got, and that's the truth."

Gregg puts a hand on his shoulder. "Easy, now, easy. The man's gone. He can't hurt anyone now."

Michael's jaw works, and his eyes blaze. "I'm not so sure of that. If a man could die twice, I swear to God, I'd see him dead again!"

"I'd be a bit careful who I talked that way around," Gregg says. "I understand the murder isn't yet solved."

"Yes, well, the police didn't suspect me before. Why would they now?"

"Perhaps because you're walking off with the man's widow, who just happens to be not only lovely, but to look at things here, rather well off. And you, my friend, are in dire financial straits."

"Not for long . . ." Michael answers, his words drifting off as they move in the opposite direction.

I turn away, my face hot. My wrists ache from the weight of the tray, and my heart thuds loudly.

"My, my. Your hero," Charlotte says softly from beside me. I have not noticed her standing there. "Do you believe me now?"

I need time to think, and I cannot think with Charlotte pushing at me. I head back towards the table and my guests. "I've got to be getting—"

She grabs my arm. "Did you *hear* it? Did you hear what Michael said about his money problems?"

"Charlotte, Michael and I have talked. He's working it out, and he doesn't want my help. Now leave it alone."

"You just don't want to face it, do you? You're hiding your head in the sand—"

It is time to turn the tables on her. "Char, what about Henry? Are you facing that? What are you doing for him?"

Her face, what is showing of it beneath the sunglasses, pales. "Henry? What on earth are you talking about?"

"His *memory*, Char. When he was here yesterday he forgot things. And you've been asking Dr. Shahi all those questions. Don't tell me you don't know what I mean."

"Well, I don't! And if you know what's good for you, you won't say anything about this—not to Henry or anyone." She grips my shoulders. "Do you hear me, Joanna? Not a word!"

"Stop it, Charlotte!" I shake her off. "I love Henry as much as you do, and if I think I can help him by saying something, I will."

Her mouth trembles, and it is only now, in trying to look into her eyes beyond the sunglasses, that I see a dark shadow around the lower rim of the glasses. With growing horror, I lift my hand to her glasses and begin gently to pull them off. She twists away. "Don't!"

"Char, take those things off. Let me see what you're hiding."

Throwing up her hands, she gives a haughty laugh. "Oh, for God's sake!" She wrenches the glasses from her face. "I ran into a cupboard door, that's all."

I stare at the mottled, brownish-green bruise. "A cupboard door."

"Yes, and I didn't want to look awful for today, so I decided to wear the glasses. Why make such an issue of it?"

"Char, this doesn't feel right. Did someone do this to you? What really happened?"

Her eyes tear. "You wouldn't believe me if I told you. You don't believe a damn thing I say anymore!"

Everyone has gone home, and we are cleaning up the kitchen. Michael is washing this time, and I am scraping. But my thoughts are with Charlotte. Directly after that scene in the garden, she gathered up Henry and left, without another word but a stiff "Thank you for a lovely day" to me.

"It was a great party, Jo," Michael says. "You're a wonderful hostess."

"I don't know about that," I say tiredly, though I appreciate his saying it. "Everyone loved your cooking, though."

"It's you they loved. You made them feel comfortable."

"Not Charlotte."

"Well, if you ask me, she makes her own troubles. She's always got something she's upset about."

"Michael, that's not fair. There's a problem with Henry."

"Really? What kind of problem?"

"She asked me not to talk about it."

"Not even to me?"

"No. Oh, Michael, I don't see any reason not to tell you. But for now, why don't we simply table it? I'm really tired."

"I'd be delighted to do just that. I'm a bit weary of the

subject of Charlotte Dean myself. Henry's a good egg, though."

"Yes. And Charlotte does love him a great deal. You've got to give her that."

"I suppose."

"Michael . . ." Exhausted as I am, I have decided to face this issue now. "What's the Red Unicorn?"

He gives a start, makes a sound of pain, and brings his hands out of the dishwater. The tip of a finger is bloody.

"Lor, you've cut yourself! Here, let me look at that."

"It's nothing, just a nick." He runs clean water over it, then drains the dishwater, which is turning pink. In the bottom of the sink lies a sharp knife with a saw-toothed edge. I pick it up.

"Is this what you cut it on? Good heavens, that must hurt."

"No, it's all right, really. Trade places with you, though. I'll dry, you wash?"

I grimace and set the nasty-looking knife out of the way on the counter top, then fill the sink with fresh soapy water. "No, sit down. Have some coffee while I finish up, it'll only take a minute."

"You know, I think I'll take you up on that." He pours, then holds the coffee pot up to me, a question in his eyes. I shake my head. "Not right now. Michael, this place . . . the Red Unicorn. What is it?"

He stirs sugar into his cup. "Where did you hear of it?"

"In the garden. When you and Gregg were talking."

He leans against the counter and sips. "How much did you hear?"

I rinse the last dish and put it in the drainer. "I heard Gregg say that he'd seen David there."

"Oh, I see . . . Well, uh, the Red Unicorn is a private club. You don't remember David mentioning it?"

"No. Is there something wrong with his having been there?"

He frowns and sets his coffee down. "Why do you ask?"

"You told Gregg it was best if I didn't know."

He pulls a handkerchief from his trouser pocket and holds it to his finger, which is bleeding again. "I suppose I just didn't want him mentioning David, when we're just about to be married. Raising old ghosts, you know. Spoiling the party, and all that."

"So that's all it was?"

"Of course. What else?" Michael smiles. "Look, might we talk about something else? I liked your Dr. Shahi. And he was most impressed by your herb garden." There is a note of humour in his voice. It has not escaped him that the herb garden was a buttering-up ploy.

"He liked you, too." I do not mention Dr. Shahi's recommendation that we wait to be married.

"And it seemed you and Gregg hit it off," Michael says.

I let the water out of the sink and dry my hands. "I liked him."

"We'll have to go up and see him work sometime. Would you like that?"

"Of course."

"Oh, and by the way, Jo. I've just about got a loan worked out to buy and fix up the gallery in London."

"Really?" I try not to show my relief. At least now I will be able to pass the word to Charlotte, and she can stop hinting at Michael's "devious motives."

"Yes, it's all but settled. There's only one small hitch." He reddens a bit and looks uneasy. "I had to tell them we're to be married shortly, and that opened up a whole can of worms. The bank would like us to join our accounts this week—before they'll sign the loan papers, that is."

"Join our accounts? How odd."

"Yes, well, it's to protect their interest. If we kept separate accounts after marriage, and I were to put all my assets into yours, they might not be able to get at them in case I defaulted. Not that I would do that, of course. But you know how stuffy and conservative lenders can be."

I am silent a moment, a bit disconcerted.

"Sweetheart, is this a problem for you? It's all right, if so. I can always look elsewhere for the loan. I just thought that since we'd be joining our accounts next week, anyway, after we're married, well, we'd be getting it over with a week early, that's all. And the fact that we use the same bank makes it fairly simple."

"Well, of course I want to do anything I can, Michael, to help you get that loan. But the thing is . . . I guess I hadn't thought about having a joint account, even after we're married."

"Oh, but Jo, we really should. Once the gallery in London is up and running properly, I should have quite a bit of income from it. I want whatever I have to be yours, and a joint account would be the easiest way to assure that, should anything happen to me."

I pour myself coffee now and sip it slowly, thinking how best to say this. "I appreciate that, Michael, and I know you mean well. But I think the reason I'm hesitating is because it's felt so good having my own money again. Managing it alone, and taking care of myself, I mean. I missed that when I was married to David."

Michael takes me in his arms and smiles. "Sweetheart, I understand that completely. And believe me, I won't intrude on that. I wouldn't think of touching your money, or trying to manage it in any way. I just want you to have mine at your disposal as well." He kisses me softly on the lips. "Tell you what. I'll leave the papers with you, and you can think about it tonight. If it doesn't feel right to you by morning, we won't do it. All right?"

"All right," I say. But I know already that I do not feel right about this, and I doubt that thinking about it will change things.

CHAPTER 16

That night it storms again. Thunder shakes the heavens, and rain beats so hard on my bedroom window I fear it will break the panes. I toss and turn, thinking about Charlotte, then Michael, then Charlotte again. When sleep finally comes I have terrible dreams. I see Charlotte on her knees, crawling down a city street to get away from something. Her knees are swollen and bruised; in fact her entire body and face are bruised, as if she's been badly beaten. I try to help her, but I haven't the strength. "Get up, get up," I cry, "you must get on your feet!" Her expression is vacant, empty. I turn and call out to Michael to lend a hand, but he and Henry are on a corner talking together, and when they look up and see our dilemma they shrug and glance away. I grab Charlotte's arm and try to fly to a safer place, pulling her with me. Her weight is too much. I cannot get us off the ground, and there is something very dark and frightening closing in.

Sometime in the night I hear a noise outside. Opening my eyes I see a shadowy figure passing by the bedroom window. With a start I jerk to a sitting position, my whole body rigid. Only then do I realise I've been sleeping, and that I must have dreamt that, too.

The shriek of a jay wakens me at dawn. Moving to turn, I find that my back and legs hurt as if I am the one who has been crawling through the streets all night. I am exhausted, lethargic. My brain feels numb. If today were my wedding day, I realise, I would not have the strength for it. As it is, I don't know how I'll manage everything I must do today. Therefore, when reminders of Charlotte and her many secrets come rushing back, I shove them away. Nor do I wish to think even of Michael and that business of our accounts. I thought about it long after he left and, in truth, I still do not feel good about it. Yet I do want to help him. Perhaps there is some other way.

Sighing, I lift the phone and ring Dr. Woolery's office. Mrs. Albicott, the doctor's receptionist, comes on. I ask her if the doctor has time in the next few days for a physical, holding my breath, rather hoping she'll say no. *"Sorry, doctor's booked. Next month, perhaps."* Then I can at least tell Dr. Shahi I tried.

But no, she checks, and yes, there has been a cancellation this morning at ten. "Will that be all right?" I glance tiredly at the clock and confirm that it will.

With far too little energy I shower, dress, and go over the list I've made and added to throughout the week. It is probably as well, I decide, that the appointment with Dr. Woolery is this morning. There will be time afterwards to finish up necessary shopping in Mevagissey. And while I'm there, I must stop by Mr. Weatherby's and remind him I'll be bringing flowers. He has offered to move things from the counters so there will be room for them, and I can help him with that. I must remember, also, to choose candles for the ceremony.

Mr. Weatherby was thrilled when I broached the idea of our being married in his shop. "To have you and Michael married here would be my greatest pleasure. It will be a fitting culmination."

A fitting culmination. Yes, I agreed. But where is my excitement for it today?

Through a front window I see Old Robert a few feet away, shielding his eyes from the sun and staring in the direction of the road. In his other hand he holds a shovel, and I see he's been setting down new peonies, but was distracted by something.

I slip out the door quietly with my coffee, thinking he may have spotted the owl we've both heard but haven't yet seen. It is an elusive thing, *hoo-ing* away at us as we work, but never showing itself. Robert has been greatly concerned since first it appeared. "An ill omen," he uttered mournfully.

I stand beside Robert and try to follow his gaze. "What is it?" I whisper. "Is it the owl?"

He shakes his head. "No owl. A man."

"The postman?"

"No. A large man, wearing a suit. Doesn't belong here."

I scan the road, but see no one. "Where is he?"

"Was behind that old oak over there. At the end of the pond." Robert nods, but doesn't point. I know he means the largest tree on the property. It stands close to the road, and has a trunk at least five feet across.

"I don't see him."

"No. I heard a car. He's gone."

But he continues to scan the horizon. After a moment we see a grey sedan crest the rise of hill to the north. It is too far away to see the make, but it's taking the back road to the village.

"I wonder what he wanted."

Robert takes his shovel and begins to dig out the peony bed again. "Nothing good."

The mystery is still not solved as I drive into the village for my appointment with Dr. Woolery. A bit uneasy, I glance down the back road as I pass, to see if a grey sedan is parked. But there are only the usual farmhouses and cows, not to mention the farmers' dogs that always bark.

I wonder if that's how Robert noticed the man? Did he hear the dogs first? They always warn of intruders on the road. But then Old Robert has his own inner radar guiding him. He wouldn't have needed dogs.

Entering the village, I still look for the car. But there are any number of grey sedans. And no one seems excessively interested in me.

The doctor's receptionist, Mrs. Albicott, says it will be only a short wait. "Doctor is removing a cast, and it's taking longer than he'd expected."

Mrs. Albicott is perhaps sixty. She is warm and motherly

and reads mystery novels at her desk when things are slow. She also keeps a large crystal bowl of boiled sweets for patients to help themselves to.

Back in the days when I was married, I came in once thinking I was pregnant, terrified of what David would do if it turned out I was right. Mrs. Albicott was very kind; looking back it seems she must have sensed my fear, no matter that I tried to hide it. Beyond that, I don't know her well. But I do know that without her, Dr. Woolery wouldn't know what to do. Patients would simply sit here waiting, growing restless and grumbling. Instead, Mrs. Albicott offers us conversation and sweets.

"How's that garden coming along?" she asks, lying her book face down and giving me all her attention.

I must have looked surprised.

"Ah, now, don't you worry. It's only Old Robert I heard it from . . . not as if the whole town's talking."

I smile. "He told you he was helping me with the weeding?"

"The other day. Comes in here and just sits sometimes. Strangest thing. Doesn't say much. He seems to like being around Luther."

"Luther?"

She waves a hand. "The old ficus over there."

In the corner is a ficus tree a good ten feet high. It branches way out to the sides and looks healthier than any I've ever seen. Not a single brown leaf on it or on the floor.

"Every now and then Old Robert goes over to Luther and stands there mumbling," Mrs. Albicott says. "Talks more to that tree than to me."

I smile. *So he's been working his magic here.* My spirits lift a bit, thinking of Robert and his ways. "He's got my roses growing like mad. The whole garden, in fact."

"That's what he said. Oh, not that he told me much. Only that you were planting lots of 'pretty little flowers.' A right nice herb garden, too, I hear."

"Yes. I . . . I've been toying with the idea of making up some tinctures."

"For healing, you mean?"

"Yes. I read a book about them in hospital. I suppose it was Henry made me think of it again."

"Henry Dean? How is the old dear?"

"Well, not too bad." It isn't my place, I think, to mention his memory loss. "He does seem rather stiff. That's why I thought perhaps an herb tincture . . . devil's claw, say. Of course, I suppose arthritis is to be expected at his age."

Mrs. Albicott shakes her head. "Henry never had arthritis before. All that gardening he does, most likely, not to mention that pretty young wife. She keeps him on the go. If he hadn't hurt that arm . . . Well, you know, he hasn't been the same since that night."

"Henry injured his arm? I didn't know that. When?"

"Oh, several months ago, it was. In fact, the same night Mr. Carr was mur—" She stops short and flushes, looking embarrassed. "I am sorry, Mrs. Carr. I didn't mean to bring up something so painful. It's only that we seldom have two emergencies in one night and, well, one tends to remember that sort of thing." She picks up her book and looks down at it, flicking pages—more to collect herself, I think, than anything.

"Henry hurt his arm the same night my husband died? You're certain?" I am startled that Charlotte never mentioned it.

Mrs. Albicott nods. "Oh yes, I remember it quite clearly. So much going on that night! We do need another doctor in this town, you know. With all these new people moving in—"

Before she can say more, Dr. Woolery's nurse is at the door, calling out my name.

The physical does not go well at all. My mind has finally wokèn up, and there are all sorts of questions running about in it since that talk with Mrs. Albicott. I am both bewildered and tense, and all I want to do now is get out of here.

"What on earth have you been doing to yourself?" Dr. Woolery demands.

He peers down at me through a squint and asks this while I've got a thermometer in my mouth. I resent so much doctors who do this. They stick that thing in your mouth and then ask questions, and you're not supposed to open your mouth to answer them, so all you can do is mumble. Have they no sense whatsoever?

For all that, I don't like doctors at all who stick things in me. The very word "probe" sends cold shivers down my spine.

This time I wait till he's good and ready to pull the thing out, and then I say, "I don't know what you mean."

"Hmpfh. Well, you've good muscle tone, I'll say that. More than I'd have expected after eight months in hospital. But Mrs. Carr, your hands are shaking. Look at this."

He grabs my hands and yanks on them so my arms are extended. Then he lets go. My hands are unsteady indeed, but more because of his arrogant attitude than anything else. I wonder what he'd think if I smacked him one.

"I'm tired," I say irritably. "That's all. I had a smallish garden party yesterday, and I overdid it a bit."

"A bit! I should say. What else have you been doing? You look a wreck. You're all drawn."

"I've been gardening and doing up the house. Not all that much." But I must admit I feel wound like a spring that is ready to snap.

He picks up a clipboard and begins to write. "See Nurse Porter. She'll draw blood for tests. We'll have the results by morning. Meanwhile, you are to go straight home and to bed. You need more rest, young woman."

I am dismissed, and as with my last visit to Woolery, I come away wondering why I ever let myself fall into his hands. If I were to go straight home, it would be to read my herbal remedy book and figure out a way to make myself well without medical interference.

Meanwhile, that conversation with Mrs. Albicott bothers me more than ever. I don't understand why Charlotte has never once mentioned that Henry injured his arm, particularly that he injured it the same night David was murdered. Can there be some connection? And if so, what? Is this at least part of what Charlotte has been hiding?

I am deciding whether to ring her and ask if I can stop by the house later when Henry himself falls into my lap, so to speak. As I leave the doctor's office I see him standing in front of Abbott's Nursery, talking to a woman I recognise as a villager, but whose name I don't know.

I start across the street and Henry spies me, waving, his face breaking into a smile. The woman, who is armed with packages and evidently shopping, drifts off, calling goodbye.

"Joanna!" Henry says as I reach him. "What a nice surprise."

"It is, isn't it? What are you doing, Henry? Are you off somewhere, or do you have a few moments?"

"I've come to see if Abbott's got the new begonias in. Charlotte dropped me off to park, and she isn't back yet. Why don't you come with me?"

I link my arm in his and we start down one of the aisles, flowers all about us, their fragrance filling the air. There are marigolds, impatiens, roses, clematis, azaleas, foxglove, jasmine. From a lattice-work roof overhead, the sun pours through hanging pots filled with ferns and blossoms of every colour. Overall there is the good, rich scent of moist earth.

"I love to simply wander through here, don't you?" Henry asks. "It's such a pleasant place to be."

"Yes. It is nice. Rather peaceful."

"I enjoyed your luncheon yesterday, as well," he says. "Pennoryn is beginning to look quite lovely. Better than ever, I'd say."

"I'm afraid I haven't enjoyed working with it as much as I might have, though. It's been rather a mad dash to get it done."

"Yes, well, with such a short season . . . Still, I always think it's the process that's the most enjoyable. The day-to-day digging about in the dirt, watching for the seed to grow." Henry stops to pick up the bloom of a bright red rose that has fallen to the ground. He holds it to his nose.

"I always felt that way, too," I agree. "It's just that there seems so much catching up to do, since I came home. And speaking of that . . . Henry, I didn't know you'd injured your arm."

He stiffens and frowns. There is a long pause before he

answers, quite angrily. "My arm . . . Well, yes, I suppose I did. But where did you learn of it?"

"From Mrs. Albicott in Dr. Woolery's office. Just now."

"Mary Albicott? Bloody hell! I thought these things were confidential between doctor and patient!"

"Oh, I'm sure they are, Henry," I say. "But Mrs. Albicott's like an old friend to both of us. I'm sure she thought I already knew."

His chin quivers. "Well, one should not make assumptions where such things are concerned. It's not professional. Not professional at all!"

"Henry, it's all right," I say soothingly, though I'm a bit bewildered—and startled—by his anger. "Really it is. And I wasn't prying. I just wonder now what had happened. Can you tell me?"

He squints into the sun, and his fingers pull distractedly at the petals of the rose. "Well, let's see, my dear . . . As I remember, I was here in town. Here at Abbott's, in fact. Two months ago? Yes, that's when it happened. I'd just purchased a bag of fertilizer, and I was lifting it into the boot of the car. It was much heavier than I'd expected, and I felt a pull . . ." He looks down at the rose, his eyes widening as if only now seeing what he's done. "My dear, my dear," he says, and lays the torn-up rose gently beside a pot of geraniums.

I cannot think how to answer. Henry's story does not at all match Mrs. Albicott's. Is it possible he doesn't remember? I wonder. And he's covering?

Furthermore, if Henry's injury did in fact happen the same night David was murdered, and he doesn't recall it, what does that tell me? Now that I think of it, I don't remember Henry ever having lapses of memory before that night. Did something traumatic happen to him, then, something that brought all this on?

Dear God. What have I stumbled across?

And who, all told, does it involve?

"Henry," I say carefully, "I would imagine Charlotte was quite upset when all this happened. I know she watches over you like a mother hen."

His eyes grow distant. "Actually, Charlotte was a bit
. . . distracted at the time."

"Distracted?"

He makes an offhand gesture. "So much going on. And I
have to protect her, as well, you know."

"Protect Charlotte? From what, Henry?"

He looks distant. "Hmm? Why, from herself, of course.
My dear, dear Charlotte. Sometimes she does things out of
passion that she later quite regrets."

"What sort of things, Henry?"

But he falls silent. His mouth goes slack. He is staring at
nothing suddenly, his eyes so blank, so empty, it seems his
entire being's shut down.

I am shaken. I don't know what to do. I look around,
remembering that Henry was waiting for Charlotte to park.
Where is she? What's taking so long? There is no one
near, no one to help.

What did people do with me, I wonder desperately,
when I was like this? What did they do? And then I remember that they simply talked to me . . . just as if I
could hear.

"Henry . . ." I say softly, bending down to lift a small
pot of roses. "Look at this." I hold the pot up. "It's the
Mrs. Miniver, named after the one in that American film
you always loved so much. You've got a Mrs. Miniver in
your garden, haven't you? Doesn't it smell wonderful?"

I hold a blossom below his nose, but not touching it.
There is no response. My eyes tear. "You know," I say, my
heart aching for him, "I remember years ago when you and
Charlotte were first married, and I was quite ill with some
bug or other. You and she came to the house in Mevagissey and rescued me. You carried me away to Fallston to get
better. Do you remember that? You insisted that you and
she would take care of me. And Henry, you did. I remember you coming up and down those great wide stairs, waiting on me, bringing me hot broth and toast . . . You were
so good to me."

*And dear God, if you've done something terrible—some-
thing you've shut out—I swear I'll protect you with my very
life.*

For I am thinking now: What if he learned that Charlotte and David were having an affair? What might this sweet, gentle man have done to "protect" her? Are we not all capable of inexplicable acts when pushed too far?

Or, it could have been an accident. Perhaps David and Henry had an argument, and—

No. An accident wouldn't account for such a vicious knifing. That could only have happened in the heat of great anger . . . a crime of passion.

"Henry—"

Then, just as suddenly as he left, he's back. Taking my hand, he pats it reassuringly, his eyes as bright and sharp as ever. "My dear, you don't look up to par. I told Charlotte when we left yesterday that you seemed a bit strained. Is everything all right?"

I blink away tears. "Yes. Yes, Henry. Everything's fine."

He smiles. "Joanna, my dear, would you accept a piece of advice from an old man?"

"You'll never be old," I say, "and I'll always listen to your advice. What is it?"

"I wouldn't waste a moment of time, my dear. Stop all this busy-work with Pennoryn and all this ruminating about the past, and just get on with it! Go to that young man of yours and tell him you love him—and then don't let him out of your sight. One never knows when happiness might be swept away."

He is gripping my hand, and for him, this is an extraordinary show of emotion. "Oh, Henry . . . I know something's wrong. Can't you tell me about it?"

But then he is looking somewhere behind me, and I turn to see Charlotte coming towards us, her face lined with worry. The sunglasses are gone, but the bruise is not. If anything, it's spread and has begun to yellow.

"Henry! Thank God. I'm so sorry, it was terrible parking, and then . . ." Her green eyes slide to mine and narrow. "What are you doing here, Joanna? What have the two of you been talking about?"

"Nothing, really." I glance down at the Mrs. Miniver. "Roses, that's all. But Char, I'd like a few words with you alone. You don't mind, do you Henry?" I am thinking only to step off to the side.

Charlotte begins to protest, but Henry beams. "No, no, not at all. You two ladies have your chat. I'll just go and check with Abbott, see if the begonias are in."

"Henry, not too far? Wait right inside for me."

"Right you are. Ta, my dear. And, Joanna—mind my words."

Taking her arm I draw Charlotte aside, out of the main aisle. "I'm worried about Henry," I say without preamble, hurrying because I know now, as she clearly does, that Henry shouldn't be left alone for long. "Char, we were standing here talking and he drifted off, just as he did yesterday—"

I am shocked when she shoves my hand from her arm. "Stay out of this! Mind your own business, Joanna. Just stay out of our lives!"

"Look, I'm sorry, but I'm only trying to help. Henry needs to see someone."

"Don't tell me about my husband! For God's sake! Go and marry your precious Michael, if that's what you want, but leave us alone. And don't come crying to me this time when you realise what a mistake you've made. I've had quite enough, do you hear?"

Her face is all but in mine, so close I can feel her anger coming at me in waves. For a brief, bizarre moment, I think she might kill me if we were anywhere else. Then she turns on her heel and rushes after Henry.

CHAPTER 17

I leave Abbott's Nursery feeling depressed at first, but then angry. I am tired of Charlotte's attitude since I've come home, tired of her thinking she knows best what is good for me and that I know nothing at all. If she could learn anything from her husband, it might be to be more objective and less judgmental. *Go to that young man and tell him you love him,* Henry said. *One never knows when happiness might be swept away.*

I can only think that given what he's now going through, Henry must know what he's talking about. As to the rest of it—his hurt arm, and how it happened—I've been given orders to keep away. And that, I decide firmly as I drive to Mevagissey, is what I'll do. Without Charlotte's approval I cannot think how I might help Henry. And raking up the night David died, uncovering secrets I can't even begin to fathom at this time, is something I don't want to face right now. None of it matters, does it? What's done is done. Learning the truth will not bring David back to life. Further, it could cause all of us considerable pain.

I am determined that for the moment I will focus on finishing up my wedding plans. That way I will not, at least, be letting Michael down.

Entering Mevagissey, I see Michael's Range Rover parked in front of the gallery. There are large narrow crates in back, and I assume these are paintings he is moving to London for the showing. I drive on, thinking I'll do my shopping and then surprise him by dropping in, as he doesn't expect to see me till tonight. I park three blocks away in front of a yarn shop that is central to all the boutiques, and sit for a moment taking a deep breath, as I am indeed weary. All that business with Charlotte and Henry is taking its toll. There are things, I think, I would be better off doing than shopping—like sitting in the garden at Pennoryn, watching my birds.

Get up! Get going, I chide myself. *Do you want to look like a matchgirl at your wedding?*

In the shops, however, it is difficult to focus on clothes. I cast aside one dress after another. Finally, moving on to some rather revealing lingerie, I find myself remembering the way I spoiled that potentially beautiful night with Michael after Lost Inn. I am both embarrassed and saddened at how consumed by fear I was. I feel I acted like a child pretending to be a woman.

Thinking this, I hold up a white silk gown, Chinese in style, with three turquoise "frog" fasteners. It is a simple classic style, more "me" than the sheer peignoirs that line the racks. I think of Michael—of our being together, and my wearing this gown for him—and suddenly I cannot wait. I imagine him touching me through the thin material, in ways he never has. I imagine myself responding. I imagine this happening now. Not three days from now, but tonight.

I'll invite him up to Pennoryn for dinner, I think. We were to meet at a restaurant—a treat after all the work of yesterday. But I will cook for him, instead. I may not be much good at it, but if I put my mind to it I can do it. It will be a gift, a way to say thank you for all the wonderful things he has done for me. I will fix something special, perhaps a small rack of lamb with roasted potatoes and fresh vegetables, steamed the way he likes them. I'll stop for a bottle of fine wine, and there will be flowers and candles on the table. I can buy the candles at Weatherby's, and the wine down the street at Parnelli's. I've not bought anything new for playing music, but I've found a good classical station on the radio, and that will be playing, and afterwards . . .

Afterwards, I will show him my new Chinese gown.

My face flushes at the thought. And I am nervous, for I am brazenly planning how tonight will end.

Relieved to have something other than Charlotte and Henry to think about, I dash through the store, buying things: a new slip, new undies, perfume, a skin-softening soap. Then in a tiny boutique at the end of the lane I find the perfect wedding dress. It is off-white cotton, mid-length, with tiny white embroidered roses around the neckline and hem. Too flowery to wear for anything again, but perfect for a small afternoon wedding. And the roses and leaves nearly match my wedding ring.

I inspect my nails. They are terrible, after all the gardening and repairs. And I still have to polish silver and clean for the reception after the wedding. Then there are table-cloths that must be pressed, and laundry to do . . .

Quickly, I pay for my dress and dash down the street to Cullender's, buying up orange sticks, buffers, files, and a bottle of nail lacquer in bright Chinese red. There are perfume bottles on a table, and I test one, spraying it on my arm and sniffing. It is light, the scent of lilacs. *Perfect.* Everything this evening must be perfect.

The traffic is heavier than usual, and as I step off the curb with my bundles a truck swerves and nearly hits me. I make a run for it to the other side of the lane. *Slow down,* I hear Dr. Shahi say. *Take time to think.* But thought has not brought me joy lately, only pain. Thought is what haunts me in the night. It makes me too cautious, too afraid. At this moment I am determined to be genuinely happy for the first time in what must be years, and I don't want that determination dampened in any way.

The Blue Swan is just ahead, and I begin running, eager to see Michael. *Come to Pennoryn tonight,* I will say. *I'll fix dinner this time. And afterwards . . .*

"Afterwards" stands outside me, like a shadow that peeks from behind a tree. I know it is there, and I am bold now, bold enough to look yet still a tiny bit afraid to see. With my heart in my throat, then, but hope in my voice, I dash across the street and into the gallery. I am balancing packages, boxes tied with string, and sacks of every size.

"Michael?" I call out. "Are you here?" I don't at first see him.

But then I do.

They are leaning against the little white desk, and they have knocked over the black orchid, so caught up are they in what they are doing. It lies on its side, unnoticed by anyone but me. Annette and Michael, their arms about each other, are kissing. At the sound of my voice they pull apart and turn to me in unison—she looking pouty, her lips swollen; Michael stunned, his jaw dropping. "J-Jo!" he stutters, his face going scarlet, then white.

For a long moment I'm unable to move either forwards or backwards. I stand absolutely still. My mouth works, but no sound comes out. Hope has caught in my throat along with my heart, and it threatens to choke me.

Michael moves. He reaches out. "This isn't . . . it isn't what it seems. Jo . . . Oh, God, don't look that way."

I hear thudding noises and realise my packages have fallen to the floor and my hands are lifeless at my sides. I am frozen, mute. I feel I've gone mad. My vision blurs. I am disappearing, the room around me fading away. Someone is speaking, but the voice becomes more and more distant. In a moment it will be gone.

This is the way it felt the night David died, I think. *And then for months . . . all of it gone.*

That is what saves me. I will not go back into that abyss. I will not let them do this to me. Not anyone—ever.

Anger floods me, and its warmth is good. I am alive, I can see, I am still on my feet. Michael is before me now, and I swing with my hand, catching him hard across the cheek. *"Liar!"* A red streak forms on pale skin, and he stumbles back. I am alert enough to see that Annette leans casually against the counter like a waiting cat, savouring the fight between two birds, knowing she will be the victor, once one of us does the other in.

That alone might have stopped me. Not wanting her to win. But the pain has cut too deep. When Michael moves to grab my shoulders I raise both arms and fling him away. "Don't touch me! Don't ever touch me again!"

"Listen to me, just listen," I hear, but it comes from far

away. In my head I am running, running through the thickets, over the stone wall, into the woods near my house— hiding from *David's* face, away from the sound of *his* voice.

I turn and stumble through the door, fumbling at the latch and catching my heel on the walk. I feel Michael's hand on my arm. It burns through the scented cologne, and I cannot wait to get home and shower, to get it off, to scrub the memory of him off my skin.

People on the street are a blur. I push someone out of my way and hear an oath, but all I want is to get to my car. It is still three blocks away, and I race until my chest hurts, but at last I am there, fumbling for the key, sliding inside, locking the doors. My breath comes so short it pains my chest.

Then suddenly it is gone completely. I cannot breathe at all. My jaw feels rigid, and there are dark spots before my eyes. *I am going to die,* I think. I clutch at my throat, my nails digging the skin, then slump against the steering wheel, tears coming, and as they begin it is like a blow to my chest, releasing my breath. I become aware that someone is banging on my window, and I see that it is Michael. "Jo, I swear, there's never been anything . . ." he cries, rattling the locked door handle. "Let me explain!" My hand shaking, I jam the key into the ignition and within moments am pulling away. The car jerks. My foot on the clutch pedal is unsteady. But the jerking is good, a jumpstart to my heart. The farther away I get, the stronger I feel.

Let her have him, he's not worth it, I say over and over in my head. I don't know who I am talking about—Michael or David. But it is David's face before me as I race home to Pennoryn.

CHAPTER 18

Scant hours have passed. I am lying on my bed, and all about me there are ghosts. Michael's face is interchangeable with David's, his sins even more so. *If he lied about Annette, what other lies might he have told?* I grasp for my childhood friend as he floats across the landscape of my heart. But then he's gone, there is nothing there.

As for David, it is as if a dam has burst. I am remembering more now, hideous dark secrets that I've locked away in some far-off corner of my mind rather than have to face them: David going up to London on weekends without me. David coming home, that strange perfume on his clothes. And then one night, David wanting me to do things . . . the most abominable things.

"Where on earth have you been?" I remember saying, watching him in the mirror as I brush my hair. I am wearing a red satin teddy and matching peignoir that I do not like, as they seem not at all me. But David has brought them home from London and asked me to wear them. We have been married only three months, and I would like to please my husband. He is staying away more and more, and I believe the fault to be mine.

"I told you where I was, Joanna. Meeting with a publisher. Why do you question me so?" He removes his grey suit jacket, draping it carefully over a chair. Flicking off his tie, he holds it loosely in one hand, all the while staring at me. I shudder, feeling a chill.

"It's just that you said you'd be home last night. I was worried."

A muscle in his jaw twitches. "Worried? Were you indeed? Well, I'm here now, my sweet. I'm here now." He comes up behind me, the tie still in his hand. His eyes are glazed, they do not focus. I feel he is seeing someone else rather than me. My mouth goes dry and my pulse beats wildly. I am deeply afraid.

"David?"

He presses against my back. His hand lightly caresses my hair, my neck. I think for a moment, It's all right, nothing to fear. He is aroused by the negligee, that is all. *I look at David in the mirror and I arrange my mouth into a smile. He smiles back. Then without warning he jerks me against him. A hand reaches down and grips my breast so hard I cry out. The other hand clamps over my mouth. I struggle but cannot move, and I cannot make a sound above a moan.*

Terrified, trapped, I claw with both hands to pull him away. But he grabs my wrists and wrenches them behind me, yanking the tie about them. He pulls it so tight my skin burns, the blood pounds in my hands. I begin to cry, and I beg him, "Don't do this, David, please don't do this." I see him in the mirror, laughing softly. "But you like it this way, don't you? You like it the way your brothers did it. It's good, isn't it—not being able to fight back."

It is a nightmare. A hand slams over my mouth again, and with the other David reaches into his shirt pocket. He pulls out something shiny—a small silver clip. It looks much like the clips he uses to hold his manuscripts together, but this one has sharp, jagged teeth in it. While I watch in horror he brings it toward my breast. I shake my head violently and try to break free. David holds me in a vise and snaps the clip onto a nipple. The pain is excruciating. I scream against his hand and begin to faint.

But then David's hand slides down between my thighs and begins to stroke me there. "You'll see," he whispers in my ear, "you'll see . . . It is so much better this way. Feel it, Joanna? Feel it coming?"

And I am horrified that I do feel it, the orgasm coming, I feel it through the pain, through the degradation. I am seeing

*us in the mirror, David stroking me, my reddening breast, and
I am feeling the pain, yet I feel the other thing, too. It is
coming upon me against my will, and it is my worst, my most
appalling humiliation.*

It is the dark, runaway train.

After that night, I learned to keep an aloe plant on the
bathroom windowsill, and when necessary, I would break
off a piece to heal my wounds. I would lie in bed those
nights staring at the ceiling, waiting for David to rise,
shower, and go into his study. I would try not to move, in
fear he might begin again. When morning came he would
waken lazily, stretching, yawning, and he would turn and
smile at me. "I never saw you come like that before,
Joanna. Didn't I tell you it was better this way?"

I cringe now as I remember this. I close my eyes hoping
to shut these pictures out, but they only become sharper,
clearer. I remember closing my eyes so that I wouldn't
have to see what David was doing. But every time they
would shut the pain deepened, and I soon learned that he
did this deliberately, that he wanted me to watch, and if I
didn't I would be punished.

This was only the beginning. The instruments of torture
—of love, as David called it—were many and diverse.
"There is a dark side to Eros," he told me in bed one
night. "The Greeks knew that love was a paradox. Jung
called Eros a 'demon'—but even he admitted it could take
us to the highest heights." The carvings of Eros on the
bedstead grinned at me, agreeing.

One day I took a book from the library, as I could not
believe that Jung had been quoted accurately. I was right.
What he actually said was, "The demon's activity extends
from the endless spaces of the heavens to the dark abysses
of hell."

I never talked to anyone about this, not even Charlotte.
I had vowed to love my husband for better or worse; therefore I pretended everything was all right. I even began to
believe that this was, in some cruel way, a normal part of
married life. My problem was that I didn't know enough,

didn't understand. David, however, with his greater experience, would teach me.

There is a knock on my door, and I am surprised to find I've been sleeping. I fight to come awake. My eyes, however, are swollen from crying; I can barely see. I turn my face to the pillow.

The knocking continues, not loud, but insistent. I am sure it is Michael. I don't want to answer, for I don't know what to say.

Finally my head hurts from worrying about it. Slipping out of bed, I pull on a robe. I walk slowly to the front door, my legs heavy, feet dragging. I am thinking all the way about Michael and what he will say. Will he apologise, make excuses, pretend? Or will he say, "Sorry, Jo, I've always had feelings for her. It finally came out, and I can't help myself?" And we'll say good-bye, nice day, and that will be that.

My hand is wet and slips on the latch. I would prefer to turn and run back to bed, forget the entire thing. But the knocking begins anew. Taking a breath I lift the latch and open the door.

It is not Michael who faces me, but Charlotte.

She sits on the bed beside me. I am limp as a dishrag and too tired to stand. Charlotte has propped pillows and made tea, placing the cup on the table at my side. It grows cold. I have told her about Michael, and she has not said, "I told you so." Instead she holds my hand sympathetically as she did when we were young, and keeps silent. Yet the torment in my head is so fierce a racket, it is a wonder she cannot hear it.

"Why did you come, Char?" I ask finally.

Her expression is gently ironic. "To tell you I was sorry . . . and that I'd be your matron of honor if you still wanted me. Joanna, I hate all this trouble between us. I've just been so worried . . ."

"About Henry?"

She strokes my hand. "Let's agree not to talk about any

of that, all right? Let's just take care of you. What else can I do?"

As if in answer a bird flies against the window, fluttering its wings on the pane. I remember I haven't filled the feeders since coming home today.

Charlotte laughs softly. It is a sound I haven't heard for a while, like a silver chime. "All right, all right," she calls out. "But hang on a bit, can't you? Joanna, I cannot believe this virtual aviary you've got. I remember you sitting on the verandah at my house when we were sixteen, and you'd seem to call them to you—not with sounds, but simply by being there. Within five minutes there would be birds of every description flying about."

I muster a smile. "You accused me of witchery."

"Well, I have since seen a man in India do the same thing. It was somewhere in the countryside, I remember, and he was sitting on the ground in typical swami fashion, garbed all in white, you know, and he only sat there silently, yet birds would flock to him. Like those stories of St. Francis."

"Dr. Shahi would say it's all energy. 'Perfectly ordinary,' he would say."

"I think he must be right. You have that energy, Joanna. You have always had a knack for making people love you."

I look at her.

"I know, I know. This is not the day to convince you of that. But don't you see, your idea of yourself has always been skewed. Of course that's no surprise, given what your family did to you."

"Please, Charlotte. Not today."

"All right. I only mean to say that you give out so much love, and it can't help but come back. Why not be happy for today, at least—with your birds and me?"

She squeezes my hand, and I meet the affection in her eyes.

"I've an idea," Charlotte says, jumping up and laughing that silver laugh again. "Remember when we were young, and one of us would be upset about something—a teacher who'd been unfair or some other girl or boy—and we would run and cry on each other's shoulders? Remember what we would do?"

I try to think back, though it takes some effort. "Bake biscuits in your mother's kitchen?"

She hoots, and for Charlotte a hoot is an astounding departure from her usual reserve. I know she is trying hard to be lively for me. "I doubt there was ever a cookie baked in my mother's kitchen!" she says.

No, I think. *It was Michael's house, Michael's mother, his kitchen.*

"Don't you remember?" she prods. "We would take buckets and spades and go down to the nearest sandy beach and build sand castles. Just like children. There is something about that, something so pure, so—so basic—it wipes all else out."

I shake my head. "I don't have time to build sand castles. I've so much to do before—"

Before the wedding. And then I remember there will be no wedding now. I have all the time in the world.

Charlotte comes and takes my hand again.

"You have me, Joanna. Let that be enough for now."

She cannot convince me to get properly dressed and drive the twenty or more minutes to a beach. But we compromise. We will go out to the pond and build our castles there. I put on old jeans and a jersey, and Charlotte borrows an ancient pair of my trousers, a shirt, and tennies. Everything is a bit too large for her, but she cinches up the pants with a belt and clomps along gamefully in the tennies, tripping only a bit on the uneven ground. We are a fine pair, looking for all the world like tramps with our tattered clothes and yellow rubber bucket that we've brought from beneath the kitchen sink.

Setting down the bucket, we scan the placid surface of the pond. Crickets are singing, and the old frog that shows up every year is voicing his loud protest at our presence. The ducks, however, are quiet. They swim lazily by, content only to make a ripple here and there.

"It's a lovely day," Charlotte says, taking a deep breath of fresh air, then blowing it out. "Not a sign of a cloud."

"Yes. It's good here in July."

She twists her hair into a knot, and somehow fixes it so it stays there. "That reminds me. You have a birthday coming up, my dear. Very soon now, in fact. Day after tomorrow?"

"How splendid of you to mention it. I've been trying to forget."

"Sorry. Still, I must get you an especially wonderful gift this year to celebrate your getting well. And we'll have lunch at a very special restaurant. Just you and me."

I kneel at the edge of the water and begin digging. "I'm not much in the mood to celebrate, Charlotte. And I'm not at all sure I'm getting well."

She kneels at my side. Attacking the dirt as if it were cookie dough, she scoops up large handfuls and pats them together. We begin the foundation for our castle. "You'll get over him, Joanna. The important thing is to keep busy."

For the next ten minutes we work without talking. Charlotte's concentration is intense. Every lookout tower, every turret, must be perfect. She finds little sticks and places them on the turrets, like flags. I am still unmotivated, and settle for patting dirt together. At one point we sit back on our heels to survey our work. "A moat," Charlotte says. "We must have a moat."

I sigh, and we begin once more to dig. Charlotte's hair has come down on the sides, and it falls about her face. The ends of my hair were drenched when I first bent over the pond to fill the bucket. We do look like children as we lift the bucket again and fill our little moat.

Water swirls round the castle. The sun fashions a rainbow bridge, one that I imagine cannot be crossed without my approval. And I am there, in that little turret window, completely protected now from the outside world. The scenes begin to fade: Michael and Annette, that horrid night with David.

"Pebbles," I say, with more vigour.

"Right you are."

We sink our fingers into the water's edge and come up with mud that is wet enough to dribble over the castle, like stones. Charlotte's nose twitches. She rubs it, and leaves mud behind. I reach over to wipe it off, but only make things worse. She laughs and twists her head to rub it on her shirt. We fall back and sit on the wet ground, admiring our castle and watching the ducks.

"Better?" Charlotte says after a while.

I look at her. The late afternoon sun is still bright, it smarts the eyes. I feel them tear. Or is it that Charlotte is back? It is good to have her back, the Charlotte I always loved. I remember now that she could be like this, that she could throw off all the airs she'd surrounded herself with since marrying Henry and just be Char again, a lovely yet somehow funny-faced kid who, even at sixteen, liked to play in the dirt.

"Almost better," I say. "Thank you."

"Each day will be easier, dear heart. You'll see."

"It just . . . It feels strange. I don't know how I could be so fooled. You tried to warn me about the two of them. Why didn't I see it?"

I am remembering that Michael had many girlfriends in school, that there was always someone flirting with him. And I hear him at Lost Inn saying that they were only distractions. *"I was going crazy, trying to stay away from you."*

Is that what today was all about? Did my reluctance to make love with Michael before marriage throw him into the arms of Annette? Or have they been together all along?

"You know, Char, I forget sometimes that Michael had his own problems, growing up. His mum wasn't beaten by his father, but the man was cold and cruel, and when he died, Michael had to take his place as head of the house. Even before that, he tried so hard to protect his mum, but she kept letting it happen, letting herself be ground down. I remember how angry he would get at his father for hurting her, but angry at her as well, because she wouldn't take a stand. And then his father died while they were out fishing, drowned right before his very eyes. That must have been so hard for him."

Charlotte is silent a moment. Then she turns to me anxiously and grabs my arm. "Joanna—dear God. Do you know what you just said?"

"No, what?"

Her fingers tighten. "You said that Michael was protective of his mother . . . that he was angry at his father for hurting her . . . and that his father died when they were out alone fishing. I never knew that."

"So? What about it?"

"For heaven's sake, Joanna, don't you think it's the least bit odd?"

"Odd, how?"

"Don't be dense! What if it wasn't an accident?"

"You think that Michael . . . Oh, really, Char. The whole thing was a terrible tragedy, and all I was saying is that it probably left Michael with a lot of bad memories that may be affecting his life today. So just don't start. *Please.*"

She drops her hand. "All right. I'm sorry I said anything. Frankly, I don't give a damn anymore what Michael Lamb did or didn't do, either to his father or anyone else. Now that you won't be seeing him anymore, and there's no way he can hurt you, it doesn't matter. But listen to me, Joanna —you're not going to go and get all soft over him again, are you?"

"Of course not. Why would I? It's obvious he doesn't want me. Char, you are so damned unrelenting."

"Am I? My dearest Joanna, you may think I do not know much, that I have lived a charmed life and all I do is have parties and travel—"

I throw up my hands and get to my feet, but she stands too and grips me by both shoulders. "No, listen to me. This much I do know. I know that neither of us can ever let *anyone* have power over us—not ever again. Do you hear me, Joanna? *Never again.*"

I am stunned by her ferocity. A dull red flush creeps up her neck to her face, and her eyes are feverish. I am reminded of the day we met at school, her anger at the bullies who tried to take her notebook away.

"For heaven's sake, what is it, Char? *Tell* me."

She shakes her head. "It doesn't matter. All that matters

is that we stick together now, that we never let each other down. *Promise me that."*

"Yes . . . yes, all right. I promise."

But a chill wind sweeps through me, and when I touch her hand it is rigid and ice cold.

Charlotte has gone. The sun is just now slipping below the hill. I sit huddled in a blanket on the sofa, and my thoughts swing from one extreme to the other, from anger, to hurt, and back again. Michael hasn't either rung me or shown up, and the thought that he might do so becomes more and more remote. I considered phoning him. There is something in the heart that wants to *know* beyond a shadow of a doubt. A tiny hopeful voice keeps saying, *Perhaps I was wrong. Perhaps he really does have some explanation, and it will suffice.* But when I reached for the phone I thought of Annette answering, that satiny voice saying, "Can't you see he doesn't love you? Why don't you leave him alone?" Worse, I thought of Michael answering and saying much the same thing.

Meanwhile, I've time now to think about that ghastly scene I've remembered with David. I understand where the red satin negligee came from. I understand, as well, the anger I've been feeling towards David since coming back to Pennoryn. What I don't understand is how I could have put up with that kind of treatment for a moment, let alone more than a year.

As for Michael, I am realising that I knew the adult man less well than I thought. And strangely, now that I don't have Charlotte throwing the idea in my face, I find I am willing to almost objectively consider the idea that Michael might have killed David.

If he had come upon a scene such as the one I've just remembered, a scene every bit as horrid as the one that day long ago on the cliffs with my brothers, might he not have done almost anything, out of an inbred need to protect me? Just as he protected his mother all those years from his father?

It would surely not have been a matter of his thinking it through, or being either "capable" or "incapable" of murder. Anyone, I believe, can kill in the heat of the moment, given due cause. The question is: Did it happen that way? Did he strike out on impulse and out of rage?

I have been thinking much this way about Henry. Why not Michael? For that matter, when I think of that ugly night with David, I wonder if I might not have reached a point where I killed him myself.

Perhaps more disconcerting than any of these possibilities is the fact that I feel now that I could accept any one of them with equal ease. Memories are flying back of other nights with David, and my anger is growing. It is like a monster released from chains, and the monster is roaring in my ear: *He deserved to die.*

I realise I am nearly echoing Michael's words to his friend Gregg: *He deserved what he got.*

I can no longer endure sitting here. Tossing off the blanket, I reach for a sweater on the rack by the door, and step outside. I don't hesitate on the porch, for I know where it is I am going. Looking neither right nor left, I cross the garden to the low stone wall that stands between me and the meadow.

Some part of me knows I am following yet another pattern. This is all too familiar—this running to the meadow when hurt or upset by David. But for me it is a safe place. Like that turret room in the sand castle, it is a place to hide from the hurt.

It is twilight now in the meadow. There are no stars, only clouds, and I wonder if I will sit here on this cold damp ground and freeze to death before I fully admit that I do not understand a thing about love.

I have never trusted it. Not even when I first met David, did I really trust it. All that *I love you, I'll love you forever, you're all that I want* business. And long before that first horrifying night with David—that night of the dark, runaway train—I knew we were done. The new skills and toys he brought home with him from London only proved how much worse things could get.

I cast back in memory and try to recall when I first suspected what I'd got into. The nettles, I think, came first

. . . and then David killing the baby mice we'd found in the attic. I knew he'd killed them when they disappeared so quickly. One moment I'd held them against my breast and loved them. The next, they were gone.

After that, it wasn't only nettles. David would do small hurtful things that seemed almost to be accidental, yet in the morning there were bruises. I learned to wear only long-sleeved, high-necked shirts.

I am also remembering now that it all began in earnest shortly after Michael came to call—the day he brought me the stone hare. David and I had been married three months, and he still didn't want people coming over. He disliked the way Charlotte would "barge in," as he called it, putting plans together for dinners he wanted no part of. Then Michael turned up, fresh from Paris, and David was jealous afterwards, asking me over and over what was said, what we did.

"You could have joined us," I answered. "We invited you." But David declined; he had a chapter to finish, and we should go on our walk without him, he said.

I came to know that he baited me that way sometimes, as if setting me up to displease him. He would then have an excuse for his anger, and whatever punishment he meted out I would take without protest, feeling guilty and to blame.

I became, finally, a wraith slipping silently about the house, hoping desperately not to be seen. *If he can't see me, he won't think of things to do to me.*

A raven croaks loudly over my head, yet another bad omen, Robert would say. I jump, that is how ragged my nerves are. Just thinking about David, and Michael, has my stomach in knots. My hands are fisted so tightly, the nails are bruising the skin. All about me now are voices, an entire Greek chorus comprised of people who presumably know me better than I know myself. Dr. Shahi begins the verse: *Women who have been abused attract men who abuse.* Charlotte chimes in with, *Don't let anyone have power over you like that—ever again.* Henry adds, in *pianissimo,* of course: *You never know when happiness might be snatched away.*

Well, I know happiness doesn't last long with me. And I damn well know who is to blame. *Me.*

All my life I've been letting people push me this way and that. I've seldom stood up for myself, until very recently. Even now I don't do enough. And I keep slipping back.

So perhaps I should phone Dr. Shahi right this minute and say, "I'll be coming out to Whitehurst, starting in the morning. I'll be there three days a week for as long as you like." We could have our nice quiet talks, and we could admire his herbs, and he could hypnotise me or whatever it is he plans to do, and perhaps in a year, or seven, we might sort it all out.

But talk is not enough for me—not now. The monster of anger consumes me; it threatens to annihilate my heart. I may not be thinking quite clearly, but I do know that before it consumes me altogether, I must do something to take back my life.

CHAPTER 19

It is half past eight when I reach Mevagissey, the dinner hour for those who work long shifts in the boatyard. I sit in my car at the foot of the hill and imagine the way it will be.

There is, of course, no way to see what is going on within. Every window is draped with faded brown curtains. My mother hung them before I was born, to keep out the cold winds from the Channel. (Or did she know even then that she would need them one day to hide what was going on within?) As I grew, it became my job to take them down each spring and wash them, and I would ask to leave them down for summer, letting in light and fresh air. My mother would not allow it. The entire town was watching our every move, she said, as indeed they may well have been. So up they went. The smallish rooms would once again become dark and rank.

I was always tripping over things, I remember. The inside lighting was poor, as my father wouldn't allow bulbs in the ceiling lights. I never knew if this was to save money, or if he too was thinking of what the neighbours might see. But the end result was that more often than not the halls were black as pitch, not only at night, but on those days when the winds were blowing and the sky was murky grey as the bottom of a bucket of swill.

I find I am angrily tapping the steering wheel with my nails. My stomach quakes, but I set my jaw for the journey in. It feels much like that—a journey back in time, back to a place I hoped I might never see again. I remove my foot from the brake and drive to the top of the hill. There I park and stand outside the car. The entrance, as is the custom here, is through the attic. There is a small door. No lights.

I reach into my pocket for the key I found in an old box of junk in my wardrobe. It protests; the lock is rusted from decades of sea air. But it turns. This is good; I may have an edge if I can take them by surprise.

The steps down through the attic are dark, narrow and winding, more treacherous even than I remember them, the odour more foul. Descending quietly, I imagine I hear my father's and brothers' boots tramping down these stairs all those years ago, night after night, *tramp, tramp, tramp*. I, at ten, eleven, twelve, would be in the kitchen trembling at the sound, wanting to run and hide, to go *anywhere* away from this place. But at that age it was impossible to run, and I would be there when they came into the kitchen. I'd be stirring a pot of something or other, setting the table, putting the kettle on for tea. I was chattel, a piece of property, invisible till they wanted me, but then I'd best have my body close at hand.

They wouldn't acknowledge me straight away, of course. First they would reach into the fridge for ale. Then they would kick their boots off, leaving them muddy and filmed with fish guts in the middle of the floor. If I didn't pick them up, Ian would kick me in the leg, behind a knee. He would do it when I least expected it, when I'd be crossing from stove to table or fridge. He had some innate sense of timing, and even when I thought I was prepared to avoid him, his foot would find its mark. My legs would buckle and I'd fall to the floor, and he'd stand there with his hands on his hips, laughing. "Seein' you're already there, how about pickin' up them boots?" he'd say, or some version of it.

My ally—anger—fails me suddenly. I am trembling precisely the way I did as a child. Each step brings me closer to the kitchen, and I am listening for Ian, waiting for him to jump out and frighten me the way he liked to do. I pause and strain my ears, but hear only a low mumble of voices. They are there, all three of them. I hear my mother's voice, but cannot make out words. Denny responds, then Joseph. They are each distinctive. Denny has a monotone, Joseph speaks softly but with a bit more strength.

Where is Ian? I wonder. I have reached the bedroom level, and still don't hear him. I have remembered where the steps squeak, and I walk on the opposite side in order to approach quietly. I smell food now: beef and vegetables. They remind me of my teenage years, when I would fix dinner before school and they would put it on to cook. When I could avoid coming home no longer I would sneak down these steps in much the same way, hoping to make it to this level and my room without them hearing me.

It is very dark here. I can almost feel those old people—that Joanna, that Ian—breathing on me. It is as if they are alive, those children, though I would swear I have long since died. I reach for the railing that runs along the wall. My hand touches cobwebs. I wipe them on my denim skirt.

Below me, the kitchen door is flung open. Ian stands there, filling the doorway. He seems a giant, ten feet wide and tall. He throws his head back and laughs an ugly laugh. "Told you it was her, din't I?"

I stop dead in fear. My foot, poised to take another step, touches air. Then I remember that it was only to Joanna the child that my brother seemed a giant. My vision clears. Ian is five feet eleven, broad-shouldered, and still much larger than I. But I am adult now, and I am here on a mission to free myself. I must not fail.

I step forward, giving Ian a shove. He registers surprise, but lets me pass. Still, he allows me less than a foot of space, and I turn sideways to squeeze through, but my chest brushes his. He laughs softly, and I can smell the alcohol. My face burns as I stumble over his foot into the kitchen, righting myself with a hand on the fridge.

"Look what chick has come home to roost," Ian jeers, following. He straddles a chair. Scooping up a bottle of ale that is half gone, he hoists it into the air as if toasting me. "Told ya she'd show up sooner or later, din't I?"

I look at Denny and Joseph, and they are staring at me.

They've been sitting at the old scarred table with Ian, and they too are drinking ale. Their hair is rumpled, as Ian's is, their clothes soiled from the day's work. I feel that if I were to come back here fifty years from now, things would be much the same.

But, no. One thing has changed. My mother, I am shocked to see, is standing at the stove. There is a large pot of what appears to be a brisket on the boil, and she's tossing in pieces of potato and carrot as she chops them, the knife flashing dully—up and down, up and down—in the dim light. She looks at me once, then away, and continues cutting. Although not by any means slender, she has lost some weight. I am astounded she is even on her feet.

For a moment I am that little girl again, reaching out. My voice catches. "How . . . how are you, Mum?"

She doesn't turn. "What are you doing here?" she says curtly.

And the little girl is gone. My chin goes up. "I want to talk with you," I say. "With all of you."

" '*I want to talk with you*,' " Ian sneers. "Like we're peasants and she's the Queen Mum come to call. Who says we want to talk to you? And what do you want, anyway? You out of money now that yer precious husband is gone? You need a place to live?"

"Quiet, Ian," Joseph says, surprising me. He flicks his reddish hair from his face and gets up, pulling out the one empty chair. "Here, Josie. You can have some dinner with us—can't she, Mum?"

My mother looks at me darkly, tosses in the last of the potatoes, and ladles scum from the brisket water. I take the seat Joseph has offered. Now that I am here I feel quite weak; I don't know how much longer I could have continued to stand.

I glance round the kitchen, noting that it looks the same. There is not a single thing that seems new. Nor has there been much cleaning done. I remember every streak on the wall, every flyspeck on the ceiling.

I remember my father laughing, fingering himself, my back bent on this very table . . . Ian and Denny on me, my hands beating at them, then finally going slack. Giving up.

I shudder, and though I feel Ian's eyes on me, I cannot bear to look at him.

My mother speaks again, harshly. "What do you want with us?"

"I . . . answers."

Ian laughs. "Answers, is it now? And where were you all that time you were married? Out there in the country with yer fancy writer husband? Oh, we heard all about it. Him murdered, you in hospital. Went loony, people said."

"What people?" I snap. "I did not go loony. Who told you that?"

"It's all about," Denny says nervously, clearing his throat. He has always followed Ian's lead. If he ever had a thought of his own, I didn't know it.

I turn on Ian. "If it *is* all about, it's because you put it there. They called you from hospital, didn't they? Called to tell my dear family I was there, because they needed family to sign the papers? And you, Mum, did you even stop and look at me while you were there? Did you stop and say hello?"

"That'll be enough!" My mother waves her skimming ladle angrily. "You made your choice three years ago when you went off to be married. You left me here—" For a moment her voice breaks. Her face begins to crumple, but then her mouth hardens. "I had to do *everything* myself, *everything*. And all the while you were having yourself a good time, trottin' off to London, buildin' yourself a fine new house, plantin' your fancy garden, buyin' them fine new china dishes—"

I have been here three minutes, and am hearing her say more to me directly than in the previous thirty years. I am stunned. But then suddenly her words poke through to my brain.

"Just a damned moment! Who told you what I was doing when I was married? Not I, certainly. You wouldn't even talk to me on the phone! And what do you know about London? How do you know about my house? My *dishes*, for God's sake?"

Her gaze slides to Ian, then away. Horrified, I turn on my brother. "You were *spying* on me? You came out to

Pennoryn? In the name of God, why?" I feel as if there is dirt all over me, dirt I will never get off. That Ian was actually at Pennoryn makes my skin crawl.

"Just checkin' up on you," he says lazily. "Seein' what the good life was all about. Nice bedroom, too, not that yer fancy husband shared it with you all that much."

My face burns, and a red haze blinds me as I remember the undraped windows that David insisted upon, hoping someone might see. Remembering, too, all the times— even these last weeks—I felt certain there was someone outside watching.

I jump to my feet. "Damn you! Damn you, Ian, you are filth, and always will be—the lot of you!" I turn on my mother, Denny, and Joseph. I feel I'm choking, and the words tumble out thinly. "You—" I point to my mother. "You knew all the while what they were doing to me, and you never stopped them, never said a word. You just sat there letting them do it! What kind of mother are you? You watched me grow up feeling cheap and dirty, as if it was all my fault—"

She turns on me, her eyes blazing. "Don't tell me your problems. I've enough of me own, thank you! Enough of me own!"

"Well, you deserve every one of them." I swing back to Ian, Denny, and Joseph. "As for you, I should have killed you years ago for what you did."

"What we did?" Ian says insolently, standing. *"What we did?"* He stabs with a finger under my chin and forces my head up. "All we did is take what was ours, and like as not the whole town sampled it as well. Here, give us a little feel, now." Before I can move, he jabs his hand under my skirt. I scream. There is movement all about us, and I see my mother scurry from the room. Denny and Joseph are standing behind Ian. I am alone with them. And Ian's hand is between my legs.

Using all my strength I wrench away, and the force sends me falling over the cooker. My face barely misses the bubbling pot. Ian moves quickly behind me, his hands at my waist. I feel him press into me, and he will do it right here, I know that. He will do it as I stand here, as he has before.

His hands yank at my skirt, and I feel him on my thighs, his fingers hard and bruising.

But even as I scream, there is something I see from the corner of my eye. It is sharp and bright. I reach for it and grab it up—my mother's cutting knife.

"No!" I scream, jabbing backwards. "No!"

Ian howls in pain and releases me. I whirl around to see that the knife has cut his arm. Blood swells from a cut. It is a small cut and for me *it is not enough.* I raise my hand to strike again.

"Josie, no!" I hear Joseph's voice, and then he and Denny are pulling Ian away. The knife strikes air, and aghast, I see myself as in a mirror, the knife in my hand dripping blood.

My brothers stare at me, dumbfounded. Ian holds his wound. "I told you," he gasps. "Din't I tell you? She killed her bloody husband!"

"I did not!" I cry. "I did not!"

"Well, look what you've bloody done to *me!*" He holds his hand up, red with blood. "You think this isn't loony? You think you're sane?"

He comes towards me, the hand outstretched, and I try to move back but am still too close to the cooker. He shoves his palm in my face and smears it with blood.

"Now you look like yourself!" he shouts as I scream and scream, rubbing at it, trying to wipe it away. *"Bloody Joanna."*

"Get away from me! Get away!" I remember the knife is still in my hands, and I start to swing with it wildly. "Back off, I tell you, or I swear to God I will kill you!"

Ian starts to laugh—big shot, not afraid of me. But I stick the point of steel beneath his chin until it plucks the skin. "I mean it, damn you. Let me out of here, or your filthy hands will never touch anyone again."

He blanches. Then he moves. Pushing past him I run from the room and take one final look back. "You are monsters, every one of you! I wish you were all dead."

Denny doesn't react, but Joseph . . . Joseph raises one hand as if beseeching. "Josie," he says, his voice filled with regret. "I . . ."

It is the last thing I hear. I am running up the stairs, out the door, and jumping into my car. Still wiping blood from my face.

Somewhere along the dark road to Pennoryn, I notice a car behind me. It doesn't pass, but keeps a steady pace. I do not at first think to be afraid. I am much too busy rubbing blood from my face with my scarf. And I am hearing over and over in my head, numbing all else, *"She killed her bloody husband."*

I see myself holding the knife and striking Ian. And I remember another knife, flashing down at David. I remember myself screaming, "No, David!"

Is Ian right? Was there no one else at Pennoryn that night but me? Did that scream come as I fought my husband off?

And if so . . . dear God, what will I do? If I tell the police, they will lock me up. I don't know how I'd survive.

But it isn't as if they've arrested someone else, some innocent person. It isn't as if telling could bring David back. It isn't as if he has a family who mourns him and would feel better, knowing.

My brain races as I drive. And now I am wiping tears away, for I see my life crumbling before me. All the years I had hoped to spend with Michael, dashed by his betrayal. And now this—to face the emptiness knowing I have raised my hand against another human being, and possibly even killed.

It is all I can think about. Therefore I do not worry about the car behind me. If anything, I believe it to be someone who lives near Pennoryn, someone who works in Mevagissey and is returning home. I also think: What more can happen this night? What could touch me after this?

But then I turn into my drive and the car behind me does not continue on the road. It follows. For one wild brief moment I believe it might be Michael. Perhaps he tried to flag me down, and I didn't see. My heart is racing, for I don't know what I will say if it is indeed he. Tell him I may have murdered my husband? That we have no future now, even if we wanted it to be?

I park and step out beside my car. The other car's head-lamps blind me; I cannot see who it is. A door opens, and someone steps out. It is not Michael. I see that straight away. A bearlike figure lumbers towards me, outlined in the beam of light—a stranger. I step back a few paces, reaching for the door handle, thinking to jump back inside should the need arise.

"Mrs. Carr? So sorry to disturb you at this hour."

"Who—"

"Inspector Goff," the gruff voice says. "We talked at the hospital. I realise it's quite late, but if it wouldn't be too much trouble, might I ask you a few questions?"

"I . . . it *is* quite late." I am thoroughly frightened now. What is he doing here? Why has he followed me? Surely police detectives don't operate this way.

"I saw you pass on the road, you see. And it came to me that since you were still up and about . . ."

"You saw me pass? Where?"

"Just this side of Mevagissey. I was there on business, and you were turning onto the Falhaven road."

Impossible, I think. "You saw in the dark it was me?"

He coughs delicately. "Actually, Mrs. Carr, you were speeding. That caught my eye. And then yes, I did see it was you."

I brush a hand over my eyes. My voice is shaky. "I don't understand. Are you ticketing me for speeding?"

"Not at all. I would like a few words with you, nothing more."

My fingers knot around the strap of my handbag. Inside is the bloody scarf I used to wipe my face of Ian's blood. "I . . . I'm really quite tired. Couldn't we do this another time?"

"Well, now, yes we could, Mrs. Carr. As a matter of fact, I've been meaning to ring you up and ask you to come to the station."

"To the . . ."

"And then I thought—when I saw you tonight, that is—that this might be more . . . well, more convenient, so to speak." He comes up to me and takes my arm in a firm

grip. "There's a bit of a chill out here. Might we go inside?"

I can't answer; my mouth is too dry for words. We go up
the steps to the porch, his hand still firmly on my arm. I
hope he cannot feel the muscles, so rigid and quivering.

"A dreadful night, wouldn't you say, Mrs. Carr? A bit of
a rain coming on."

Turning my key, I open the door and we step inside.
"Yes," I say. "A dreadful night indeed."

CHAPTER 20

Inspector Goff is wearing a dark raincoat and hat, and now that we're inside he removes the hat. His greyish hair is rumpled, and the stark overhead light I've flicked on reveals a bald spot right on top. This might have given him a harmless look, like someone's grandfather, if it weren't for the eyes. They are far too watchful, too bright.

I move through the front room turning on lamps, then snap off the overhead light. "Take off your coat, Inspector, please take a seat, can I get you something?" I am saying nervously all the while.

"A hot cup of tea would be nice."

"Of course. I'll put the kettle on."

I see him making himself at home, removing his coat and draping it on a chair, as I disappear into the kitchen.

I reach for the kettle but my hand fumbles, and I lean against the sink, feeling unwell. Jumbled thoughts run through my head: Was he outside the house in Mevagissey? Did he hear the commotion? Does he know what went on?

I wonder too if he has followed me before this, and I simply haven't known. If so, what might I have done that I wouldn't have wanted him to see?

Charlotte said he'd been to talk with her, asking questions about that night. And it must be he whom Robert saw on the road the other day, out beyond the duck pond.

I feel certain he is going to arrest me. He thinks I killed

David, and somehow he's got the evidence these past few days to back him up.

But then surely, I think, I'd be in handcuffs by now, not making tea at the kitchen sink.

I turn the water on and splash my face with it. Drying off with a towel, I see myself reflected in the window glass. I look pale and frightened. Filling the kettle, I plug it in to boil. Closing my mind to anything else, I take two china cups and saucers from the cupboard and set them on the counter. My hands are shaking, the cups clatter. Going to the fridge I take out lemon and milk and set everything, along with the teapot and cosy, on a tray. My movements are slow, I am stalling. I do not want to go back in there. What will I say?

"Lemon or milk, Inspector?"

"Milk, please."

I lean forward and pour. The rain has begun. It patters on the roof, and louder droplets strike the birdhouse outside the bay window. I must remember to move it to a drier spot tomorrow.

Provided I am here tomorrow. Should I be taken away, will Robert feed my birds? I can't bear to break their trust, now that I've got it. There must be food every day.

"Been thinking of moving to a warmer climate, I have," the inspector says.

"Well, yes, I can see why. It's never warm for long here."

"Expensive, though. Moving."

"Yes," I answer automatically, still thinking what I must ask people to do for me when I'm arrested. Charlotte will close the house up, of course—again. Robert might keep up the garden this time. Michael . . .

I focus on the inspector rather than think about Michael. "Sorry. What was that?"

"I was remembering last year. How crisp and clear it was the night your husband was murdered."

I look at him. "Yes, I remember. You said you were here."

"Assigned to the case from the beginning," he says, sipping his tea. "I can picture it as if it were yesterday, you lying on the floor there, not a mark on you . . ."

I shift uncomfortably. "I understood there was a bruise."

"On the forehead, yes, of course. I'm thinking more that it's rather unusual, you know. Someone breaks in, kills the husband of the house, he won't ordinarily leave anyone alive. Certainly not covered up like that. And why does he break in, in the first place? Money, perhaps? Silver? Jewelry? You never reported anything missing."

I open my mouth, but he cuts me off.

"Of course, you were in hospital, you wouldn't know if anything were missing. Still, you've been home awhile now. I take it you've found nothing gone?"

"No . . ."

"No, of course not, otherwise you'd have rung us up to report it, isn't that so? Well, then, rape. A person breaks in to rape." His eyes stare right through me. "But you were not raped, were you, Mrs. Carr?"

He rubs his heavy hands together, as if pleased with his deduction. "Well, all right, then! So now there's the other theory—that murder often begins in the home."

I am full-out frightened now, but I can't let him see it. I try to cover with a false stab at amusement. "What are you saying, Inspector? That I killed my husband, then bashed myself over the head?"

Saying it aloud, this is the first time since Ian accused me that I've remembered I couldn't possibly have done it. *I did not bash myself on the head.*

The inspector smiles. "Actually, Mrs. Carr, I have never believed that you killed your husband."

"You haven't."

"No, no, not at all. In the first place, there wasn't a drop of blood on you—not even a sign of it being washed off. There were tests done, of course. And one doesn't . . ." He pauses, seeming to choose his words carefully. "One doesn't knife someone to death without there being blood. On the clothes, in the hair, under the nails. No matter how hard you try to wash it off, traces remain. Nor were there traces in your shower, as there certainly would have been under close examination. Furthermore, the very idea of you murdering your husband in such a bloody manner, then running to shower and change clothes, hiding the whole mess, lying on the floor to knock yourself unconscious . . . well, it's ludicrous, to say the least. Don't you think?" He beams. "And what did you strike yourself with? There was nothing nearby."

"I . . . well, yes, of course, you're right."

"Precisely! Therefore, you did not murder your husband, Mrs. Carr."

I am so relieved to hear him pronounce my innocence, I nearly laugh out loud.

"No, Mrs. Carr . . . it was your friend, Michael Lamb, who 'did the dirty deed,' as they say. Your fiancé now, I gather."

The laugh dies on my lips.

"I've been doing a bit of checking, you see. You and Michael Lamb have been close since childhood. You were close, in fact, right up to the time you married David Carr."

"Yes, but I hardly see . . ."

"Ah, but, your marriage wasn't a happy one, was it, Mrs. Carr? I understand you and Mr. Lamb are to be married in two day's time."

"Just a moment. Who in the name of God told you all this?"

"I don't think that matters at present. The point is, Michael Lamb set himself up long ago to be your protector, didn't he? And when he saw your trouble with your husband, he took steps to end it."

I force myself to smile. "Really, Inspector. I had no trouble with my husband. You're making this whole thing up!"

He sighs and reaches into a pocket of his coat. "I thought you might say that. Mrs. Carr, I've brought along a few photos. I'd like to show them to you."

He holds them out, a thin stack, perhaps ten, all Polaroid color shots. I take them, sit back down, and look at the one on top. My heart begins to race. I feel hot then cold, both embarrassed and horrified by what I see: David naked above two women, who lie on a bed. The women are in bondage, and there are all manner of instruments of torture about, which David is using—

My hand goes to my mouth. Without fully realising what I'm doing, I scatter the photos to the floor and run to the bathroom. Leaning over the toilet I retch and retch. When I am done I am weak, my ribs sore.

Finally, I wash my face and dry it, then stare at myself in the mirror. To have lived with a man like that, to have let him do the things he did, and not left him—to have put up with it over and over, and not even realise that there must be so much more.

And what about Michael? What does the inspector know? Has he facts?

I go back into the living room to face him. The inspector has picked up the photographs and they now rest in a stack on the table. I do not look at them again. I sit on the sofa and wrap my arms round myself to keep warm.

"Where did they come from?" I ask, though I think I already know.

"They were taken in London, Mrs. Carr—at a private 'sex club,' as they call it. The Red Unicorn."

"I see. All right, Inspector, I will admit that my husband had certain . . . appetites I could not fill. But it is quite a leap from that to your suspicions that Michael Lamb killed him. Why on earth would he do such a thing?"

The inspector smiles. I do not like his smile; it reminds me of my neighbour's cat creeping up on my birds.

"Why, out of jealousy, of course. Please don't insult my intelligence, Mrs. Carr. I've built a rather solid circumstantial case against your friend, you see. His alibi for the night of the murder is not precisely above question, given that it comes from so close an associate as Miss Bower. And I've a rather solid witness to his . . . habit, shall we say, of leaping to your defence. Threats made in the past against your own family, in fact."

Relief floods me—and anger. *My brother!* Ian—he's your witness, the one who set you against Michael."

I should have known, and I don't need the inspector's caught-out look to confirm it. "But don't you understand, he's always hated Michael, he'd do anything to hurt him!"

Inspector Goff sighs. "I understand, of course, that you would like to believe the best of Michael Lamb. And certainly I've no desire to spoil your new life, Mrs. Carr. It's been a difficult year for you, has it not? As for us all." The smile becomes confidential, the voice lowers. "I may have mentioned, I've been bothered rather a lot by the cold this year. There is nothing I would like better than to forget all this nasty business, move to a warmer climate and retire. Unfortunately, that would require a bit of cash."

I sit there, dumbfounded. Am I hearing what I think I am hearing?

"How much do you want?" I manage at last. "I haven't a lot."

"Ah, yes, yes, as to that, I know precisely how much you have, Mrs. Carr. I've spoken with your bank. But you know, I'm not a greedy man. Let us say the price of an airline ticket . . . and a small stipend each month for the next three years. For my services, so to speak."

"Services!"

The smile disappears, the face hardens. "Perhaps you would prefer I remain on the job and issue a warrant for Michael Lamb's arrest."

No, I would prefer to kill you, I think. For one mad moment I wonder how he would respond if I were to dash to the kitchen, grab a large knife, and run back in here with it. What if I were to hold it to his heart and threaten to shove it in—just as I did with Ian?

What if, in fact, I did shove it in? I would like to see that smug look wiped from his face.

"How can I know you'll leave Michael alone if I give you all this?" I demand.

"Well, now I suppose you can't know, Mrs. Carr. You'll simply have to trust me, won't you?"

CHAPTER 21

It is the next morning, and I am thinking, *Ironic. I finally am forced to trust a man, and it's got to be a blackmailer.*

And why, I wonder, did I rush so quickly to Michael's defence? Why do I even care about protecting him from all this? Is it a part of my illness? Am I taking the blame on myself for his trouble?

Perhaps. But it is, I think, more that I feel quite certain now that Michael is not guilty of David's murder. And regardless of what's happened between us, regardless of anything he might have done to betray me these past few days, I owe him for years of kindness. I cannot allow him to be destroyed by Inspector Goff's greed.

The inspector did not want a check. He wanted cash, which I did not have, and I've agreed to meet him at two this afternoon, outside my bank. I will withdraw the sum he has demanded and it will nearly wipe me out. I will have to get a job. Even that will not cover the inspector's three-year "stipend." But with any luck he'll go off to his island or wherever he must to follow the sun, and Michael will be left in peace.

That's the catch, of course—with any luck. Perhaps he won't go away at all. He could turn up on my doorstep, or Michael's, any time he wishes, demanding more.

I stoop to pull a weed from my herb garden and think that there is only one effective solution to this. If the real killer were uncovered and charged, my blackmailing po-

liceman would have no power over either of us—none at
all.

The real killer . . .

I think I now know who that is. But can I use that knowledge to save Michael . . . without hurting someone I
love?

I come upon her quietly, on her terrace. She is sunning
herself, the dark glasses reflecting a dusting of gossamer
clouds. The sun won't last; another rain is forecast, and
already a stiff breeze is moving in from the sea. It skitters
through treetops surrounding the lawn, turning the leaves
to silver-grey. Tiny waves skip over the river that bends and
twists at the foot of the hill.

Charlotte, however, is protected from the vicissitudes of
climate here on her terrace, just as she's been protected
from so many things, since marrying Henry.

I stand to the side watching her a moment. She moves
not a muscle, but smiles. "I hear you there, Joanna. Are
you sneaking up on me?" She lazily extends a hand.
"Come, sit beside me."

I take her hand and sit on the edge of the chaise. Her
skin is very warm, but dry. Charlotte seldom perspires, I
remember now. Beside her, on a small table, is a half-
empty glass of white wine, and next to that, a bottle.

"How did you know it was me?" I say.

"I felt your presence. I always do." She strokes my bare
arm. "Dear Joanna. I'm so happy you're here."

"I thought you might not mind if I just stopped by."

"Of course I don't." She pushes the sunglasses back on
her head. "But there's something in your voice. What's
wrong?"

"He came to see me last night. Inspector Goff."

Her hand tenses on my arm and she wriggles to a sitting
position, frowning. "What did he want?"

"Money."

"*Money?* What on earth—"

"For his silence."

"Dear God! Oh, dear God, Joanna. He threatened to
arrest you?"

"Not me. Michael."

She stares at me a moment. Then she sits back, sighing with relief. "Oh, well, then. Surely you didn't give him anything."

"No. But I said I would. Today."

She grabs me again. "No! No, you can't do that! You mustn't!"

"Really? Why not, Char? Do you hate Michael so much, you want to see him go to jail for something he didn't do?"

"I . . ."

"He didn't, did he, Char? He didn't kill David."

She pales and looks away.

"What was going on between you and David, Char?"

She flinches. "Me and David? Nothing! Nothing at all!"

I pull from my pocket the note I discovered weeks ago in David's jacket. The parchment is perhaps a bit more rumpled than when I found it. I read it over and over that first week, shoving it away in a drawer finally so I wouldn't have to think about it.

Charlotte reaches for the note. "What . . . ?" Mystified, she begins to read it aloud. *"David, I cannot keep on with this charade . . . I must see you . . . meet me in the meadow . . ."*

Her eyes close briefly. Her hands and the note fall limply to her lap. "Where did you find this?" she says tiredly.

"In David's jacket, the first night I got home."

"And you never said anything? Never asked me about it?"

"For the longest while, I don't think I really wanted to know."

"But God, Joanna, you've been thinking we had an affair? You thought I'd betrayed you?"

I don't answer.

Charlotte looks away again. Her face is slack, bone-weary. "I haven't wanted to tell you. I kept thinking that with him dead, and you not remembering . . . I thought we might just forget the whole thing, and we'd never have to talk about it at all."

I stand and walk to the low brick wall that surrounds the

terrace. "Well, we do have to talk about it. I want to hear all of it," I say, anger flaring. *"Right now."*

Her green eyes turn to me, brimming with tears. "Oh, Joanna. It was nothing like what you're thinking, I swear to you. He . . . David made advances to me. He did it all the time, and I hated it! I threatened to tell you, and he said that if I did he would make certain I never saw you again." She rises and comes to stand before me, wringing her hands. "I didn't know what he meant by that, but by this time I believed he might do anything, anything at all. I was so afraid." She places both cold hands on my face. "Oh, please tell me you believe me."

I remove her hands. "I would like to. But the 'charade,' Charlotte. What about that?"

She turns back to the lounge, picking up her wine and taking a deep draught. Her hand shakes. "Don't you see, that was what it felt like, having to sit with the two of you over dinner, or even be in the same house with him and not tell you. And it wasn't as if he *stopped,* you know. He kept on and on, and I didn't dare tell Henry. I knew it would upset him, and I couldn't risk that. Henry's health was still relatively good then, but at his age . . ."

"So you wrote David this note. Why?"

She flutters a hand and gives a tremulous laugh. "Oh, I thought foolishly that it might do some good. I wanted to threaten him once and for all that I'd tell you. I wanted to tell him that if he hurt either of us, I would go to the police. Joanna, I really was so afraid. Even before you told me what he was doing to you, David frightened me to death. But I didn't know what else to do."

"And he met with you?"

"Yes."

"What did he say?"

Her voice is bitter, slurring a bit. "Laughed in my face— said you woul'n't believe me. Said he had you wrapped round his little finger, and you'd only turn against me."

"Char . . . you believed him?"

She gives me a look. And now it is my turn to glance away. My friend, who has known me half my life, is right.

David had so much power over me then, I might well have believed him over her.

My shoulders slump with weariness, and she comes and sits beside me, stroking my hair where it lies on my shoulder. Her hand is unsteady, and for the first time I realise she must have been drinking quite some time. "I'm so sorry," she croons. "I should have told you. I just loved you too much to risk losing you." She takes my face between her hands again and, turning me to her, kisses me on the mouth. It is not a friendship kiss. It is lingering, passionate, sensual.

Shaken, I draw back. "Char . . . ?"

Her trembling fingers caress my face. "Just let me love you, Joanna. Just this once. Please, dear, I've waited so long." ·

"No!" I push her away. "Stop!" There is a sudden roaring in my head, and all about me now float images—images of Charlotte, of David, of me. They fly helter-skelter through my brain, no sense, no order. They strike and confuse me, and I grab at one, try to fasten it to the spot. But it's elusive, it runs, then rushes back to taunt.

Charlotte, in my bed at Pennoryn, lying with me side by side. I am wearing the red peignoir, and she is on the bed kissing me—not like a friend but a lover. I see David—David walking in and finding us that way. The memory tears through my head with hurricane force, and I am hearing my husband say as if from a great distance, "My two little sluts. Did you plan this nice party for me?"

I grasp Charlotte's arm for support. "I *remember*," I say. "Oh, God, I remember the night David died!"

CHAPTER 22

Charlotte and I sit quietly. Her arm is about me, and I am glad for that, as she gives me comfort and warmth. I don't know how I would have got through this alone. She rocks me gently, holding me close. "Tell me what you remember," she whispers.

"Oh, Char. It began after dinner that night. It was cold, even for early December. I remember the wind came blowing through the hills and down the chimney. David made me dress in that hideous red thing. I stood before the mirror in it and hated it. But I hated myself more. I felt if I had to go through another night like the ones before, I might kill myself."

I knot my hands together, staring down at them. "I threatened to leave David. I told him if he didn't get out, I would. We had a horrible fight, and he hit me, then he stormed from the house. Shortly after that you came. You found me in bed, crying. You lay beside me on the bed, just consoling me, the way we always did when we were kids. One moment it was like that, and then . . ."

I look at her in wonderment. "Char, you turned and kissed me . . . the way you just did. I was startled, I didn't know what to do or how to respond, because I never knew you felt that way. But then David walked in and he saw us, and . . ." I cannot say it. *It turned him on.*

She grimaces. "He was so bloody evil. *'Did you plan this little scene just for me?'* he said. Then he started to come at us, the most dreadful look in his eyes. I remember every word as if it were happening now. *'My two little sluts. My, my, my. Show me how the two of you do it.'* "

The memories rush back quickly now. "We tried to get off the bed," I say, "but he grabbed me. He grabbed me by the front of the red teddy I'd worn beneath the negligee, and ripped it wide open. I remember the sound, that awful sound." My eyes sting. "Oh, Char, it's all coming back now. You tried to get him off me, but he slapped you so hard it knocked you down. And he kept saying things, telling you to take off your clothes, saying how he'd had you already, there was nothing to hide."

Charlotte hugs me tight. "He was lying, Joanna. I swear to God. David was vile. He kept at me, over and over, but I kept fending him off. He wanted you to doubt me. He wanted to break us apart, that's all."

I grip her hands. "I remember him knocking you down, then yanking you to your feet and dragging you to the door. You kept screaming at him, hitting him, then I was on him. I beat on his back, and I kept yelling at him to stop, but he had so much strength."

"As if he'd gone mad," Charlotte agrees, shivering. "He shrugged you off as if you were no more than a flea. Then he dragged me outside, threw me on the ground, and kicked me. Oh, Joanna, I've never been so afraid in my life, not for myself, but for you. He yelled at me, 'Get out of here! Don't ever come near my wife again!' and I got up and ran across the garden, then the meadow, looking for that farmhouse down the road. I thought I might call for the police, but no one was home and everything was locked up tight. So I ran back to your driveway and jumped into my car, and raced home to phone them from there."

Charlotte stands, reaches for the bottle of wine, and fills her now-empty glass. She holds it up to me first, but I shake my head. She downs it in two swift gulps, then places the glass on the table. She misses by an inch, and the glass tumbles to the terrace, breaking. She barely notices.

"By the time I got home I was in such a state, I couldn't keep what had happened from Henry. I didn't tell him everything, only that David was in a rage. And Henry said,

'Well, why don't we go to Pennoryn ourselves and just see.' "

She passes a hand over her eyes. "Dear Henry, he means well, but he's old-fashioned that way, he doesn't like to involve himself in other people's business. I let him talk me into not calling the police." Her green eyes seem to avoid mine. "I didn't know, you see. I didn't really know what you would want me to do. I know it sounds crazy, but I thought—oh God, Joanna, I'm sorry, but I thought you might be all right once I'd gone, that David might have calmed down, and the two of you . . ."

"Well," I say, "you couldn't have known."

"And I felt so guilty, you see, for kissing you. I felt I'd caused it. All the way back to Pennoryn with Henry, I kept running it through my mind, how I'd never meant to hurt you with what I did. And I thought if the police were called and David told them he saw me kissing you, Henry would learn of it. It would be all over for me."

She covers her face and weeps. It is I who now stand and comfort her, patting her back. "It's all right, Char. Really, it's all right."

Her voice rises, high and bewildered like a little girl's. "But when we got back to Pennoryn, the front door was wide open. And you were lying so quietly there on the floor. It was quite strange, Joanna, just as the inspector said. You were lying there with that blanket over you, and I almost believed for a moment you were sleeping. Then I saw the blood all about the hearth, and David with all that blood on him, and my heart nearly stopped. I thought you were both dead." She pulls back and takes me by the shoulders. "Joanna, what in the name of God happened? Do you remember that?"

"Yes." The film plays itself out on the screen of my mind —everything sharp and clear. I see David and Charlotte. I see me. I hear every word, every inflection. "I am running out onto the porch and I see you run across the garden. Then I see David go round to the side of the house. I know he isn't following you, so you're safe, you've got away. I run back into the living room to call the police, but David comes through from the kitchen and reaches me first. He throws the phone on the floor. He has the stone hare in his other hand, the one Michael gave us as a wedding gift. He's brought it in from the garden. He holds it up. 'I've always hated this, did you know that?' he says, and I just stand there terrified and shake my head. 'It was always Michael, wasn't it?' he rages. 'And now *her*. Never me. You've never had any real passion for me!'

" 'That's not true,' I cry. 'It was good with us in the beginning. It was good . . . till you spoiled it.'

" '*I* spoiled it!' he shouts. 'You with your proper little ways of making love, you with your constant hounding, *I want a baby, David*. And all the while you were mooning over your sweet little artist friend. Or so I thought.' "

I give a shudder. "He threw back his head and laughed then, Char, and my very bones went cold. 'If I'd known you had a girlfriend all the while,' he said, 'we might have had some fun.' Then he came at me, and he backed me up against the sofa. He started to kiss me, and his hands were all over me. I started to scream and scream, and I remember I didn't know whose hands they were—David's, or my brothers'. But it didn't matter. I'd had all I could stand. I . . ."

Suddenly, my voice fails.

"What?" Charlotte says urgently. "For God's sake, *what?*"

"Someone was there. I see someone there."

Her voice trembles. "Can you see who?"

"I don't know. A figure." But I cannot grasp it. It won't come through.

Charlotte looks so strained, so anxious.

"Char . . ." I swallow hard, hating to say it, but it's why I've come here today. It's the only thing that makes sense. "You know who it was—don't you?"

"No, I—"

"Please tell me. It was Henry, wasn't it?"

She draws back, stricken. Both hands go to her cheeks.

"Listen to me, Char. Henry hurt his arm that same night. He told me he'd hurt it at Abbott's, lifting bags of fertilizer. But Mrs. Albicott at the doctor's office distinctly said he'd hurt it that night. I can't imagine why Henry lied about when it happened, unless . . . Char, I thought you and David were having an affair. Did Henry think that as well? Did he come to Pennoryn that night and kill David, either out of jealousy or thinking to protect you from him?"

Charlotte moves away from me. She stands, turns away, and her hand goes out blindly, as if to clutch the air for support. I am shocked at how feeble, how pale she seems suddenly. The huge diamond wedding ring glints in the sunlight, and then it is gone as Charlotte clutches herself about the waist.

"No . . ." she sobs, "no, it can't have been Henry. He couldn't . . ."

She spins back to me, clearly in pain. Her face is twisted, flushed. "If only you hadn't remembered any of it! I tried so hard to get you to just forget the whole thing. I even tried to make you believe Michael had killed David, when I didn't half believe it myself . . ."

"Wait a minute, Char. Are you saying you honestly don't know for sure? You don't *know* if Henry did it?"

She shakes her head back and forth, back and forth, her eyes streaming with tears. Then it all tumbles out. "He . . . oh, God, it didn't happen the way I told you! Henry wasn't at Fallston that night when I got home."

"He wasn't here? Where was he?"

"That's just it, I don't know. He was just beginning to have these episodes of wandering off and forgetting what he'd done, and I was worried sick when I got home and he wasn't there. I was worried about you as well, of course. I wanted to get back to Pennoryn and make sure you were all right. But I couldn't just leave without finding Henry. I went crazy driving up all the little country lanes around here, looking for that damned Morris. I was getting ready to phone the police, both about Henry and you, when he came through the door. He didn't know where he'd been." Again, her voice catches on a sob. "Didn't even remember being gone, just getting out of the Morris in the driveway. I was so relieved to see him, I scooped him right up and we hurried back to Pennoryn to get you and take you out of there. But then when we arrived . . ." She falls silent.

"You saw what had happened, and thought Henry might have done it but not remembered it?"

"Yes. God help me, that's what I thought. I thought if he'd happened to come to Pennoryn looking for me, and seen from the road what David did, the way he threw me out—that perhaps instead of coming after me, he might have gone inside and—"

"Killed David," I finish for her.

Charlotte's eyes fill with tears. I hold her close. "Poor Char. And you still don't know?"

She shakes her head. "Dr. Woolery's seen Henry. He called in a specialist, and we got the diagnosis a few weeks ago. It's Alzheimer's. Joanna, Henry will never recall that night, and unless you remember . . . don't you see, no one will ever know!"

I pull back. "Yet you deliberately tried to make me suspect Michael."

She looks away, flushing. "I've just been so afraid. I'm losing Henry, Joanna. There's no telling how long we'll have before he's simply—gone. Then you came home, and I thought, well, at least I'll still have Joanna. But no sooner did I think it than you were deciding to marry Michael . . ."

"And you thought you would lose me, too."

She looks away. "I'm sorry. I'm not proud of it."

I pace back and forth on the terrace, thinking it through. "You know," I say finally, "I came here today thinking the police needed another suspect to divert their attention from Michael. I was reasonably certain Henry was guilty, and that you were covering for him. I thought if I could prove it . . ." I look at her. "But I don't really want to hurt Henry, Char. I don't want to hurt either of you."

Her expression is so hopeful yet timid, so unlike my friend as I've known her, it makes me want to cry. "What are you going to do, then?" she asks.

"I don't know, Char. I just don't know." I glance at my watch. "I've really got to get to the bank. Until I can figure this out, I should keep to the inspector's plan."

A bit of her toughness comes back, and there is that narrowing of the eyes I know so well. "Dear heart . . . if it weren't for him, you know, our troubles would be over. It doesn't really matter now who killed David, does it? So long as the police never find out? We could just let the whole thing go and get on with our lives."

I cross over to her and touch lightly the remaining discoloration beneath her eye. "Can you get on with your life that easily, Char? Henry did this, didn't he?"

She flushes.

"The other day at Abbott's," I tell her, "he lost his temper quite suddenly. Does he do that often?"

"He . . . no, not when he's in his right mind, so to speak. Only when he has these episodes. I try to stop him from going off somewhere, and he fights me off. The other day . . . Well, it was an accident, of course. But he got me in the eye with his elbow."

"Char, I'm so sorry. Is there nothing the doctors can do?"

"Live with it, they say. Or put him in a home." Her chin goes up. "Can you see me doing that?"

"No, I can't. But Char, you may have to one day."

"Not as long as I'm breathing," she says fiercely. "Oh, my dear . . ." She wraps her arms around me. "Promise me that even if things end up turning out all right with Michael, you won't leave me. I swear I won't give you so much grief in the future."

I hug her tight, stroking her thin back. "I won't leave you, Char. I love you."

Her hot tears burn my cheek.

CHAPTER 23

I leave Charlotte and drive to the village. There is less than an hour before I'm to meet Inspector Goff, and I am anxious. I must do one more thing before the bank. Looking in, I see a long queue.

Across the lane, in front of the news agency, is a telephone. I cross to it. Gathering up my courage, I try Michael at his cottage, hoping he'll be there. The phone rings and rings. *Please don't make me deal with Annette at the gallery,* I am praying. Then, just as I'm about to hang up, Michael answers.

"Yes, hello," he says, out of breath.

"Michael, it's Joanna."

"Jo! God, I am so glad you called. I've just been out to the house, looking for you. Sweetheart, I'm so sorry about yesterday. I wanted to explain, but right after you ran off I had a call from the gallery in London. The pipes finally burst, and we had a flood. I had to get right up there and pack up paintings before they were destroyed. I've been up all night, and I'm just now back, but I came out to Pennoryn to tell you—"

I lean against the phone booth, weak and confused. "Michael, please stop. I haven't time for this right now, it isn't important."

"No, let me talk—please. Jo, Annette was jealous of you. She's always had feelings for me, but there's never been anything between us. Please believe me. When she looked through the window and saw you coming yesterday, she grabbed me, and I know it must have looked awful, but—"

I can't help it; I must point out the obvious. "Michael, you were kissing her."

"I *wasn't* kissing her. She was kissing me. There's a difference. Jo, we need to see each other and talk face to face. I've got to get right back up to London now, but what about tonight? It's your birthday, isn't it? How about letting me take you to dinner?"

The flurry of words is confusing me, and I don't know what to say or even what to believe. I can see through the bank windows from here, and the queue is getting longer. I've got to get in there and out before the inspector arrives at two. And the clock outside, above the doors, tells me it is already 1:40.

"Michael, this isn't at all why I called, and I'm in a bit of a hurry. A lot has happened since last night. I thought you should know about it."

I tell him about Inspector Goff's visit, and his blackmailing scheme. "I thought at first I wouldn't mention it to you, as I'm handling it. But he might come to you about it. You should be prepared to deal with it calmly." I can just see Michael losing his temper and putting the inspector into retirement—forever.

But oddly, he doesn't seem upset. "Jo . . . I can't believe you would do this for me. And I love you for it. But I won't have you giving that bloody vermin your money."

"Michael, there's no other way that I can see right now. I think it's best for all concerned to just get rid of him, send him packing, so to speak. Otherwise, he'll be poking about in all our lives."

"I do see what you're saying. But Jo, let me think a moment. There must be something . . ."

I wait anxiously, watching the clock over the bank. Just as I'm about to tell him I must hang up, he says, "Sweetheart, have you got those papers with you? The ones for the joint account?"

"I think so . . . yes. I stuck them in my bag when you gave them to me the other night so I wouldn't lose them. Why?"

"All right. First of all, I've worked out a loan without our having to do all that. I knew you didn't feel right about it, and I'd never want you to do something that isn't right for you. But Jo, will you trust me on this? Sign those papers now, anyway, and turn them into the bank. *Don't* take out any cash. And when the inspector arrives, tell him we joined our accounts yesterday, and that the papers went through faster than you'd expected. Tell him you can't take anything out without my signature as well. That way he'll have to come to me."

"But, Michael—"

"Please, Jo. I don't want you having anything more to do with this dirty business. Will you trust me? As soon as I've dealt with the inspector, I'll sign it all back to you. I promise."

"It's not that I don't trust you, Michael. I just don't know if he'll settle for that."

"But don't you see, he'll have to. If he has access to bank records, he'll know soon enough that you've told him the truth. And there won't be a thing he can do about it. He'll have to come to me."

"I suppose you're right . . ."

"I am. Believe me. Hurry now, Jo. And will you meet me tonight at The Blue Swan? I'll be driving down late from London, but I'm fairly certain I can be here by ten. We can talk more about all this. And after that, we'll have a midnight celebration. Something special for your birthday."

I can hear the smile in his voice . . . and the seduction. He is trying to woo me back. "Oh, Michael, I don't know."

"Jo, please say yes. We'll have a long talk, and we'll work things out. All this business about the inspector and Annette, it can all be put to rights, you'll see."

Finally, I agree. "All right, I'll see you at The Blue Swan at ten. But I'm not making any promises."

Again I hear that smile. "You are a hard woman, my love. But follow my lead on this. It'll soon be over. I promise."

The clock over the teller's counter says 1:53, and they always make you wait when you've any changes to make on an account. If I'm not in front of the bank at two sharp, will the inspector think I've changed my mind and leave? Will he report what he suspects, and have Michael picked up? There are still three people in the queue before me.

The clock hands move, and I lick my lips, tasting bile, as the elderly woman just ahead of me chats with the teller about her grandchildren. Just when I think she's through she starts on her cat. I clear my throat, and the two women look at me. I smile, but my message is clear. *Hurry up.* The customer gathers up her cash and puts it carefully into a tattered needlepoint bag. An assortment of odds and ends tumble out onto the floor: money-off coupons, letters, bills. She stoops to pick them up but she is terribly stiff, and I kneel to help her. "Oh, dear, I'm so sorry," she apologises, flustered. "I don't know why I carry so many things, but then if I don't keep them with me at all times, I forget I've got them . . ."

I am desperate now about the time, but I say, "Don't worry, it's all right," as I hand her several items. She takes them with a hand that shakes, and I see she is confused and quite tired. I reassure her that she hasn't been dumb to drop her things, or even to carry them with her. The woman thanks me and leaves, walking at a bit of a tilt because of the heavy bag.

I slip the joint account papers out of my bag and glance at them as I set them on the counter. Michael has already filled in his information and signed, I see. I take the counter pen and sign my own name and account number above his. "I'd like to change my account," I say. "I'm being married, and my fiancé and I would like our accounts joined."

The teller looks at the papers, then up at me. "It will take a few minutes. You'll need to talk to the accounts manager."

"No, please, I don't have time for that. Can't I just leave these papers with you? I've an urgent meeting at two."

Sweat pops out on my forehead; I watch the clock as the teller steps to a desk in back and speaks to a supervisor.

They haven't seen me in here for a while. They look me up and down. The clock hands move to 1:59. "Please hurry," I say, forcing a smile, though my voice shakes. "I really must go." They both come back to the window, and the supervisor asks me to show identification. I half dump my bag, giving them my driver's licence, anything they want. They scan it, look me up and down once more, and finally the supervisor nods and leaves.

"Your fiancé?" the teller says, typing information into a computer. "His account is here as well?"

"Yes," I answer irritably. "Michael Lamb. It's all here, everything you need." I point to the papers.

She pauses as the computer screen brings up records. Arching a brow, she looks at me. "You're certain you want to do this, Mrs. Carr?"

"Yes—yes, of course I'm sure! Why do you ask?"

"It's only that you've rather a large sum deposited, and your fiancé, Mr. Lamb . . ."

Has rather a small one. She doesn't need to tell me. "Look, what does it matter? This really is not your business, is it? Can't you just do your job and get on with it?"

She gives an offended shrug. "Whatever you say." There is another flurry of taps and pauses, and finally she sets me free with a slip of paper that shows Michael's and my accounts have been joined. I glance at the clock.

2:11. Dear God. So late. But surely—

I exit the bank and stand on the sidewalk, off to the side of the door. The inspector is nowhere in sight. I look up the street and down, but see no sign of him. Inching back against the brick wall of the bank, I try to appear casual, as if merely waiting for a friend.

At half past two I am not only tired, but greatly disturbed. I cannot believe the greedy inspector would give up his pot of gold merely because I was eleven minutes late. I check my watch, though I've done so several times in the past fifteen minutes. 2:36.

I wait, my legs weary from standing. The sun moves behind the news agent's building across the street. There is an odour of fish from the restaurant just beside it. They are preparing for the evening meal. My stomach growls; I have eaten only a piece of fruit today. Women pass with packages, others with young children, all of them hurrying, no doubt to get home.

A quarter past three, and I am growing angry now, rather than anxious. What am I doing, I wonder, letting this blackmailing policeman control me this way? Michael was right. I was crazy to agree to pay him in the first place, crazy to come here. And now I am truly insane if I continue to wait.

Whatever his game is, I no longer wish to play.

I return to my car, still half expecting him to come along, call out to me, rush to catch me. But there is no loud voice, no sound of running feet. I slide into my car, toss my handbag onto the seat, and head home.

The inspector's failure to show is a puzzle, but I am so all-in and my mind so muddled from hunger, I cannot decipher it. By now I am more than willing to let Michael deal with him, if and when he does show up again. I need to get home and rest.

Meanwhile, a more important question nags. I've tried to shove it away since Charlotte's, but it jumps in now as I'm driving home. *Remember that night*, it says. *Who else was at Pennoryn that night?*

I cannot remember. All I get are random thoughts, and I could put something together with them, but it would be largely imagination.

The problem with that is I manage to be wrong about so many things.

I have turned west on the road to Pennoryn, and the scene is surreal. An incoming fog slips through clefts in the hills. Tendrils of it slide like a snake into the valley, hugging the ground. Green farmlands on either side disappear, and only the cows are left visible, as if standing on clouds. I have to squint to see, and barely miss a farmer walking along the side of the road with his dog. I swerve, check the rearview mirror to make sure he's all right, and he shakes his fist at me, but moves along. There is something about him that reminds me of someone, a tilt of the head, perhaps, or . . . no, the walk. The walk reminds me of Ian.

Ian, my dear devoted brother, who told Inspector Goff about Michael and me. Ian, who told him Michael had it in him to murder.

I tap the wheel, thinking. Why would Ian have done that? Out of spite? To get even with me for cutting him the night before? Or was there more to it?

I would like to confront Ian with this. In truth, I would like to beat his bloody brains in.

I am still thinking as much when I reach Pennoryn and pull into the drive. The late afternoon sun turns the windows to gold, and the gardens are so beautiful they nearly make me cry.

Old Robert's truck is gone, I see. I've been after him to take a day off, or at least to leave early. He works much too hard. I draw up to the front door, park and get out, my eye caught by something on the porch—deep red roses, in a green glass vase.

I run up the steps and bend down, finding a card nestled among the thorns. I pull it out carefully and see a fancy scroll across the top: *Happy Birthday!* Below that is a hand-printed message:

Dearest Jo, I can't wait to see you tonight. I love you . . . Michael.

I hold the roses up, sniffing their lush scent, and cannot believe he's done this. He must have phoned the order in right after talking with me. And all the while I was standing in that bank, pooling all my assets with his, largely to protect him—

It is more difficult than one supposes to break old habits of caring.

I wonder if Michael's already left for London. I should tell him that the inspector never showed up, if not. And I would like to thank him for the roses.

Again his phone rings and rings, and this time an out-of-breath Annette answers. I am surprised she's in his cottage, and almost hang up. I must force myself to keep my voice crisp, impersonal. "This is Joanna Carr. Has Michael left yet?"

"Michael?" she says stiffly. "Yes, he's gone. Hold a moment, please. I've got my arms full of paintings, and I must set them down."

I hear her lay the phone down, and faint noises in the background. Moments later she comes back on.

"Shall I take a message?" she asks, her tone still hostile.

"Yes, will you? Please tell him I have urgent news, and to phone me if he can. If not, I'll just see him tonight."

A brief pause. "See him? In London, you mean?"

I grit my teeth. "No, Mevagissey."

"But Michael's not coming back here tonight," she says with a hint of triumph that she knows something I don't. "Didn't he tell you? He's staying up in London. There's been some trouble, you know."

"Yes, I heard. The plumbing. He said he'd be back rather late."

"No, not the plumbing. He's had bad news about the financing for the new gallery up there." But then she wavers. "Of course, if he said . . . He's supposed to meet you here tonight, you say? At the gallery?"

"Yes. At ten. We talked only a while ago."

"Oh. Well, then. I suppose he forgot to mention it to me."

"He was hurried. I'm sure he simply forgot."

I'm surprised to find I'm feeling a bit sorry for her. I know what it is to love Michael, and to lose him. The fact that we're meeting tonight—and that Michael didn't tell her about it—can't be easy for her.

"I doubt I'll be hearing from him, but if I do, I'll give him your message," she says. Her tone leaves me with little hope.

"Mrs. Carr?"

"Yes?"

"There's something I really must say."

I grip the receiver hard. "All right."

"You know, it hasn't been easy for Michael since you came home. It's bad enough he's got all these troubles with the gallery, but to have to worry about you, too—"

"Pardon me?" I interrupt. "Michael does not have to worry about me."

"Well, he feels he does. He neglected his work, you know, when you were in hospital. That's why he's got all these troubles in the first place. And now with all this business of the financing falling through . . . I would hate to see his entire business go down the drain."

"The entire business? I didn't know it was that serious."

"Well, it is. And really, he'd be much better off if you'd just let him go."

"You know," I say angrily, "you are out of bounds. First you drive Michael into the ground financially, and then you blame me for doing it."

"I did not drive him into the ground!"

"Oh, no? Michael himself told me the improvements to the gallery were all your idea. He also told me you faked that little 'romantic' scene in the gallery for my benefit. *You're* the one who should get out of his life. At least I'm trying to help him."

"You hateful, rotten bitch!" she says. "I've done more for him than you ever could! I was keeping him alive here while you were in hospital pining over your dead husband. Furthermore, as for helping Michael, at least I've never tried to buy his love. And as to that—how does it feel to know you're now worth more to him dead than alive?"

Waiting restlessly for night to come, I think about Annette's parting words. I wish I hadn't heard them. It's hard to get that sort of thing out of one's head. And though I don't for a minute believe that Michael would rather have me dead than alive, it is also just as true that if anything were to happen to me before we could cancel that joint account, my money would be all his.

But how did Annette find out about it?

Well, she probably saw the papers lying about before Michael brought them to me. Or—and, of course, this is it —he discussed it with her. She has been managing his books, after all. She'd have to know what he was doing to secure that loan.

I wonder if she's given him my message. I think not or he would have phoned by now. I go about the house looking for things to do so the time will pass quickly. First on my list is closing all the curtains in the house. Since learning about Ian's nasty little "visits," I feel I'm in a goldfish bowl when they're open. It angers me to do this, as I've always enjoyed seeing the sun go down beyond the hill. I like watching the birds as they take their final meal of the evening, then tuck themselves into their wings to sleep.

I am angry again, too, about Inspector Goff. What was all that business last night about? Was he only trying to frighten me? Or was he testing, to see if I'd admit to anything?

When I'm done with the busywork and can find nothing more to do, I settle in the parlour in front of the telly, too on edge to read, and weary of thinking about it all.

The news is on, and I turn up the sound to hear the weather. "Yet another storm front by morning . . . gale warnings along the coast . . ."

My eyelids become heavy; they close. I can still hear the telly, and the weather report droning on. Then the anchor begins a news story. My eyelids drift open lazily. The words "Mevagissey Murder" flash across the screen. Startled, I come awake and reach for the remote, cranking the volume up even more. There is very little crime in that tiny hamlet. What can it be?

". . . car was apparently run off the road by someone who fled the scene of the crime," the anchor says. "The police as yet have no leads. Inspector Horace Goff was due to retire . . ."

In the upper left-hand corner a small photo appears, an old photo, as he looks much younger, but it undoubtedly is the Inspector Goff I know.

"When?" I wonder aloud. "My God, when did this happen?" But that news has apparently already been given, and the anchor is moving on now to a story about an armed robbery in Liverpool.

I flick the telly off, and sit quite still, feeling dazed. Inspector Goff—dead.

But who killed him? *Run off the road . . . someone who fled the scene of the crime.* Who would do this?

The answer does not bear inspection. Aside from me, there are at least three people I know whose lives might be simplified by Inspector Goff's death—all three of whom I love.

CHAPTER 24

I walk about like a robot, dressing, and end up finally in jeans with boots and a large white pullover sweater. I top the sweater with a black leather jacket I haven't worn in years and climb into the car, still bewildered and quite anxious. There is a light fog coming in. It is nothing compared to the fog in my brain.

Which one of you did it? I am asking myself over and over as I drive. *Which one?*

"I'll handle the inspector," Michael said. *"It'll all be over soon."*

No . . . Please, God, don't let it be Michael. One does not get away with killing a policeman.

Could it possibly have been Henry? *"I never know what he might do these days,"* Charlotte said. *"He's got a terrible temper."*

Or Charlotte herself? *"If it weren't for him, you know, our troubles would be over."*

I shake my head to rid myself of the images. *I've got to get to Michael. I've got to know if it was him.*

And if so, then what? a small voice says.

I don't know, I don't know. The fog won't leave my brain.

I reach Mevagissey shortly before ten. Shops have closed for the night, and there are few people on the streets. Music drifts from a pub a block north of The Blue Swan.

Michael's cottage is dark, and there is only a small light on in the gallery, at the back. It's quite dim in there and, looking in, I don't see Michael. Nor have I seen his car parked on the street. Both halves of the Dutch door are closed, and at first I think to wait on the sidewalk until he arrives. But then I try the door, and it opens.

"Michael?" I call out, stepping inside.

There is no answer, and I decide that perhaps he is in the cottage, or even in the alley in back, either loading or unloading the Range Rover of paintings he's brought down from London. Several new paintings line the floor along the walls, and several are on easels throughout the room. It's quite crowded in here now, nearly impossible to see to the back wall. The tiny lamp on Annette's desk does little to dispel the gloom. I can see dark and light on the paintings, but little colour, and in some cases, only outlines of frames.

I reach for the light switch, remembering it's by the front door, and flick it. Nothing happens.

"Michael?" I call again, a bit nervous now. "Are you here?"

I notice that the air in the room is cold. If Michael had been here I would know it, I think. There would be some hint of warmth.

I begin to feel afraid. Why doesn't the electricity work? There are tracks of indirect lighting around the ceiling; it should have come on.

I begin to walk towards the back, past the easels, and that is when I hear it—a sound of breathing close by. A scrape, as of a shoe on the floor. I whirl to the left, my heart pounding. "Michael . . . ?"

The beam of a torch strikes my face. "Happy Birthday," an insolent voice says. "Welcome to the celebration."

A hand grabs my arm, another covers my mouth to stifle my scream. The torch falls to the floor, and all is dark. Even the lamp on the desk has been extinguished. I struggle, kicking backwards, clawing at the hand on my mouth. An arm grips me around the waist. I smell fish on the breath, and ale. It is all too familiar. It fills me with terror.

Ian.

"Teach you to cut me, you little bitch."

Reminded, I go for the wound on his arm and tear at it, digging with my nails. Ian mutters a violent oath but only tightens his grip. His arm crushes my ribs. He begins to carry me against him that way towards the back. I try to bite at the hand on my mouth. It's too tight, there's no room. I can't breathe, my chest blossoms with pain.

But my arms are still free. As we pass the little desk I reach for the delicate vase holding the orchid and grab it, swinging it back towards Ian's head. The glass shatters, falling all around us. Ian howls and loosens his grip. I squirm away and start to run. I make it halfway to the front door before he catches me. But this time I am ready. I still have the neck of the shattered vase in my hand, and I whirl around, jabbing it at his neck. He screams and slaps me hard. But he's let go, and I am at the front door before I feel the blow to my head. My vision blurs, and I am falling, falling onto the dark floor.

I open my eyes. We are in the alley behind The Blue Swan. I am on the ground, just outside a circle of light from the lamp over the service door. I am bound hand and foot, and Ian is opening the back of a grey van. There is a name written across the doors. My blurry vision can barely make it out, but the right-hand door bears the partial word, "hew's." *Mayhew's,* I think. He's stolen the van from the boatyard.

My mouth is taped, and I scream in my throat, hoping to call attention. But there is no one back here to see, only the rear entrances to shops that are closed. *If only Michael would come.*

I turn my head to see, and pain ricochets from one side to the next. But there is light from Michael's cottage. A shaft of it cuts through the hedge between the garden and the gallery.

It takes every ounce of strength I can muster, but I lift my bound feet and kick at Ian's legs, thinking to knock him down, make him yell out. But he is built like a rock; he makes only a muffled angry sound. He turns from the van and hauls me up by an arm, shoving me onto the bare metal floor. My face slides on splinters, my head strikes a pile of lumber. I am on my stomach, and I slam down with the toe of my boots, striking the floor of the van over and over, making what noise I can. Again, I scream against the tape. But no one comes.

With mounting panic, I remember that Michael always leaves a light on by the kitchen door when he's gone. He's in London tonight, just as Annette said. His plans changed, and he forgot to tell me.

Ian slams the van doors and I am in the dark alone. I hear him race to the front and get behind the wheel, and the next minute he is gunning the engine and speeding away. My face bumps against the metal floor at every rut; lumber falls down on me. I am buried beneath it, unable to move.

I am buried far more deeply in fear.

The van finally comes to a stop. At first I hear only the ticking of the hot engine, and I wonder what Ian is doing. I hear him moving about in front. The glove compartment opens and closes. There's a metallic sound. He gets out, comes round to the back. The doors open. Ian climbs up and pulls the lumber off me. He is breathing heavily and his hands are agitated, hurrying. He mutters things beneath his breath and I cannot make them out, but I know they are oaths, and they are laced with my name.

He drags me from the van. My chin bumps against something and catches. I feel it cut. He yanks harder, and pain sears through my jaw. Finally he's got me out, and my face hits the ground. He rolls me over and I feel hot blood run down my chin, onto my throat. In my mouth is the taste of blood and dirt. Ian lifts me and carries me like a sack, over his shoulder. It is then I see where we are: on the cliffs.

I have not been to this isolated spot since my thirteenth birthday. But I recognise a particular gnarled tree. My brothers tied me to this tree that day, and I shall never forget it as long as I live.

I am weak with fear now, unable to fight back. Ian drops me to the wet, stony ground. The mist is thick, and the only sound is of the foghorns wailing outside the harbour. There is no light save from the torch Ian carries, the kind with a handle for hanging it up while one is busy at other things. I hear a rattle, and see that looped around Ian's arm are chains.

He laughs harshly. "It's been a bit of a wait, now, hasn't it? Eighteen years. Isn't it nice your little boyfriend couldn't make it tonight."

I am confused; it must show in my eyes.

"Oh, he sent you a sweet note, he did—with the roses. 'Jo, I'm so sorry. I won't be able to meet you at the gallery at ten. I'll ring you from London. Much love, Michael.' Or somethin' like that." He smiles an ugly smile. "Just lucky I happened along right when the flower truck did. That girl, the one that delivered them flowers? Pretty little thing. Gave me a nice new blank card to write on. Said I must be a real romantic."

My eyes close briefly in despair.

"Now let's see if you're worth all the trouble, slut."

Ian hangs the torch on a limb of the tree. His hands reach down and yank me to my feet. He pushes me against the tree and holds me there with his own body. Sheer terror gives me strength to resist, squirming to get away. But I've made matters worse. As Ian loops the chain around the trunk, I feel him grow hard against me. I try to move back, but my wrists, still bound behind me, cut as they scrape along the tree. My knees burn as he twists the thin chain around my legs. I am crying now, and I cannot stop.

Ian rips the tape from my mouth. "No one around t'hear ya. Cry all y'want. Then y'can tell me how y'like it, girl. Tell me the way y'told that husband of yours, all those nights I was standin' outside yer window."

Through my panic, hope comes. *Has my brother unwittingly given me the way out?*

I bide my time. I close my eyes tight as he lifts my cotton jersey with those ugly hands, and I try not to scream when his fingers, then his mouth, close over my breast. He is making horrid gulping sounds, and his hair smells as if it hasn't been washed in weeks. I feel sick, but I hold it back, swallowing over and over. He rips the top buttons on my jeans, pushing them down around my hips. Then he stands back, takes the torch from the branch, and shines it on me, up and down.

"Now, will you look at that. What a pretty little sight. You've grown a bit, haven't you, girl?"

I am quaking so hard, I can hardly speak. I lick my lips, forcing out words I remember from the past, words that saved me from even worse pain. "Untie me, Ian . . . I can make it good for you."

He laughs. Then he says uncertainly, "Y'think I'd fall for that? Y'must think I'm really dumb."

"Ian, be reasonable. What can I do? You're stronger than me, I'd never get away." I lower my voice, trying to make it seductive. "Ian . . . if you watched us, you know. You know what David and I did."

I can see it working on him: images from those nights he spied on us through the window. Things I did for David, things he made me do.

He shakes his head, but he's thinking about it. I cannot see his eyes in the dark, but I know. This is Ian, and I know.

"You can have it that way, Ian," I say softly, "or I can fight you. If I have to fight you, it'll leave marks. I'll go to the police the minute you let me go." And then I think, *the inspector.* Even dead, he may be worth something.

"Ian, there's a police inspector asking questions. I'll tell him about this. I'll tell him you killed David. He'll come after you, they'll lock you up."

My brother makes a scornful sound. "Y'can forget yer bloody inspector. He's bloody well dead."

Then he laughs at my expression. "Thought you could bluff me, did you? Well, he's dead as yesterday's fish. Tried t' pin the murder on me, he did. Said a witness saw me out there at yer house that night. Wanted me to pay 'im to keep silent."

My God. The inspector was making his rounds with more than me. "You killed him?" I say.

"Gave his car a little push off the road, that's all. Right after he left you last night. Thought I'd scare him off, but the bloody bastard drove into a tree."

He is sweeping the torch up and down my body as he

talks, and it's like a cold hand, touching me. There is fog all around us, and I shiver. My nipples harden from the cold. Ian's breath begins to quicken. He steps closer.

"Oh God, Ian—don't. Please don't." My voice shakes, and my fear, as always, only makes him worse. His voice becomes soft, the edges blurred.

"I use to watch you and him . . . him touchin' you all over, doin' things. I wondered how it'd feel . . ."

More words come to me from the past, words that saved me from David. They gained me freedom from the bonds, at least.

"Ian, it's like you said. I'm not a little girl anymore." I brush myself against him, as much as I can with so little room.

Ian draws in a harsh breath and goes rigid. His hand plunges between my legs, and I arch my back and moan. "That's good, that's good . . ." I whisper urgently. "Oh, Ian, that's so good. Get me out of these clothes!"

He is on another plane now, the way he was in my childhood, the way David used to be. I would stare at the ceiling and pretend, and if they thought it would be better, they'd do what I asked. I would save myself a minute—or five—of pain.

Groaning, Ian's arms dart around me, behind the tree. He struggles with the chains, grunting. Finally they come loose. Weak with relief, I slide to the ground. In a split second Ian is there beside me, cutting with his knife at the rope round my ankles. He is cursing, pulling, jerking, and at last they come free. He starts on my hands. I lie there limp and passive, not fighting. At one point he meets my eyes, and I smile, letting my legs fall open, inviting. He goes back to the knots with renewed fervour.

Give me one moment, I pray. *One moment when he's so caught up, he forgets the knife.*

But then suddenly he freezes, his eyes snapping up to the road. I turn my head and see lights approaching.

"Bloody hell!" Ian says, rocking back on his heels. "Who . . . ?"

The car is racing, barrelling towards us. When it gets to within fifty yards it leaves the road and swerves across the rutted track. Less than twenty yards from us it screeches to a halt, and I can make it out now—a black Range Rover.

Ian springs to his feet. He backs off and starts to run, but Michael leaps from the car and is after him. The ropes round my wrists are loose, and I use my teeth to get them off. I grab the chain from the ground and jump up, running after the two of them. Ian heads along the cliff-edge to the south, and I see him stumble over rocks. Michael is on him in seconds, a foot shoving him face down, then holding him to the ground. He lifts a fist and rams it into the back of Ian's neck.

"Get away from him!" I yell, running up and pushing Michael aside with all the strength I've got. "Get away!"

Michael stumbles back, bewilderment on his face. I stand above Ian and swing with the chain, striking him on the back. He tries to get up, but I swing again—and again, and again. Ian falls flat and screams. I see blood on his skull, and still I raise my arm. Michael grabs my wrist, yelling, "That's enough, Jo! For God's sake, that's enough!"

I stand back, breathing heavily, my hands shaking like palsy. Sweat streams down my face. I look at my brother, this monster, and I think: *No—it is not enough, it will never be enough.* But now I can barely stand. I am crying, sobbing, and Michael is putting his arms around me. "I'm here," he murmurs, "it's all right."

And it might have been all right, except that at that moment Ian rises to his knees, bent over and moving slowly as if he's barely got any strength at all. He is moaning, and Michael, stricken with guilt as I would not have been, reaches to help him. Quick as a flash Ian draws his knife from inside his jacket and slashes at Michael's gut. The blade barely misses, and Ian comes at him again. I still have the chain, and I turn and hurl it with all my might, screaming, "No!" and catch Ian straight across the face. He is knocked back, shrieking, holding his hands to the blood that courses down.

Then he rallies and is on me, his bloody fingers round my throat. Michael grabs for his neck, and he turns on Michael and smashes his fist into his face.

I shove Ian sideways. He staggers but keeps to his feet. Turning away, he begins to run. I race after him, but the fog swallows him up and I lose all sense of direction. I think he's gone to the right, in fact I can almost feel him there. I turn that way and hear Michael behind me, yelling at me, "Jo, watch out!" But I don't see it until I'm upon it, and by then my foot has gone into the crevice and I'm falling into open space. The sea beats against the rocks hundreds of feet below. It roars in my ears, and the last thing I see is Michael's face above me in the fog, his hand reaching out. But then he is gone, and so am I.

CHAPTER 25

I sense, vaguely, that I lie with my back against a cold, hard slab. Across the screen of my closed eyelids the hideous film plays again.

"I see you've been so involved with your girlfriend you've let the fire go out," David says.

Charlotte has run, and David has torn the phone from my hands as I tried to call the police. He puts a log on, acting as if nothing has happened. I see him kneeling there, his handsome face flushed by the flames. Then he stands and turns to me, removing his belt. He comes towards me holding the belt out, and when he gets to me he knocks me to the floor. Then he nudges me with a foot—not hard, he wants no bruises— but enough that I know to turn onto my stomach, which I obediently do. He lashes the belt round my wrists.

I am still in the red peignoir, and beneath it is the teddy he ripped when Charlotte was here. David's hand strays to a buttock and strokes it beneath the high cut of satin. I cringe. "Get up, my sweet." He pulls me by an elbow. My feet slip from under me and he pulls harder until I am upright. He walks me back into the bedroom, shoving me down on the bed. Pushing the torn remnants of the teddy aside, he studies every inch of my flesh, touching me here and there.

"At least she left no marks," he says of Charlotte, and I plead with him, "I swear to you, David, it wasn't like that! Please don't hurt me." He ignores me and reaches into the nightstand, pulling out long strips of scarlet silk. He flips me onto my stomach again, removes the belt from my wrists, and

*with the silk he ties my hands to the Eros bedposts, and then
my legs. I lie still, not fighting it; I know by now it will do no
good. David has improved his skills in London. Not only has
he been working out and grown strong, but he knows precisely
how to hold a woman down.*

*I should be accustomed to this now, but I am always afraid
on my stomach. It is a terrifying feeling when you cannot see
it coming—when there is pain, and you don't know what is
causing it or how terrible it might get. All you know is that
there are sounds, sounds of metal and perhaps glass, sounds
of things you can only imagine in your worst nightmares—
and then the fiery, excruciating contact. You scream, and the
mind scrabbles for a way out, but you can only think: What
next, what next? The imagination runs wild, and soon you are
screaming against the pillow as both pain and fear over-
whelm.*

*David always said that the screaming made it better. Once
I was bold enough to shout at him, "If you think that, then let
me do it to you! You be the one feeling pain, damn you!" He
slapped me so hard he left a bruise that time. I stayed indoors
for a week, afraid to let anyone see.*

*So I lie there and let him do what he will, and I plead with
God to let me die. God seems to answer, for I am whisked off
to a plateau above the clouds, and all I can feel there is the
soft wing of an angel enfolding me, holding me safe. The
angel's face is golden, luminous. She hums a tender lullaby
and rocks me gently side to side, until—with a soft, child-like
sob—I sleep.*

*There is a sound. I hear it from far off, and the angel wings
disperse as I come awake. I hear them whir, like the wings of
a dove.* Come back! *I cry,* don't leave me. *But they are gone.
A sharp, unbearable sadness pierces my heart.*

*David sits beside me on the bed; my hands and feet are
free. The red peignoir lies on the floor, and he strokes my
naked body softly, gently, making tiny noises in his throat.
"My sweet little Joanna," he murmurs, "that was so good. Tell
me you liked it, too."*

I taste blood on my lips. "I liked it, too," I say dully.

"You know, once you give in to it, you are always so good.

Your passion ignites me, my sweet. I can't think of another thing but having you."

I stare at the ceiling. I am sore all over, and my throat burns. A wave of depression engulfs me as David lifts me into his arms and carries me into the living room. He sets me down on the sofa before the fire. My punishment, I know, has only begun.

I lie still, awaiting his next move. My head to the side, I see the stone hare on the floor by my limp hand, where David dropped it earlier. I think of Michael, and I remember his goodness, his kind heart. If he were to see what I've become . . . after all he did to keep me safe . . .

A rage begins to grow. It pushes the depression aside and fills every inch of my being, every cell, every nerve. Soon it is all there is—rage slicing through me, cutting at my dead mind, my humiliated skin. In my ears begins the roar of a choir of angels, their outraged wings beating at my heart.

David bends over the fire again. He holds something in his hand. When he turns back to me I see it is a thin brown European cigarette. He has lit it in the flames, and I know he doesn't smoke, nor ever has. He stands, crosses over to me, and kneels, bringing the red-hot tip towards me. The angel wings beat harder and harder, they are furious now, and their whirring screams a dictum in my ears: Fight back, fight back!

My fingers close over the stone hare. With a fierce guttural yell I grab it up and half rise, aiming for David's skull.

Stunned, he falls back. But I've missed, I've only grazed his shoulder. His eyes swing to me, and the astonishment, the absolute hatred there, tells me I am about to die. Terrified, I struggle to my feet and run for the door. But David is right behind me, and he grabs my hand that still holds the hare. We wrestle with it, but David wins. He's got the hare and he raises it, his face mottled with fury. I scream, throwing up a hand. The heavy stone image crashes down on my head. My vision darkens, and nausea swells my throat as I start to slip away.

I am on the floor. My limbs are useless, they are numb. I hear a sound, and at first I believe it to be that host of angels, come to carry me away.

It is not the angels—it is a knife cutting through air. Through my half-closed eyes I see its bright blade as someone

behind David slashes down. The knife strikes him in the
back, over and over. Blood spurts. David's face registers
shock, he claws at air. As he falls to the floor, my eyes, glued
to him until now, rise . . . and I see the face of his killer.

There is pain in my left leg. My head throbs. I try to raise
myself up, but fall back, dizzy. The fog has turned to a
heavy mizzle and the winds are fierce. I remember chasing
after Ian and falling. I know I must be somewhere on the
cliffs, but I cannot see farther than my hand.

A voice calls; it seems to come from above. "Jo?"

"Michael! Is that you?"

There is silence. "Michael?" I call again.

"Yes, sweetheart, it's me. Are you all right?"

"I'm not sure." I make to stand, and my back hurts. My
boot scrapes against rock.

"Wait there, love," I hear. "I'm coming down."

A tremor of fear goes through me. "Michael, I can't see
anything. Where am I?"

"You fell on a ledge—not too far down. I saw it happen,
but then the fog closed in. Jo, I'm right above you. There's
a fissure here—just enough for a toehold, but it goes at
least as far as that ledge. I'm on my way down. I've brought
ropes from the car." Stones rattle down the cliff and I hear
him grunt.

I stretch out my left arm to see how much room I've got,
and there is nothing but empty space. I hear the waves
now, crashing below, and feel spray. I extend my right hand
and it slides in something slick. Guano, I think. I rub it on
my jeans, then feel for the cliff-side. "Michael . . ." My
voice shakes. "This ledge isn't very wide. Three feet at
most."

"I know. I saw. Can you stand? Is there anything to get a
hold on once I'm there?"

I run my fingers along the cliff-side again. It feels sheer,
not a jutting rock anywhere. Then I find a crevice running
horizontally at about waist-height, were I on my feet. The
crevice itself is perhaps four inches in height and as long as
I can reach in length. I turn sideways to slide my fingers in,
but with the motion pain shoots through my left leg, so

much I can't help but yell out. I fall back, breathing heavily.

Michael calls down. "Jo, what's wrong?"

"My leg. I don't think I can move it."

A small silence. "Is it broken?"

"I'm not sure. I don't know. Michael, I'm afraid."

He doesn't answer. I hear his boots strike rock and the light slap of a rope. The wind picks up and rain begins, tearing at my hair and clothes. Needles of it sting my face like a thousand hungry birds plucking about for food. The minutes drag by and, despite the fact that Michael is here, I feel entirely alone in a hostile world. There is a fear in my gut that has nothing to do with being on this ledge, but with something else, as if there is something ugly still walking the cliffs this night, something I am about to discover that will alter my life forever. I feel as if the devil himself stands nearby.

"Michael?" In my tone is a plea for reassurance.

Why doesn't he answer?

He is not, I think, a climber. Michael is strong and in good shape, but if he has ever done any climbing, I don't know about it. Over the years, experienced hikers have been killed on these cliffs. When the tide comes in, pounding waves reach up and snatch everything within reach.

I strain my ears to hear him, but all sound has stopped. I call out again, alarmed. "Michael?"

He answers, closer now. "Yes, Jo."

I shiver. There is something in his voice—I've never heard that tone before, one of absolute determination and even desperation. I am more frightened than ever suddenly. I don't know why, but I am frightened of Michael. I feel trapped on this ledge, unable to move. And I don't want him here.

"Michael . . . listen to me, I want you to leave me here. Go back up. Go to Mevagissey and get help." There is a huge lump of fear in my throat.

He laughs softly. "I don't think so, my dear. We have a bit of unfinished business."

His boots slap down, and I feel the thud vibrate through the stone ledge beneath my back.

* * *

It is quite dark, but I can see him now through the driving rain. There is an emergency torch attached to his belt; it casts a bright circle of light from the waist up. He is standing at my feet, clinging to the bald cliff face. In the bobbing light I see a line tied to his waist, and a second one over his shoulder. Both hang down from above, and they hang perhaps three feet away from the face of the cliff, telling me that the granite juts out somewhere above.

Michael shouts over the roar of wind and wave. "Put this about your waist." He tosses an end of rope. It falls against my legs—a slim coil but strong, the kind he uses for binding crates. There are knots at three-foot intervals.

"The knots are for toe-holds," he says, leaning closer. "I've got both lines tied to the Range Rover."

I stare at the rope. Again, I shiver, and my hand shrinks from touching it. There is danger here—terrible danger— and I need to stay free. This is all I can think.

"Take the rope, Jo!"

I cannot see his face; it is shadowed. But I hear his anger. "Mi-Michael, my leg's no good. It won't take my weight. I can't stand."

"Get the bloody rope about you, then worry about that!" He points the torch directly in my face. "Bloody hell—*do* it, Jo!"

I shrink against the granite cliff, trembling.

"Jo . . ." His voice lowers, becomes soft, almost deadly. "If you don't do as I say, I am going to push you off the damn cliff myself."

I am more terrified than ever. In my ear there is a whisper, and the whisper is Annette's. It tells me, *Don't you know you're worth more to him dead than alive?*

And I think, *He has to make it look good. Has to make it seem he tried to rescue me. But he'll get me tied to this rope, get me dangling, then cut—*

That's why he didn't leave me here and go for help. He doesn't want help.

Through my panic comes Michael's voice, more reasonable now, cajoling. "Look, Jo, I'm sorry. I didn't mean to frighten you. I wouldn't hurt you, love, I'm just worried for you. Please take the rope."

"I c-can't."

"Yes, love, you can. Listen to me. The ledge we're on ends about twenty yards to the left, and only a few feet to the right. But there's another ledge, ten feet above us. It leads to that old cove, the one we hid in from your brothers that day. Sweetheart, you remember that day, don't you? Remember how afraid you were, and then I came, and I took care of you? I'll take care of you now, Jo. I'll climb up to the ledge first, then I'll pull you up. We'll inch our way along to the cove, then take the path to the top. Jo, you trust me, don't you? I would never let you down."

My teeth are chattering. I am so frightened that every inch of me shakes. But I want to believe him. What he says makes sense—and Michael *wouldn't* ever hurt me, would he? That's what I've been telling Charlotte, over and over —that no matter how desperate to save his sinking fortunes, he wouldn't hurt me . . .

Then why am I so afraid now, as if something terrible is about to happen?

Old patterns. Of course. Annette planted that kernel of fear, and I, who have learned not to trust, am feeding off it. I've been foolish.

Gritting my teeth, I center most of my weight on my right side, using stomach muscles to lift my shoulders and sore back. I manage to get the rope about me, but the pain to my left knee is intense. I cry out, and my foot jerks and slides on the slick wet stone, going over the edge. Grabbing the crevice with my fingers I hang on for dear life to keep my entire body from following.

Michael catches my right ankle, steadying me. The fierce throbbing flares, then recedes. "Are you all right?" he asks.

"Yes."

"Good. Can you knot the rope?"

I secure it several times. Both the rope and my fingers are wet, and I fumble at it. I cannot help the small cry of frustration that escapes my lips.

"That's just fine, Jo. You're doing great. Now wrap it a few times round your chest, just beneath your shoulders.

It'll give you better balance." He pays the rope out so there's more to work with.

It is awkward, but I manage. I am bound, finally—trussed from waist to chest. There is no going back.

"Perfect," Michael says. He stands again and the winds gust, nearly carrying his words away. "Now get a purchase in that crack again, and I'll pull on the rope and help you to your feet. You'll have to be careful not to come down on that left foot, that's all."

I slide the fingers of my right hand into the crevice. With my left hand I press down just a bit behind me, and with that hand I push, while with the other I pull, testing.

"Ready?" Michael says.

"Ready." I brace myself.

Michael twists the rope round his hand and begins to draw me towards him. The cord tightens about my waist and strains at my chest. My upper body rises to a thirty-degree angle. But then a gust of wind catches me, and I begin to swing out, away from the cliff. My hand slips from the cleft in the rock.

I try to throw myself back towards the cliff. "Michael!" I reach for his hand, but it isn't there.

A wave of dizziness strikes me. Before my eyes tumbles the image of that boy at Lost Inn. His jeering face haunts me. *"You're stupid lady, stupid. Why'd you listen to me? Why'd you go through that stone the wrong way? Bad luck, now, lady. Bad, bad luck all the rest of your life."*

And Annette: *". . . worth more dead than alive."*

With a mighty thrust I fling myself forward, grabbing the rope. In the next second I am falling towards Michael. I strike up against him, and we both sway from the force. We balance precariously, then settle for a moment against the cliff. But the wind blasts into us again, and we are still off-balance. Michael's foot slips, rock crumbles, and he takes me with him—out away from the cliff, over the sea. Together we are like a pendulum; we have weight, and we swing farther than we might have alone. That same weight sends us flying back towards the cliff. Michael's arm is fast about me, and mine about him. He yells something into my ear, and I'm not certain I understand but I think he is telling me to twist about so that our legs are in front, to absorb the impact as we hit. We are like children on a swing, heading for the trunk of a tree. At the last minute I bend my left knee back and brace myself for the right foot to jar. We slam up hard, and I feel the pain shoot up both legs to my head. We bounce away slightly, not far. But this time the winds and rain are against us, they toss us like rag dolls in the sky. When we swing back we are turned in such a way that I will hit first, and the last thing I see, or rather feel, is Michael making a powerful effort to turn himself to take the brunt of the crash. His shoulder and head strike the granite wall, absorbing the impact for me. I feel him go slack, and there is blood pouring down his face, black as the night. I grab for any small cleft, any crack or nub. There is nothing—and worse, we have stopped below the ledge and are dangling in air, no foothold at all.

It is then I hear an evil laugh from above. "Couldn't've asked for better if I'd planned it m'self," Ian says.

And I know now why I felt the devil walked the cliffs this night.

CHAPTER 26

I grab for Michael's torch, which dangles on a cord from his belt. Fumbling, I push the rubbery button to turn it on. It flickers, goes out. I jam the button again and again, and finally the light holds. I shine it upward and see Ian on the ledge Michael spoke of, the one that leads to the cove. He is pointing his torch down at us. He is laughing, but the sound is eerie, as if issuing from someone quite mad.

The wind explodes around us, and Michael's dead weight pulls on me. The thin ropes round my waist and chest threaten to cut me in half. "Michael! Michael, wake up!" His breath is faint on my cheek, but I cannot rouse him. I reach up and feel the ledge we fell from, close enough to just get a hand-hold. "Michael . . . oh, please, you've got to be all right. I can't pull us both up."

I scream up to Ian, "For God's sake, help us!"

He laughs. "And now how would I be doin' that, little girl?"

"We're tied to the Range Rover, you can get back up there and pull us with it."

He laughs. "And *why* would I be doin' that?" He flicks the beam of light along the ledge, and sees my hand there. "Y'could do it yerself, y'know. Hoist yerself up, that is. Have to cut yer little boyfriend loose, of course. Y'want my knife?" He holds it out. It's the kind of serrated blade that's used to gut fish at the docks.

"You bastard! Go to hell."

"Mmm. That's what I thought. Well, then . . ."

He points the light at our ropes, which hang straight before him, only inches from each other. In his other hand he holds the knife, and he brings it to the ropes. My blood freezes.

"You wouldn't! Even you aren't that murderous!" But he is. I know this in my heart: my brother is going to kill us.

"Ian, listen—listen, I know you hate me now. But get us out of this and I swear I'll do anything you want."

"You'd be makin' it good for me, is that what yer sayin'?" A chilling laugh. "Like y'did up there a bit ago?"

"No—no, that was a mistake. You frightened me, that's all. Ian, get us up and I'll do anything. I'll even come back home to live. I'll be there all the time for you, you can do anything. Just help us, for God's sake!"

"Y'know, I've been thinkin', little girl. Yer really more trouble than yer worth." He begins to saw at one of the lines with his knife.

I shake Michael frantically. If we can only reach our own ledge—

He groans, but his eyes remain closed. Our weight is stretching the wet ropes now, and we begin to slide down the face of the cliff. Desperate, I drop the torch and lunge for the ledge, grabbing it with both hands, tugging as hard as I can. I strain and strain, but am able to lift us only a few inches. I feel for a knot by my dangling feet, hoping to push against it. But the rain has made my boots too slick. They grab, grab again, then slide away.

Sirens sound in the distance. Suddenly, Ian jerks his head around, and I sense a dark figure in the shadows behind him. I cannot make it out. There is astonishment, however, in Ian's voice.

"Ah, no . . . no, y'wouldn't . . ." he cries, and it is, I think, the sort of cry one makes when facing Death.

Another movement, dark against dark, and Ian seems yanked backwards. There is a scuffle, stones fall over the edge and strike us. I hear muttered oaths, a voice I do not recognise as the wind and the shrieking of sirens whip it away. Then I hear a cry, and in the next moment Ian comes tumbling from his ledge, flying like a bird, arms outstretched over the sea. I have only a glimpse as he falls past

us, an impression of a face white with fear, the mouth in
rictus as screams spew forth. Then all sound is muffled by
the crashing waves.

I cling to the rope and to Michael, looking up, but can
see no one on the ledge. Far above that, at the top of the
cliff, is a glow of flashing red lights. I hear shouts from
there. "Hullo! Someone down there? Can you hear us?"

"Yes!" I call back. "We're down here on the ledge."

"How many of you?"

"Two . . ." I hesitate. "No, three." There is movement
above, on the ledge Ian was on. A pale countenance appears. A smallish, dark-clothed figure perches there.

"I didn't mean to push him over," it says, crying. "I just
tried to get his knife, Josie, so's he couldn't hurt you anymore."

"I know," I say softly, "I know."

"I followed you and him out here, and I went back and
called the police."

I can hear them on two-way radios, and the clank of the
rescue climbers' gear, the thunk of lines being tossed over.
My chest and underarms burn from Michael's weight on
the ropes; my entire body is racked with pain. But we'll be
all right now. I can last till they come.

My brother Joseph rubs his eyes. "I'm sorry for what I
did to you, Josie. I tried to make up for it. I killed him so
he couldn't do those things to you anymore."

"Yes," I say. "I remember."

We are no longer talking about Ian, but David.

My brother kneels on the edge of the cliff, a small, dark
avenging angel. "It'll be all right now," he says. "You're
safe. We're all safe now."

EPILOGUE

Several months have passed since all that happened, and my brother Joseph is serving a three-year sentence for having killed David. He turned himself in that night on the cliffs, and he would have taken responsibility for Ian's death as well, but I wouldn't let him. As an eyewitness I testified that Ian had slipped, it was an accident. There'd been enough grief, I felt. Why compound it with more?

As for David's murder, I gave the police an edited version of what I'd remembered about that night. "My brother saved my life," I told them. "And his own. It was self-defence."

It was strange at the jail the next morning, seeing my brother behind a wall of glass. All those years I'd prayed for some sort of protective barrier between us, and then to have it like that. Joseph's eyes were bloodshot from tears and lack of sleep, his red hair dirty and mussed. He looked no more than a helpless lad as he told me, chin trembling, how it had been a stone on his heart—the way he, Denny, and Ian had used me. "On me like the hand of God, a giant weight, I swear."

Then he said something odd. "I kept thinkin' how y'never liked them red shoes."

I thought he'd gone round the bend with that. But then he explained that he too remembered that special day when I was six and he took me to see *The Wizard of Oz.*

"When we got out, I asked you how you liked them

shoes. And you said if you was Dorothy, you'd have stayed there. You'd never've clicked your heels and gone home."

I didn't remember that, but I believe it. Even at six, the witch's castle must have seemed far better than the way things were at home.

Joseph told me that the night David died, he'd come up to Pennoryn to tell me, finally, that Ian was spying on me. I think he also wanted to talk about Mum. But then he saw through the window what David was doing to me, and all those years of guilt rose up. Hardly knowing what he was doing, he struck David down.

As to Mum, Joseph's story was so horrifying I cannot relate it here in its entirety. It had to do with Ian and Denny using our mother after I left to marry David. That was why she turned on me that night, crying, "I had to do *everything*." I should have remembered that Joseph was the only one in the house with any conscience at all. He didn't always participate in Ian and Denny's little games with me, and never, he said, with our mum. Yet he couldn't take action against them; he was too afraid for that. Like our mother, he would turn his face and run.

I can no longer find it in my heart to hate them for that; it was their way of finding safety, while mine was hiding in the meadow or dreaming of turrets in the sky.

To this day, whenever I think of the night David died, I believe there were angels amongst us. Nothing will convince me otherwise. Else why would Joseph have been there just then at all? And why would he have had the grace and kindness to cover me with that blanket? "I couldn't leave you like that," was his simple explanation, "so bare, and so cold."

He even took the stone hare away and pitched it over a cliff. Remembering the old superstition, he feared David's soul would enter the hare and linger on at Pennoryn.

It was Joseph who'd read me that story of the white hare as a child. I remember now bringing the book home from school.

I think sometimes about my family and wonder how I managed to survive. According to Dr. Shahi, I may have been "reconstructing" all along, without even knowing it.

Take Pennoryn, for instance. Isn't that what David and I both did—building a gentler past for ourselves with our house? Perhaps we'd hoped to convince ourselves that Pennoryn was the kind of world we'd sprung from. I had my gardens, and David . . .

What happened to David, I'll never know. He may have meant well when first we met. He may have genuinely wanted the kind of life we planned at Pennoryn—and at the same time been unable to live it.

One day I asked my good doctor: "How could I have thought we were soul mates? Was I that hopelessly romantic, that blind?" And he told me, "Soul mates are not always good people. Often their only purpose in this particular life is to force us to grow."

As to Dr. Shahi's theory about reconstructing one's past, now that I've had a bit of practise with it, I think it's a good one. Certainly reconstructing that day of my thirteenth birthday helped. He had me imagine in hypnosis that my whole family—not to mention numerous friends—were out there on the cliffs, bringing me love and no harm. I even imagined Ian never touching me, not once in my entire life. Instead, he was good and kind, the nicest brother one could ever want.

Well, that was a bit of a stretch, I'll say. But I did my best, and strangely enough, I no longer feel fear when I think of that day, or that place on the cliffs. I no longer tremble when I think of Ian. But the proof of the pudding is not how I feel about Ian, but my relationship with Michael.

It is good. It is so good, I sometimes sit in our little cottage garden watching the butterflies play about the fuchsia plant, and cry. They are tears of joy, and they cleanse. Everything about me now looks bright and new, and I take joy from so many things: the head of lettuce that we grow for our evening meal, the herb garden I've expanded, a new radiant bud on the clematis vine. In good weather Michael and I sit here with our tea or coffee. In bad, we nestle inside and I might read while Michael paints, or perhaps we'll simply talk.

I like living here at the cottage, and being in town. I've made at least three new friends with nearby shopkeepers, and I even have a part-time job. Michael would have had me work in The Blue Swan, but I wanted something that was all my own. So I'm back at Morley's, the gallery I worked at before I met David. They've got me setting up showings, and Michael teases me about being a competitor, but in truth he doesn't mind. I also have my own private bank account—never once touched for the gallery in London, as Michael insisted on working those finances out himself.

As for Annette, I am pleased to say she's moved on. Michael found her a job in Paris at my urging, when he would have just as soon let her go. It was Annette, after all, who phoned Michael that day in London and screamed at him jealously, "What are you doing, telling me one thing and her another?" When he'd calmed her down, he realised that the note I'd found on my doorstep with the roses was different from the one he'd written—and that I was walking into a trap. We can thank Annette for that phone call, at least. God only knows what otherwise might have happened on those cliffs.

My brother Denny has run off somewhere. A neighbour said she saw him in Liverpool on the street, and that he didn't look well. I have tried to feel some responsibility for him, even a grain of sympathy. But I must admit that even with "reconstructing" my past, this is a sticking point for me. Dr. Shahi says the emotions take time to heal, and forgiveness will come. The best I can do for now is not think of Denny at all. Meanwhile, with my brothers gone, my mother slipped back into sitting in her chair and withdrawing. We had to put her in a home, and Joseph, once he's served his sentence, will most likely live in that house alone.

I asked Michael: "Why did you replace my childhood house with trees in that painting at Harbourside?"

"I didn't want you reminded of your past every time you looked at it," he said. Michael, too, is having to learn to let go. He's not nearly so overly protective of me now.

I've sold Pennoryn. Yet I think of it often. I remember the two hills that form that valley, that gentle *V.* I think of how that valley became my abyss—a chasm so wide, it is a wonder I've made it back across. Robert is still there, tending the gardens for the new owners. They're down from London, a nice couple, and they looked a bit askance when I told them to think nothing of it if he mentions needing a pint of rum or the eye of a bat. They'll learn in time that life is so much richer for the differences between us all. I feel that way about Charlotte, as well. While I cannot return the kinds of feelings she has for me, I can accept that she has them and still be her friend. That, I think, is a kind of love.

As for Henry, he is deteriorating rapidly now. I visit him often, and Charlotte has vowed to be with him to the end.

I would like to believe that Michael and I will be happy together to the end . . . forever, as it says on my wedding ring. But I am still working through it. I still have those nightmarish moments when the past rushes in and happens all over again. They are, however, becoming less and less. One day Dr. Shahi had me in hypnosis, traipsing blithely down a street in Mevagissey with my mother, both of us with fancy parasols in our hands, it being a hot summer's day. She was buying me a nice new frock and we were having lunch afterwards at one of the better restaurants. My mother was holding my hand lovingly and smiling.

That in itself was so ludicrous, so far from the truth, I burst out laughing in the middle of the session. Afterwards, however, I did not feel so bitter towards my mother, nor so untrusting. It was almost as if we actually did those things —loved each other, laughed, and had good times—but on some other plane. Now and then at home I sit in the garden and cross over to that plane, and there she is, waiting, her hand held out, welcoming and loving.

We'll be starting on my brothers again next week. God knows what Dr. Shahi may concoct for them. A Sunday sail down the Thames?

I laugh about it, but there are things I've learned the past year—good things—that will be with me always. One is that Mrs. Rimes was right. Only a man in love sends postcards to a woman even when she is senseless.

Another is that when people are meant to find each other, even though it may take a lifetime, they do.

The Dollmaker was a serial killer who stalked Los
Angeles and left a grisly calling card on the faces of his
female victims. With a single faultless shot, Detective
Harry Bosch thought he had ended the city's nightmare.

Now, the dead man's widow is suing Harry and the LAPD
for killing the wrong man—an accusation that rings terri-
fyingly true when a new victim is discovered with the
Dollmaker's macabre signature.

Now, for the second time, Harry must hunt down a death-
dealer who is very much alive, before he strikes again. It's
a blood-tracked quest that will take Harry from the hard
edges of the L.A. night to the last place he ever wanted
to go—the darkness of his own heart.

"Exceptional...A stylish blend of grit and elegance."
—Nelson DeMille

In prison, they call her the Sculptress for the strange figurines she carves—symbols of the day she hacked her mother and sister to pieces and reassembled them in a blood-drenched jigsaw. Sullen, menacing, grotesquely fat, Olive Martin is burned-out journalist Rosalind Leigh's only hope of getting a new book published.

But as she interviews Olive in her cell, Roz finds flaws in the Sculptress's confession. Is she really guilty as she insists? Drawn into Olive's world of obsessional lies and love, nothing can stop Roz's pursuit of the chilling, convoluted truth. Not the tidy suburbanites who'd rather forget the murders, not a volatile ex-policeman and her own erotic response to him, not an attack on her life.

MINETTE WALTERS
THE SCULPTRESS

"Creepy but compulsive...The assured British stylist doesn't let up on her sensitive probing of two tortured souls...Hard to put down."
—*The New York Times Book Review*

They met at Sarah Lawrence College, at a time
when the world seemed to shine with possibility—
flamboyant and fabulously beautiful Delphine; poor
but talented Daisy; plain, practical Gina; and gentle
Franca. Four bright, brave and spirited women
determined to defy convention, to have it all—to
lead glorious lives and build brilliant careers, and
most of all, never to stand in any man's shadow.

But times change, and through the years, their
dreams of independence give way to passionate
new longings. Which of them will make stunning
sacrifices in the name of love?

WOMEN LIKE US
Erica Abeel
_____ 95506-5 $5.99 U.S./$6.99 Can.

They were called the class from Hell—thirty-four
inner-city sophomores she inherited from a teacher
who'd been "pushed over the edge." She was told
"those kids have tasted blood. They're dangerous."

But LouAnne Johnson had a different idea. Where the
school system saw thirty-four unreachable kids, she
saw young men and women with intelligence and
dreams. When others gave up on them, she broke the
rules to give them the best things a teacher can give—
hope and belief in themselves. When statistics showed
the chances were they'd never graduate, she fought to
beat the odds.

This is her remarkable true story—and theirs.

DANGEROUS MINDS

LOUANNE JOHNSON

NOW A MAJOR MOTION PICTURE FROM HOLLYWOOD PICTURES STARRING

MICHELLE PFEIFFER